The Secret Diary of Mrs. John Quincy Adams

Wife of the Sixth President of the United States

The Secret Diary of Mrs. John Quincy Adams

Wife of the Sixth President of the United States

Beatrice Fairbanks Cayzer

Legacies Books
Palm Beach, Florida

Also by Beatrice Fairbanks Cayzer*

TALES OF PALM BEACH (as Beatrice de Holguin)

THE PRINCE AND PRINCESS OF WALES

ROYAL ECCENTRICS (with Barbara Cartland)

ROYAL LOVERS (with Barbara Cartland)

THE ROYAL WORLD OF ANIMALS

DIANE (PRINCESSE DE POLIGNAC)

MURDER BY MEDICINE

THE HAPPY HARROW MURDER TRILOGY

MURDER TO MUSIC

MURDERED MOTHERS

MURDER IN MARRIAGE

VAMPIRE MURDERS

LOVE LOVE IN DARFUR

THE HARROW QUARTET

MURDER FOR NUMITIONS

MODELS MURDERED IN MILAN

MOCKING MURDERS IN MADRID

MEXICO'S MOVIELAND MURDERS

MURDER FOR BEAUTY

THE SECRET DIARY OF MRS. JOHN QUINCY ADAMS

TO SAVE A CHILD

AWARD-WINNING AUTHOR

Beatrice Fairbanks Cayzer

Beatrice Fairbanks Cayzer was photographed in the Caribbean after boarding an authentic slave ship called "GHOST". As a daughter of a United States Ambassador to Ethiopia she has always been deeply troubled by slavery existing anywhere. Her roots to the Adams-Fairbanks family have enflamed this interest when she learned that both Louisa and John Quincy Adams had such a great part in ending slavery in the United States. Beatrice being the god-daughter of a First Lady of Ecuador, Dona Elena de Arroyo del Rio lived with her god-mother when President Carlos Arroyo del Rio was in exile, thereby gaining an insight into the latter years of a President being out of office. Beatrice takes you on a journey to the countries where John Quincy Adams served as Ambassador, then on to his negotiating treaties and entering a political life and his entrance into the turmoil of Washington politics.

Legacies Books
a division of Humanics Publishing Group

The Secret Diary of Mrs. John Quincy Adams
© 2015 by Beatrice F. Cayzer
© 2015 Green Dragon Books. All rights reserved.
A Legacies Books Publication
First Edition

This book is licensed for your personal enjoyment only. This book may not be resold or given away to other people. If you would like to share this book with another person, please ask them to purchase their own copy. Thank you for respecting intellectual property rights.

No part of this book may be reproduced or transmitted in any form or by any means, electronic or mechanical, including photocopying, recording, or by any information storage and retrieval system, without written permission from the publisher. For information, address Brumby.

Legacies Books is an imprint of and published by Green Dragon Books™, a division of Brumby Holdings, Inc. Its trademark, consisting of the words "Legacies Books" and the portrayal of a sextant, is registered with the U.S. Patent and Trademark Office and in other countries.

Brumby Holdings, Inc.
Green Dragon Books
2875 S. Ocean Blvd., Ste 200
Palm Beach, FL 33480

Printed in the United States of America and the United Kingdom

ISBN (Hardcover) 978162386-011-0
ISBN (Paperback) 978162386-021-9

Library of Congress Cataloging-in-Publication Data 201464206

This novel is based on a true story:
there are some fictionalized parts
enhanced for dramatization.

This book is dedicated to

Mrs. William Roosevelt,

granddaughter-in-law of

President Franklin D. Roosevelt

Samadhi:
The state of deep undifferentiated awareness
(in) which there is only the self
within a transcendent observing entity.
In this state unconditional love
is the organizing principle of that Universe.

—Dr. Edgar Mitchell
Astronaut, Sixth Man On The Moon.

London, November 11, 1795

I am sitting at my little Chippendale-designed desk on a London autumn morning contemplating Maman's invitation to have Johnny Adams dine with us this evening, I remember how he was a victim to my independent ways when, as a young girl of four, I gave him dog biscuits to eat!

What struck me first upon meeting Johnny Adams that day in 1779 was a stink of traveler that blasted from his clothes. Without bathing or changing his shirt, he came straight to our house after arriving in Nantes from Paris. His stink was bad, but not as bad as what I'd smelled from the ships that arrived there from Africa, making Nantes the Capital of France's Slave Trade. And I'd seen African slaves herded from ships, where the close-packed people stank because they were covered in each other's human waste and blood from suffering in close quarters.

My Maryland-born tobacco-broker father, Joshua Johnson, brought our family out of his base in England to take refuge in Nantes during the American Revolution.

Johnny's father, the famous John Adams, had come to visit us with Benjamin Franklin because my father was known to be a supporter of our Revolution.

Having prospered from importing tobacco through

Nantes, Papa accumulated a fleet of ships that gave him a certain prestige with the French Navy. This connection to the French Navy caught the attention of both Mr. Adams and Mr. Franklin.

After Father welcomed Mr. Franklin in our front hall, I heard Mr. Adams say, "Our Yorktown army needs help with back-up by a fleet of the French Navy. There is one off of Rhode Island that would be very useful."

Benjamin Franklin nodded. He added. "I've spoken to the Marquis de Bonvouloir requesting engineers for our army. He promised to recruit what he could."

Whilst the two gentlemen followed Father into the garden for secret talks, my mother welcomed Johnny Adams and introduced Nancy and me.

"Bonjour, je veux vous presenter mes deux filles aînées."

My mother, Maman, insisted on speaking in French when we were in France, and she never missed a chance to push us forward with any visitor. I felt very grown up to be introduced as one of the older girls, even though I was only four.

"Enchanté, Madame," Johnny Adams replied and gave a courtly bow, European style.

He'd traveled with the two eminent gentlemen, but stood abandoned in the hall, not included in their business. Johnny, at twelve, had completed his studies and traveled far with his father. But there were limits to what access Benjamin Franklin permitted him.

Mr. Franklin had impressed my father with political successes reaped in Paris; Father had previously praised Mr. Franklin at our family suppers. Whatever Mr. Franklin wanted he would get in our house. Apparently Mr. Franklin wanted this Johnny Adams be left indoors with Father's children.

Nancy and I gave Johnny a quick look-over. He wasn't handsome, but he had a decent, rounded chin and slim, long fingers. Nancy's mouth curled, signaling she disliked his clothes. He wore a cut-down version of his father's embroidered silk shirt, brocade vest, satin coat, and tight knee pants. And he had that smell.

Clothes matter to me. Nancy and I wore perfect imitations of Maman's wide pannier skirt with our waists pinched in, thanks to silk sashes. Our flat chests didn't suit the style of her dipping bertha, but Maman had beautiful breasts, and Papa was proud to have her show their tops to advantage as was the style both in London and in Paris. Maman had given birth to four children, but her breasts remained perky and pleasing. She was still nursing the youngest, but the color of her breasts was of a flawless ivory.

Maman also had exquisite posture and a graceful way of gliding along our marble floors as if she were dancing. My posture was a constant problem. The nuns at my convent school complained about it all the time. I truly wanted to stand up straight because my auburn ringlets flew every which way when I curved my back. Posture was no problem for Johnny. He had perfect posture. I didn't like him.

Johnny Adams was so full of himself, showing off his grasp of foreign languages, boasting that he could speak three, and claiming he was proficient in both Latin and Greek. He did have a good Parisian accent in French. I'd been scolded by our convent's nuns because I'd adopted the Nantes harsh "r" and wasn't comfortable with the cut-crystal Parisian vowels.

This Johnny launched into crowing about his latest experience in Paris, where he'd seen the first experiment of the flying globe. I'd heard before how excited the Parisians were who'd seen the balloon and its basket containing a human being.

Johnny commented, "A Mr. Montgolfier has discovered that if one fills a ball with inflammable air—that is, lighter than common air—the ball itself will go up to an immense height. If it succeeds, it could become very useful to mankind."

Maman sensed that Nancy and I were not overwhelmed by Johnny. She led him into our library with us trailing behind. As a mark of favoring him, she switched to English. "I'm told we're to call you Johnny," she began in her warmest tones, "and that you are fond of reading."

Johnny straightened, his lips in a mute encouragement.

Maman persisted, "Would you like to read to us from one of our books?" She handed him a leatherbound copy of Shakespeare's As

You Like It. "In the letter of introduction about you, I learned that you adore the theatre."

At that, Johnny opened his mouth and never shut it again until Maman called a servant to bring croquettes to tide him over until dinner would be served. Always an excellent hostess, Maman guessed that a growing boy would have a healthy appetite and made sure he'd not regret abandoning a reading for food.

Whilst Johnny exchanged the book for a dish of croquettes, I noticed that under a side table there was a plate full of the biscuits Maman had prepared earlier for my spaniel puppy, Blackie. While Blackie had been banished outside the house for the arrival of the visitors from Paris, the dish remained full. Ah! What a chance that gave me for a bit of fun! When Johnny had finished off the dish of croquettes, I replaced it with that plate of dog biscuits.

Johnny ate every one of them.

Maman said nothing. It was always her policy to say nothing about anything that was less than agreeable. Anyway, she knew that her recipe for those biscuits contained good quality flour, fresh butter, and chocolate drops.

The secret talks ended, and we went in to dinner where Johnny proved he hadn't lost his appetite. Over dinner he was encouraged to speak about his studies at Leyden University.

Nancy and I were permitted to join the grown-ups. As an Englishwoman, Maman disapproved of children in formal rooms. She believed in the saying, "Children should be seen but not heard." That day she added, "Children should eat in the nursery."

Father didn't agree. "I like our American ways of gathering a family together at meals. Teach the young ones civilized conversation. And manners."

He didn't address that last remark to Johnny. He should have because Johnny was not only gulping down his food, but he was speaking with his mouth full. If I'd done that at the convent school I later attended, the nuns would have rapped my fingers, or worse, my bottom!

Whilst talking, eating, or boasting this Johnny Adams didn't appeal to me at all. I was relieved when that threesome continued their journey. In our front hall I curtsied properly to all three, but I winked at Nancy when Johnny was eased out the door carrying a basket full of croquettes to feed him on his way, even though Mr. Adams and his son weren't planning to go far.

I was disappointed in Maman. She pushed Nancy forward, urging her to kiss Johnny Adams goodbye. Nancy pretended to lose a shoe and leaned away from him.

I thought, "Oh, Maman, how could you push Nancy on to that unattractive Johnny?"

I dearly loved Maman, Nancy, and my spaniel

Blackie, in that order. Nancy and my spaniel were perfect, but although I placed her at the top of our totem pole, Maman had her odd moments. I could not call her perfect. I believed she gave everyone too much food because she wasn't given enough when she was young. I enjoyed watching our chef follow instructions for her recipes, but I didn't want to have to eat everything she had ordered, unless there was chocolate in the mix.

I did not love Father. I was afraid of him. Maman warned me that I must always obey him or else he might leave us.

It was a relief when the visitors' carriage trundled away and we two girls were allowed to join our little sisters in the nursery. It was such a trial to be put on display at that age. I hated trying to be on good behavior for guests, particularly if they were boys or men. What I really liked was to be with children, playing or being naughty, and that bit of mischief with Johnny had brought me much delight!

I did not mention my ruminations on Johnny from sixteen years ago in my official diary. All I wrote was, "I perfectly remember the elegance of the mansion in which we resided," to describe our Nantes home. Actually, it was practically a castle.

But it has been a relief to come back to England. We returned as soon as the hostilities in America ended. We won our Revolution! My father was subsequently named Consul in London for the United States.

In the 1780s, Johnny's father was Minister to the Court of St. James from the United States. At that time, he and Mrs. Adams often came for dinner to our London home. But latterly they had more important places to dine, in the United States, where Mr. Adams has become its first Vice-President.

Some time earlier Johnny was named Minister Plenipotentiary to Holland, thanks to the intervention of President George Washington. A year later he showed up in London to help ratify the "Jay Treaty." At least, that was his official reason for the trip from the Netherlands, but in fact, the treaty had already been signed by a legation secretary.

Johnny came straight to our home from his ship with the excuse he wanted to have his mail collected here. This time there was no travel-smell about him or from his clothes. I surmise he has learned more about hygiene in Holland, a nation famous for cleanliness. Maman invited him to return for dinner.

London, November 12, 1795

After eating two servings of every course, Johnny stayed on last night to listen to a family concert put on by two of my sisters and me. Nancy, Mary Ann, and I had orders from Father to entertain him with music by Handel. I have become quite proficient on the pianoforte and the harp, but I certainly had no intention of singing for Johnny Adams no matter how much Father prodded! However, it seemed easier to comply rather than to cause a row.

This morning, I again made no mention of Johnny in my official diary. Instead, I continued reminiscences about my school days, which I shall include here as well.

Maman, who retained the French way of naming one's mother, found a boarding school near London where Nancy and I were promptly enrolled. We were permitted to come home on weekends, and it was far less strict than the French convent. But I hated its hideous uniform: brown in winter, green in summer. Brown to hide dirt. Green to blend in stains from the leaves in which we rolled. I recruited a group of students to march in formation on our empty playing fields. I called that group my Amazon Army.

We played pranks on our teachers—innocent ones, like changing salt for sugar in the sugar bowls.

I asked to be addressed as Duchess by my classmates, but the girls complained. One girl accused me of being a snob, which I most certainly wasn't! Some of the girls made fun of the French accents that Nancy and I had acquired. But they used French expressions, too, particularly the naughty words. However, there was no malice towards me, and I left the school in good form with friends I would retain for almost a decade.

Nancy and I were launched into Father's diplomatic circle as soon as we were rid of that hideous school uniform. We danced into the early hours in the ballroom of the London house on Tower Hill Papa had leased. We sat for a portrait artist, who made two very flattering oil paintings. A tutor was hired to teach us to sing and to play several musical instruments. We took cooking lessons too, as future chatelaines who should be able to instruct a chef what to make for parties. And such was the breadth and depth of our schooling.

Since the conclusion of our formal studies, we older sisters have been placed on pedestals by Father, who shows us off with great pride. But there have been no proposals of marriage for Nancy or me as of yet.

London, February 23, 1796

The question of whether or not Nancy and I are to become spinsters has been weighing heavily on our family. Maman has been becoming alarmed that we would end up without husbands. Her eager eyes have been studying the bachelors who come to her extravagant dinners.

Johnny, as the eldest son of the Vice President of the United States, looked a prime "catch." Maman polished up her matchmaking skills. She was quick to point him out as a possible suitor for Nancy, reminding her that she had met him as a six-year-old in Nantes.

Johnny appeared to enjoy Nancy's company. I was left outside their nightly two-some conversation, but I was able to make jokes and speak out very frankly to Johnny. How I wish things had remained that way!

One evening after another of Maman's fabulous dinners, Nancy made a remark to Johnny about his clothes being messy. "Your jacket needs ironing, and so does your cravat." Fury raged in Johnny's eyes, and–having eaten his dinner–he marched out our front door.

Nancy, no fool, had caught him off guard. That evening Johnny had given us a preview of his foul temper.

"Never would I put up with a temper like that," she told me. Never was our favorite word at that time.

I hadn't reckoned on what a perilous situation I was in, now that Nancy felt nothing except disgust for Johnny, because now I was chosen to be the lamb brought to slaughter. That was due to the disastrous financial situation which had befallen my father's monetary affairs. I knew a little about the situation, but I hadn't guessed how terribly that could affect my life. Going from riches to poverty can bring about very horrible changes. Father was temporarily able to disguise his business's collapse. However he wanted one less daughter on his hands, and I was the one to go.

My father, who had been a lucky merchant in London before the Revolutionary War, and again after, was a big spender. He never—yes never!—said "no" to any of Maman's luxurious parties. She could use expensive imported fruits, the finest Jamaican sugar, and aged brandy in her recipes for the delicious treats she served. All eight of us children wore the finest silks in the newest fashions. Our home was open to all the promising young Americans in London, and they swarmed there nightly. Even Johnny Adams remarked on the expensive wines that were served. Perhaps our lives would have continued in that luxurious manner if one of Father's partners hadn't disappeared with company funds. That calamity was slow to surface, and Father used "the quiet before the storm" to rid himself of at least one daughter. Me!

Father's brother, now the first Governor of Maryland, wrote father a letter chiding him for allowing us to be so visibly on the marriage market. "They should take up with proper American men," Governor Johnson had cautioned.

Father paid due attention to his letter, and after Johnny Adams was spurned by Nancy, our Papa pushed Johnny on me. Certainly, he had several reasons for doing so. When I reached twenty-one, I would be four years beyond debutante age. My younger sisters were worried that there would be no dowry money left for them if I didn't marry soon. Mary Ann blurted out during a music lesson, "I'm going to hate you if I don't get a husband!"

I'm a great believer in family harmony. I love reading the novels written by Jane Austin. In particular, I relate to Elizabeth, "Lizzie" in Pride and Prejudice, and to her concerns for her younger sisters. They were five, and we are seven to be married off. Actually, I love all of Jane Austin's books. With such solid wisdom inherent in them, I should never have become engaged to Mr. Adams if I'd heeded her advice—with or without Father's insistence.

When Father dug deep into his nearly-empty pockets to give a ball for my twenty-first birthday, which was held last night, I failed to clue to what he had in mind. After the lavish supper he complimented Johnny on his position as Minister to Holland, rumbled on about how much he admired Johnny's father, and then lowered the boom by firmly placing my right hand on Johnny's arm and shoving us into the parade of engaged couples circling the ballroom. In our part of England, an unmarried girl circling a main room on the arm of a gentleman means you are engaged.

Oh, yes, Johnny had blurted out a hint of what could happen when we'd attended a play at a Drury Lane theater some nights earlier. But, a proposal of marriage? To me? I felt hit by a thunderbolt. I'd believed he was only interested in Nancy, even after her obvious dislike for him. I'd always considered Nancy the pretty one, the talented one, the smart one among the daughters of our family. Me? Me! Me a bride, getting married before Miss Johnson: the eldest sister? And to marry someone I disliked? Whom both Nancy and I disliked!

London, March 20, 1796

Johnny proved not so easy for Father to entrap. He began to backslide like a man fighting an avalanche. Johnny had said before on various occasions that he considered me too forward, too independent. That, from the son of a signer of the Declaration of Independence! Johnny definitely showed signs he'd had "second thoughts."

Maman took the situation in hand and made comment after comment about what an ideal couple we looked. More, she said that Father was thinking about buying a little house for me. When we were in a park and a baby buggy was pushed by a nanny nearby, Maman would coo, "Won't Louisa make a lovely mother?"

Johnny, on the rebound from Nancy's rejection, finally had the "serious talk" with Father, who said he would give five hundred pounds sterling for my dowry.

I knew better than that. What with seven girls to marry off? That could amount to thirty-five hundred by the time he settled all seven of us with husbands. Never!

With Father having financial difficulties, how could he have promised Johnny five hundred? Never. But he did.

Johnny did not "go down on bended knee" to me. He left England.

London, April 17, 1796

From his post in Holland, Johnny sent me a list of books I should read "to improve my mind." That, although months ago he had been heard at dinner to say he did not believe in higher education for women. I am to study those books until we meet again, "which might be in one year or in seven." Good grief, how can I face my school friends, most already married and with children? I have no ring from Johnny—nothing, from him but a series of grumpy letters.

Father insisted I speak up and suggest to Johnny we marry during his next scheduled trip to London. I did, following orders, and Johnny said, "No," very brusquely, without any chance for me to argue for a prompt wedding date. I suppose my asking that outright was an example of what he called my "forward ways." But it wasn't fair for me to get a scolding. That suggestion of an early wedding date had originated with Father, not from me.

God knows I don't want to marry him.

As a Londoner I could hardly escape all the gossip concerning the misery caused to both the Prince and the Princess of Wales because they had been forced into their disastrous marriage. "Prinny's" father, old King George the Third, had wearied of all the scandalous sexual affairs his eldest son had embarked on these past years—first with widowed Mrs. Fitzherbert, then latterly to Lady Jersey and two well-known actresses. "Prinny" had acquiesced to undergo a marriage to Princess Caroline of Brunswick in exchange for having his enormous debts paid off.

The Princess was his first cousin, the daughter of one of King George's sisters She was already a spinster at the age of twenty-six. Princess Caroline had been pushed into the marriage with promises she would have an elevated position and enjoy the luxuries of the British Court.

From their wedding night forward, “Prinnie” and Caroline hated each other. They had rival Courts and sniped at each other viciously, exchanging odious and too-revealing letters that were printed in newspapers to the public’s distress. Even the birth of their child this past January could not keep them together. This story is not one to encourage me to hope for happiness in marriage, and much less in one that would tie me to Johnny Adams.

London, August 14, 1796

On one of Johnny's later trips I felt relieved to believe I would be lucky and left a spinster when I learned that he had hidden from his parents that he had asked me to marry him and that I—at Father's command—had accepted. He had also talked dowry with my father, but said nothing about that to his parents.

His forceful mother—about whom I had heard what a "wonder" she was considered by all those privileged to meet her—had written to him that she was against a match with a woman born and bred in England and partly educated in France. Abigail wrote to him in no uncertain terms, and I am sorry to relate that I saw the letter. Abigail's opinion was clear enough in her words. "I would hope for the love

I bear my country that the Siren is at least half-blood." By half-blood in this context Abigail meant that I was half-American, which indeed I was and am.

London, June 3, 1797

From his post as Minister to The Hague, Johnny wrote to my parents late last year that he had been transferred as Minister to Portugal. Father spent a small fortune on a trousseau for me, all in light lawn cotton, so that I should be able to tolerate the heat in that country. Trunks were packed and ready when Johnny wrote from Holland to announce that he is not going to Portugal. His newer posting is to Prussia, and I know how cold that country could be. I've met merchants who have spent frozen winters in Berlin, its capital.

I am never to use my lovely lawn gowns in Portugal. Never.

In his next letter Johnny finally agreed to marry me when he next arrives in London. It came written in a most frigid style, in no doubt I would submit.

London, July 10, 1797

I have spent a great deal of time fretting over my wedding outfit during the back-and-forth of negotiating for the event itself. I am not to wear a gown or a tiara. Too un-American. Johnny has already informed me that we will be walking together for our marriage to All Hallows Barking on Tower Hill near where I live. Instead of worrying that my outfit will be ruined by not taking a carriage to the church, I should have thought more about the marital bed, though some thinking about it I have done.

Maman, daughter of a mother with twenty-two children and herself the mother of nine, has told me nothing of how babies are made. Yes, she can coo at them all neatly dressed in a carriage, but never has she whispered one word about what will happen inside me in the marital bed to get a baby. She took a more subtle approach instead.

Maman, in her inimitable zest for parties, often organizes picnics, hoping that we girls will learn the facts of life by observing farm animals. During past summers, we would be driven in several carriages to nearby meadows and pretend we were rustics. Not farmers—because we were not dressed as the family of a gentleman farmer would be—but as farmhands' girls, rather in the style that unfortunate Queen Marie Antoinette had adopted, as well as Lady Sarah Lennox when she was trying to catch the eye of King George.

Now that I am twenty-two, I wore one of the useless lawn dresses for this escapade. Usually I was not terribly interested in what clothes I wore for a picnic, but this time I wanted to meld into the landscape. I had a hidden reason; I wanted to use the opportunity of being at a farm to observe the cows with a bull, or if Fortune be with me, a mare being covered by a stallion.

No luck. All I witnessed was a stray dog going at a bitch. He had a very pink thing like a finger that stuck out from his hairy pouch. He thrust that thing into the underside of the bitch. They stayed like that for a while with the male bouncing on top until Father angrily shooed them out of sight of his seven daughters. There was an expression on my brother's face that I had never seen there before. Never. Lewd, and he laughed too loudly. His school friends did the same. What was funny?

I reminisced about the times we'd been alone, trying to relate it to what my wedding day might hold in store. After he arrived from Holland, Johnny never kissed me on the lips. Once, when I tripped over a puppy and twisted my ankle, he pressed his lips to the top of my head to make it appear he was comforting me. But it was less than I would have shown a kitten with an injured paw. That kiss certainly didn't set me on fire or produce any of those vast emotions I read about in the poems over which I panted.

Johnny must feel trapped. He can no longer sail back to his post in Holland. His father, now President, was who had arranged for him to take up the post of Minister to Prussia, with a stopover in London. I am trapped as well. I am yet left to face my former school friends with no wedding ring on my finger and, until he'd arrived, with only a series of cold letters from Johnny giving vague mentions of a future in Berlin. I vacillate between feeling sad or glad.

When there was still no wedding ring on my finger, and before he arrived back in London, Maman wrote to Johnny and demanded he "do the right thing" and marry me.

Johnny wrote again. And again he ordered me to discipline myself, without giving a date for our wedding. I didn't rebel. I am twenty-two and will soon be written off for the marriage stakes. Not that such a future would be any calamity in my mind. But it does mean a great deal to Maman, and she was not to give up on Johnny. Was she beginning to count how many mouths there are to be fed? That with me married, there would be one less? Oh, Maman is very aware that Johnny is the only one of those young American blades who has actually considered marriage to me. I know I could not do better. Not since Johnny's father became President of the United States. I assume the senior Adamses have money, and I will be well cared for.

Johnny eventually complied with my mother's demand and returned to London to give me an opportunity to set a date for our wedding. However, after arriving, like a skittish horse he figuratively reared up and again tried to get out of the nuptials. Maman reined him in! I was prompted to choose a date. I obliged, and the wedding is to take place in two weeks' time.

London and a countryside honeymoon, August 1, 1797

On July 26, 1797, Johnny and I walked to the Tower Bridge Church of All Hallows with my parents and one witness, and I became Mrs. John Quincy Adams. Oh, and I am not to call him Johnny anymore. From then on I am only to address him as Mr. Adams.

My parents took us to view a stately home and then gave a supper in our honor to which they invited Reverend John Hewlett, who had married us. Shortly after that lavish meal, we left in a public stagecoach. We didn't travel alone. We were accompanied on the honeymoon by my personal maid and Mr. Adams' brother, Thomas.

In the terrible, suffocating heat inside that coach, Mr. Adams looked out for a bed-and-breakfast inn where we could put up for the night. I'd made the unfortunate suggestion we should take pot luck and had urged Mr. Adams not to book ahead. Fanning myself, feeling I might become ill or faint from the heat in that airless coach, I, too, stared out at high hedges or plowed fields trying to single out a suitable lodging.

The four of us were crammed in with two other paying passengers. The crowded box rocked worse than a boat in a gale on the Thames River. Finally, when the coach stopped to give the passengers a chance to be refreshed, we settled on the first hostelry we discovered. The place was probably originally designed as a stop for carriages to change horses. It was seedy, flea-infested, and definitely third class.

What happened on the wedding night? Nothing special. We were both exhausted from our long walks to and from the church and then all the toasts at the wedding supper, in addition to the coach drive into the countryside to search for an inn.

There was a great to-do about single or double rooms. Thomas couldn't share a room with my maid.

I felt frightened to be alone with my new husband. As I'd been told to address him as Mr. Adams now that we were married, I took special note of his first words to me in our disgusting little bedroom. All he said was, "You will enjoy the landscapes we pass tomorrow."

Not a good start. Love was not mentioned. He climbed into the poor, tiny bed, mumbled something, and then turned his back to me to go to sleep.

At least he hadn't spoken of the five hundred pounds written into our marriage contract. Father's five hundred pounds sterling had not been produced in time for our very belated wedding, but he'd kept promising it would be forthcoming. I knew that would never happen. I dreaded to think about it and what shame I would have to endure when Mr. Adams realized that those five hundred would never come.

Before sleeping he did mumble about "five hundred something-something," but never came right out with a complaint. I do believe he suspected that the promised five hundred would not appear, so why waste any breath?

Very early the next morning, Mr. Adams was dressed and ready to continue our journey into the countryside. London had been unseasonably hot, so Father had ruled we should travel in the countryside for our honeymoon, to be refreshed in shady forests and glens. What a mistake!

The next public stagecoach we boarded was even more crowded. It carried four passengers in addition to our party, so our maid had to climb up top with the coachman. Again, the heat was oppressive. But this time I had come prepared with my handkerchief soaked in lavender water.

At the first opportunity, Thomas suggested we leave the public transport and rest at a country bed-and-breakfast hostelry. With any luck we could find a hostelry converted from a manor house by people who had fallen on hard times, hoping the fees charged would save their manor's roof by offering hospitality to Londoners.

When next there was a call to change horses, we four left the stagecoach and asked for the nearest upscale bed-and-breakfast. We used a succession of such places for the next empty nights. They were horrible inns.

During those empty nights I lay awake recalling an unpleasant afternoon that doubled my fears of marriage. Maman had been busy overseeing a pre-wedding banquet for us and had sent me to the drawing room to offer a cup of tea to our gossipy neighbor, Lady Johnson. She had full lips that protruded like a frog's. She rarely combed her hair, preferring the old style of slapping on a powdered wig. Hers was usually untidy, needing a wash. On one occasion a tiny mouse had jumped out of that day's wig. On this afternoon she'd brought worse than a mouse to our home. She carried news of yet another marital battle between the Prince and Princess of Wales.

Settling herself in Papa's favorite chair, the red one upholstered in red brocade, Lady Johnson began, "Thank you for the tea, my dear, but never put in milk first. That's what the lower classes do. Well, I hear you're to be married next week. Pity. I hear you've chosen an American, one of those revolutionaries, and that he's taking you from London to Prussia. Awful place, Prussia, so cold. The poor Princess of Wales was born in Brunswick, not far away. She has never adjusted to London. Not even after the Prince of Wales spent so many thousands of pounds having her rooms decorated especially. Never works to marry your first cousin. He loves London, loves Carlton House."

"First cousins," I echoed.

"Yes, my dear. Where have you been that you didn't know that? Pity you don't go to Court or to balls other than the ones in your own house. His father's sister is Princess Caroline's mother. But from the tasteless way she dresses and her ghastly table manners, I'd never have believed her mother was an English princess if I hadn't been presented at Court when we were both girls. Recently I was commanded to go to Windsor and saw the two battlers trying to avoid each other all evening. The Prince of Wales, so dashing in his uniform, which he wears all the time, although unlike his brothers he has never heard a shot fired. The Princess of Wales is getting as fat as her husband. I hear they both adore their little daughter Charlotte, but I wager that since she was conceived there has been no activity in the marital bedroom."

Maman appeared in the drawing room at that moment and pressed a cautionary finger to her lips to silence Lady Johnson.

Lady Johnson, shaking her head to complain that her tea had grown cold, took no notice of Maman's protesting finger. "Tea's grown cold. Hate cold tea. Yes, no action in the marital bed, I repeat. No action, too much action, or dirty action—the result is always a bad marriage."

There was a plate of cookies on the near table, and Maman pushed them on to Lady Johnson, just as I'd pushed dog biscuits on to Johnny all those years ago in Nantes. The gambit had worked then and worked again that afternoon. Lady Johnson stopped gossiping and ate all the biscuits.

After Lady Johnson had left, and I was in my virginal bed, I couldn't help replaying every word she'd said. "No action in the marital bed. No action, too much action, or dirty action," made no sense to me. Surely beds were made to sleep in. From what I'd seen of any action between men and women, the action had been played out on the ballroom floor, or in the card game room, or on the hunting field. What could she have meant? Was I supposed to act like the dogs I had seen?

I felt afraid. The unknown has always frightened me. Beads of perspiration broke out on my forehead and in my armpits as I lay both in my solitary bed and in my torturous nights next to a snoring Mr. Adams, dreading what he might have in mind for me.

In the mornings my maid had searched for my nightdresses for some evidence of a consummated marriage. None! My mother had whispered to me on the morning of my wedding that there was a membrane guarding my private parts which would be broken on penetration. That was the first I'd heard of any penetration. And there was none on those first four nights.

Finally, on our fifth day we came to just such a rundown manor house as Thomas had described. It was there I lost my virginity. We'd struggled up cobblestones to a Cotswold yellowstone manor belonging to a young couple of our age, who were attempting to draw in paying guests. Thomas had carried Mr. Adams' case, while my maid was burdened with her own small bag in addition to my finery. Fragile as she was, the poor girl swung my hatboxes by their straps and the traveling trunk by its top handle, right up the three flights of stairs to the top floor master bedroom.

Mr. Adams downed three glasses of Madeira wine after supper, and hurried upstairs with a gesture that I was to follow. There had been a dainty pianoforte in the manor's hall, and I would have liked to tickle its keys, but from my maid's pleading facial expression I could see that she was hoping to avoid being part of a scene that would surely follow if I didn't obey my husband and go to bed.

She helped me to undress, as usual. I disliked the bare master bedroom, where hard times had compelled its owner to sell all the furniture except the ancient double bed. Mr. Adams was making strange throaty noises out in the corridor. When my maid had braided my hair neatly and I was modestly clothed in a silk nightgown, she left me alone. Mr. Adams strode straight to the bed.

His night robe was ghastly—its style something from the last century. He let it fall to the floor. I saw his flat buttocks that had hair on them. He climbed into the bed and looked at me without a word. The look gave an order, "Come to bed."

No kiss. No sweet compliments. No endearing bits of poetry. I tried not to stare at his naked body. I'd never seen a man naked. I didn't expect there to be an organ outside his body, but there was one and it was upstanding.

There were two mahogany steps to reach the sheets. A dusty, very old damask drapery fell from a coronet against the wall above the headboard, with two curtains reaching to the floor on either side. I wanted to hide in one of the curtains as I used to do in France when I was a little girl. Instead, I lay down on my stomach, remembering the position the dogs had taken that day when I watched them coupling during the picnic.

"If brains make a garden, yours must be a sandy desert," Mr. Adams groaned and pulled my body around so that I was facing him. He placed a hand between my thighs and opened my legs, like a table needing planks. I had never had my legs opened before. Once, when I had gone fishing for salmon I'd had to hop from one rock to another, and that was the only time I'd opened my legs so wide. Oh, oh, I shouldn't refer to my legs as legs; Maman always insists we call them our "limbs."

Without any semblance of affection Mr. Adams thrust that organ between my legs and broke something inside of me, a sharp but not-too-bad pain followed, and then he moved above and inside of me with a rhythm as if he was dancing. I had never expected anything like that. Never.

A grunt from him, and then I felt a spurt of liquid inside of me. He withdrew that organ, turned over on his side and fell asleep.

He snored. I had never expected to hear that noise all night long. Never.

After the awful coupling I lay awake in misery trembling like a frond in a hurricane. Shakily, I wondered what would a lifetime of couplings bring? Misery, forever?

Perhaps I shouldn't have described my wedding night and honeymoon so graphically, but I feel as if I must release the experience, if only to a book my eyes alone will see. To a girl her wedding night is very important. She may have dreamed of it or dreaded it. Whichever, she would certainly have given it considerable thought. In my own case, I hadn't thought enough about the honeymoon nights. I should have! Before July 26, I had spent most time dreaming about what a lovely wedding dress I would get.

Mr. Adams's cold words on our first night of coupling remain engraved on my mind like the legend written in stone on a pylon beside a battlefield. This morning, my maid found the evidence of our coupling on my gown, a bright red stain as shocking as the experience itself.

London, September 7, 1797

Much of the space in my traveling trunk had been taken over by some of Benjamin Franklin's disposable pads for my monthly courses. I was prone to suffer with a flow equal to that of the buckshot wounds for which the pads had been designed, and I didn't want to soil any of the new dresses in my trousseau. Never happened! It will be many months before I will need a sanitary napkin. I was pregnant from that week on following the fifth night after our wedding.

I wrote in my official diary that "hanging and marriage were strongly assimilated." The nightly test some people call "lovemaking" creaked on when we returned to London, where we spend most of our time simply waiting to leave for Prussia. I compare my body to the chamber pot Mr. Adams uses for his urine and excrement, except that I am a pot for that other liquid that he shoots into me.

Thomas, Mr. Adams's younger brother, continually tries to ease my distress. As he had in those dreadful carriage journeys around the steaming countryside, he keeps telling jokes, creating puns, and making me laugh. Thank God for Thomas!

So the days aren't so horrible. And as Thomas, a heavy drinker, stays downstairs with the wine bottles when I go up to the marital bed with Mr. Adams, dear Thomas has little idea what happens there.

Relations with his brother are cordial, but not so close as to permit Thomas to ask Mr. Adams what his experiences were in the marital bed, and Mr. Adams is certainly not one to volunteer the information that his bride is not enthralled with what happened there. I play the part of a contented wife so well that dear Thomas told me in my London hotel room that he'd written to Quincy to relate to his parents what a loving person I've proven to be.

"Dear Louisa, you are a charmer. How I envy my brother!" Thomas trilled one late afternoon, when he was already in his cups after a meal well-fortified with wines. Thomas had come into my bedroom to collect a ticket for the play he was to attend that night with all my family. He acted as affectionate as a puppy but instead of trying to lick me he tried to hug me. I cringed, smiling but firm. No hugs, please. None. That was not acceptable, even though he was my brother-in-law.

I certainly long for affection, but not at the price of one of my husband's horrible temper tantrums. And he would most certainly disapprove of a show of affection from any other man, even if the man is his brother.

Maman quickly guessed that matters are not going well. She tried with her usual gambit to ease the situation by giving more parties in the Tower Hill house to bring cheer into my life.

Father bought tickets to concerts and to operas for us. No help. Gloom is the rule for us.

Before my marriage there were operas considered too-concerned with lovemaking for an unmarried girl to attend, and now I choose to see those above all others. Is there not some way I can learn to enjoy "lovemaking" since so much poetry and so many novels describe it as "rapture?"

Hell was what I consider it.

London, September 18, 1797

The so incorrectly termed "lovemaking" has continued without any show of affection. Still, no "I love you" nor even "You are very pretty" or "I like your nightgown." Why? Is there some part of me missing? Is that the reason for no words of endearment? Or even a tender look?

Did I lose my innocence that one evening in the park when my adored first admirer caressed me so deliciously? Does Mr. Adams know that I was the object of another American's ardor? That he was a respectable member of my father's consulate corps? And that he called me "wife!" and seemed very eager to marry me? But nothing more came of that first admirer's protestations of love. Oh yes! He said he loved me!

Then one day my admirer left England, went across the Atlantic, back to the United States to another job. Did he become privy to information concerning my father's coming bankruptcy? Or was he present when one of Father's creditors accused him of juggling the bills of lading of some of the shipments from the United States? The man shouted out that tobacco had been priced at a higher cost when reaching London than when it left American docks, which was tantamount to accusing my father of pocketing the difference!

Or did he merely get what he had desired from me and was satiated?

When he left, I felt as miserable as when all my hair was shaved from my head after I caught typhoid at seventeen. No, I felt worse. When my head was shaved, I knew my hair would grow back.

I can't have done anything too seriously wrong with him because I didn't get pregnant. One of my school friends told me a girl can get pregnant by kissing a boy. But I didn't, although I have kissed several.

Or was Mr. Adams' total lack of any show of affection due to my terrible secret? I have a disgrace buried in my family's past, which may have destroyed any love he might have felt for me when we were courting in London. I torture myself with fear he knows the secret and that it is what keeps him from putting love into lovemaking.

Sometimes I long to speak the words aloud. I am illegitimate. I was born a bastard. I was born out of wedlock. Certainly, the specter of illegitimacy, though unspoken, haunted me every night of those "honeymoon" ordeals. But no one speaks of such things. "Illegitimate" is one word never heard in my parents' house. Never. But I know both my mother and grandmother were born illegitimate too.

Father has never invited my grandmother, Miss Mary Young, to be part of our family. My grandmother, Miss Mary Young, never married although she bore Mr. Nust twenty-two children. She sent most of them to an orphanage because Mr. Nust objected to their puking and squalling. Mean, he didn't want to spend money on food or clothes for any of his children he kept in his house.

Maman was not sent to an orphanage because she has such a lovable personality. Father met her when she was fifteen. Nancy was born that same year. I came along two years later, followed by a sister who died in France, and my four younger sisters. When Maman believed she was expecting a son, Father married her, with my five sisters and me attending the wedding.

Mr. Adams knows nothing of this. The family secret has been carefully guarded. But a few days ago, merely six weeks after our honeymoon ended and we returned to Mr. Adams' room at London's Osborne Hotel, I endured a terrible scene which threatened to reveal my secret.

Father became old and ill-looking during the time we spent on our so-misnamed honeymoon. One of his ships vanished coming to England from the East Indies. Pirates? A typhoon? No vestige of that ship has been found. Almost simultaneously Father's consignment of four hundred and twenty-nine pipes of French brandy was smashed up on Guernsey's rocks when another of his ships came to grief in a storm between France and Southampton. Father resolved to escape to America before he could end up with no credit.

On the same day that Father and Maman took my six sisters and my brother to abscond to America, a surge—like a tidal wave—of his creditors appeared at the Osborne Hotel. All of them demanded Mr. Adams pay them what my father owed. Of course, Mr. Adams did no such thing. Why should he? My father's debts were my father's.

These creditors hurled horrible insults and accusations.

I took refuge in the hotel's smoking room, because I imagined that no one would think of looking for a lady there. Our old servant Chivers did. He knew my ways and guessed exactly where I would go. He faced me down, claiming quite rightly that he had not been paid his wages for the past three months and he, in his turn, would be thrown into debtors prison because he had not paid his shoemaker or laundress. His usually ingratiating expression had turned into a shark's hateful, hungry, toothy sneer.

"Mrs. Adams," he hissed, "I know all your family's secrets because I have been with the Johnsons for thirteen years. I was present in 1785 when your father finally married your mother, holding their latest babe with you standing next to him, all of nine years old. Two of your sisters, Miss Nancy and Miss Mary Ann, eleven and six, must remember it well. I am sure you do. Sure, and I know your father had the six born before 1785 inscribed as legitimate on their baptismal certificates. Four of you at St. Botolph without Aldgate. Two in Nantes, when we were all in France. Your mother calling herself Dame Catherine Nuth on one, and Catherine Young on the others. She was illegitimate. None of you early ones were legitimate. Bastards, the mother, the grandmother, and all of you first six children. Only the last two weren't bastards."

I went pale, as if a vampire had sucked all the blood from my face. Of course I remember every aspect of my parents' embarrassing wedding ceremony. It was quick and untidy with the baby shrieking and puking, but the worst for me was when I read brass plaques in the wall that stated there were parishioners buried in the churchyard who had died of the Plague. All their names were listed. I had read Samuel Pepys' diary and knew about the Bubonic Plague, and I felt terrified that, even though more than a century had elapsed, I could still contract the Plague there. My memory of that day is of horror.

"I want my guineas," Chivers spat out.

Chivers' words were instruments of torture as bad as any the Spanish Inquisition had used. But like some of the Spanish nobles, I bought my way out, giving in to his blackmailing scheme by offering him my jewelry. I stripped off the diamond rings my parents had given me, keeping only the plain gold circlet that was from Mr. Adams. For my wedding gift, my grandmother had sent a brooch with emeralds, and I unpinned that from my silk jacket's left breast to surrender it to Chivers.

In the end, Chivers scuttled away like a cockroach. But will he try to wring more valuables out of Mr. Adams by hinting at what he knows?

I followed Chivers to where the other creditors were still banging on our bedroom door. Mr. Adams opened it slightly to permit me to enter, and the bottom of that space was quickly filled by Chivers's foot.

"I want my guineas," he repeated to Mr. Adams, but without the horrible prelude about my illegitimacy.

Coldly, in the stern tones of a disciplinarian, Mr. Adams refused to give him any money. "Chivers, you were employed by Consul Johnson, not by me. You will have to collect what is owed to you from him."

Without another word Mr. Adams pushed shut our door, forcing Chivers to pull away his foot or have it crushed.

I haven't learned whether or not Chivers managed later to push his way again through the clamoring creditors to reveal my secret and offer to keep quiet about my illegitimacy in exchange for currency or more jewelry. Did he?

Berlin, November 28, 1798

During the intervening weeks before our ship was due to take us to Prussia, I caught looks from Mr. Adams that caused my heart to tremble, fearful that he knew my secret and would cast me aside.

Because my parents left England for America, and my grandmother Miss Young recently passed on, there was nobody remaining in England who would take me in!

Stories appeared in newspapers claiming that I had been privy to my father's insolvency, and that together—father and daughter—we had schemed to entrap the son of the American President to pay the Johnson family debts.

Mr. Adams certainly wore a very dour expression for our final days in London. He was so overwrought that we arrived too late at the dock to catch our ship before it sailed for Prussia, and he had to pay extra for a skiff to ferry us out to it to catch up. We did. The ship had anchored for the night, before attempting the Channel crossing and the Baltic Sea.

Pay extra! His most hated expression. It always brought out more sour looks from Mr. Adams, like a head cold ends in a coughing spell. I was learning how much he hated spending any money that he hadn't budgeted for.

Pregnant, I was ill all the way to Prussia. Our ship had a normal crossing; I was not seasick. I was ill because I was pregnant. Mr. Adams didn't show any emotion over my news of a baby on the way. No doubt he'd expected me to start a family immediately.

From our ship we transferred to a coach for the long, bumpy road to Berlin. I was ill in the coach, too, even though I'd learned, how much Mr. Adams detested the stink of bile. There was nothing I could do to stop the vomiting.

Berlin was quite a revelation. It was no London—not as beautiful, but it certainly had a grandeur of its own. I particularly enjoyed the drive under its famous Linden trees.

There were several outstanding palaces belonging to royal princes and imposing boulevards with graceful parks leading to them. But we didn't go to live in any lovely building with a park. Mr. Adams chose a cheap lodging to stay within budget.

The hotel was disgusting. Cramped, with tiny rooms, it had an unpleasant smell of boiling cabbage that lingered even at breakfast time. That provoked more illness in me.

The food was awful. It came as part of the price of the rooms we took—sausages that smelled rancid, boiled potatoes with no flavor, and knockwurst. I couldn't keep any of it down.

I am very much looking forward to my stomach and ourselves being more permanently settled.

Berlin, March 4, 1798

Within six weeks of arrival in Prussia, I had a miscarriage. Another six weeks, after only one menstrual period, and I was pregnant again. Obviously, Mr. Adams believes he should fulfill a marital duty, or else he gets some pleasure from sexual intercourse and thinks that as he has a wife, he might as well use her.

There are fine jewelry shops and ready-to-wear clothing emporiums in Berlin. Mr. Adams never takes me to buy anything. Never. But there are other pleasures I have found for myself here.

Mr. Adams had to present his diplomatic credentials promptly, and did so on December 5. The old king had died, and young King Frederick wanted to show that he was instituting a modern reign by a speedy acceptance of the new envoy from America. Summoned to Court, Mr. Adams ordered me to accompany him as far as the outside corridor to the throne room. By a miracle I didn't become ill there. Shifting feet and sending embarrassed glances at the foot guards on duty, I failed to notice the arrival of a young mother surrounded by sleepy children. One of the little boys slipped on the polished floor. I bent to pick him up, and the woman immediately took a fancy to me. The woman was Queen Luise!

One year younger than I, she had already given King Frederick two healthy babes and one stillborn with yet another on the way. She gave me a huge grin, as if we were girls together going to a ball, and invited me to follow her into a delicately furnished room beyond the hall. She spoke to me in German, and when I shook my head all smiles, she switched to a fine Parisian French and invited me to sit down opposite her at a whist table. Instant friendship!

We giggled, and from her pocket she gave me a wet piece of chocolate that could have been lathered with a child's spit. Somehow I managed to swallow that without feeling queasy.

The children were carried off to bed; the cards for whist appeared. She inquired with arched eyebrows if I was familiar with this card game. When I nodded encouragingly, she dealt from a pack of new cards, and we began to play. She is a far better whist player than I am, but I managed to hold my own.

When Mr. Adams re-appeared from the throne room, he seemed astonished at the sight of his insignificant wife playing cards with the Queen. He had to use all his diplomatic skill to control a temper tantrum. When Her Majesty suggested he return alone to our hotel, offering to send me there later in the royal carriage, he sputtered like a tea kettle ready to boil.

The Queen and I became and are yet fast friends. After all, we do have the same name. I called her "Luise," not "Votre Majeste" nor "Reine Luise," and she gives me an extra smile every time I do.

For weeks that have stretched into months I continue to play whist with Queen Luise. Apparently she enjoys beating me at cards, even though she knows in advance I am the less talented whist player.

I have been elevated to a favored position at Court, and when I finally had a miscarriage that cost me a great loss of blood, the dear Queen insisted on sending me her own personal physician. The person who gave me lovely gifts was the Queen, not Mr. Adams. Both the King and Queen felt sad for me that I had miscarried in their capital. Although it was in the depths of winter, I received gifts of fruit and sweetmeats. I liked best the apples that must have been kept in storage and the cherry-filled chocolates. Wonderful!

And, while I have to address my husband as Mr. Adams, the King said I should call him "Freddy." His Majesty's Court has also noticed that I am in favor. I have become popular, and with Mr. Adams, I am often invited to many private homes outside the diplomatic circle.

Berlin, September 17, 1799

I've lost weight. Mr. Adams scolds me, complaining I choose to wear ridiculous dresses that are cut too high under the bust, accentuating my fallen stomach. We argue about my shoes too. He declares their pointed toes will cramp my feet and I won't be able to take long walks with him. When does he invite me to do that?

Our worst domestic battle erupted this past summer because Queen Luise sent over a pot of rouge to help me look less pale. Rouge is all the fashion at her Court. The next time we were invited to a ball at the royal palace I applied the rouge to my sunken cheeks.

I should never have done that. Never.

Mr. Adams burst into the most awful rage. He went into the washroom, got a cloth, wet it with cold water, returned to where I was seated on our horrible marital bed, and proceeded to scrub my cheeks raw to remove all the offending rouge. After that, I was obliged to accompany him to the royal palace as if we were on the best of terms. Diplomatically, I managed. At least my cheeks were fashionably red from all that scrubbing.

Perhaps, Mr. Adams felt remorse for flying into a temper. Days later he invited me to hear a concert featuring a new symphony by Ludwig von Beethoven. It was glorious. I adored the music and bought a harp to practice learning the theme. It was inspired by a Schiller poem, and I love poetry, but it was the music that had calmed tremulous fears for my sanity.

I know Mr. Adams secretly burns with shame for having such a towering temper. I watch when he tries to control it in front of a fellow diplomat or a visitor from America. He usually manages, and then takes out his furies on me.

Unthinking, I applied rouge again for the first party I would attend with Mr. Adams after my lying-in. I did not want to look a fright amidst that splendor. Mr. Adams followed that simple act with another volcanic outburst. He shouted at me to remove the rouge myself. I refused. So Mr. Adams left me in our miserable marital bed while he went alone to the party.

Did I suffer this time? Never! I found the cache where we stored our savings. I put on the dress Mr. Adams had ordered I discard, called for another carriage, gave directions to the coachman for the principal concert hall, bought a ticket at the door, and enjoyed the most glorious evening listening to Handel's music. This was a sublime performance of the Messiah. My earlier distress was cured by those ringing repetitions of "Alleluia, Alleluia," accenting its fabulous mix of choral and instrument sounds.

I resolve that in future I will do as I please, wear rouge if I like, and go to concerts alone. I am going to be daring. I will never submit to bullying again. Never!

Berlin, April 2, 1801

These past two years have been a whirlwind of social engagements and attempts at starting a family with Mr. Adams. And while I should have reveled in my ascendancy into high society, I could not. This is a society where the culture accepts lascivious behavior. Many of the nobles have illegitimate children. The ladies of the court take lovers openly, dancing with them at the royal balls. All the talk is how few of the great families can be sure that the heirs to titles were actually the sons of the husbands of certain ladies who took lovers indiscriminately. A Saxe-Coburg wife was said to be sleeping with her husband's Jewish tailor.

With all that gossip about who is legitimate and who is not, I constantly wonder: Can my own secret be kept under wraps? And when Mr. Adams treats me so coldly, is it because he was told my secret by Chivers?

Sleep evades me. Night after night I lie awake worrying. Mr. Adams scolds me even for my sleeplessness.

He complains it keeps him from a good night's rest.

What does he not complain about? He complains about every little thing!

With all my worry, is it any wonder I have had three additional miscarriages? Each time, when the gushes of blood ended a pregnancy, Queen Luise sent her personal doctor and servants to inquire about my health.

At last, I am close to bringing a pregnancy full term. If

God favors me, I will soon final y bear Mr. Adams a child.

Berlin, April 17, 1801

On April 12, after Mr. Adams had recorded in his diary about the days of excruciating pains I had to endure, I delivered a son. When I was well enough to take a peek into his diary, I saw that Mr. Adams has big plans for our little tyke.

For instance, when we went to the British Embassy for his baptism. Mr. Adams declared to Lord and Lady Carysfort that our son must be christened George Washington. Why? Oh, he gave a "diplomatic" reason. But the truth is: He intends to suck up more to see what else he can wrest from that great gentleman who is our ex-President. It wasn't enough his having initiated Mr. Adams's diplomatic career by having given him the post of Minister to Holland?

I also worried that Mr. Adams' father might find it offensive that the baby hadn't been named for him.

I was not permitted to suggest a name—certainly not my father's since he's become a bankrupt, fleeing back to Maryland to scrounge a living.

Not a little thing—not at all—is the way Mr. Adams harps on how we must discipline our child. That tiny bundle, so vulnerable in his cradle, has already caused Mr. Adams to write out plans for his behavior and education.

There were not many gifts forthcoming from Mr. Adams for the poor little dear. I barely manage on the pittance Mr. Adams gives me to buy cloth for his clothes and diapers. Our babe's crib is second-hand. His blanket was a gift from the English Ambassador's wife.

Mr. Adams furthers his own agenda. He works hard at agreements to use the Prussian ports for America's merchant ships. He gives constant reports to the State Department about the rise of Napoleon Bonaparte. He also goes frequently to the "Casino," which is a center for literary discussions and a repository of the latest newspapers and magazines.

To his mother he not only sent news of his firstborn's arrival, he recorded stirrings of love for me. "It will, I am very sure, give you pleasure when I assure you that I find her more deserving of my affection, I will not indulge myself in the pyrogenics which my inclination dictates."

Queen Luise showered my little George with exquisite gifts. Beautiful ones like Dresden porcelain monkeys, but not the practical ones I need so badly.

We still converse in French. She has that marvelous Parisian accent, while I am stuck with my provincial Nantes vowels. Never mind. I am learning to speak German. And quite well!

When I was presented at Court, Queen Luise was having a pastel sketch made by Madame Vigee Le Brun. This talented woman—such a great portraitist of the French royal family—had somehow managed to escape the hordes of revolutionaries. They guillotined her main patrons, Queen Marie Antoinette and King Louis XVI, but Madame Vigee Le Brun arrived safely in Berlin to shimmer like a star.

Her portraits are an immense success. The one she made of Queen Luise is an absolute delight. The King adores it!

Berlin, May 5, 1801

Mr. Adams is out of a job! His father, who has lost his bid for re-election to a Second Term as President of the United States having been defeated by Thomas Jefferson, has made it a point to end his dear son Johnny's absence from Abigail's side.

She wrote he was needed at home for, "His light will shine before men."

Mr. Adams had to present his letters of recall to King Frederick at Potsdam today. Queen Luise pronounced she was devastated at losing her special companion, but showered me with more lovely gifts.

This has all happened so fast! With me feeling in robust good health, Mr. Adams had decided we could give a large dinner party for the many friends we had found in Prussia. However, if Mr. Adams spent the money for a party assuming we would be around for plenty of return invitations, things did not turn out as he had imagined. Instead, on April 26, he received the news he had been recalled to Washington. We have had to decline any and all invitations while we prepare to cross the Atlantic.

All the valuable gifts that the King and Queen sent to my baby are not to go with us. I have already begun parceling out many lovely Meissen porcelains to Berlin friends when Mr. Adams ordered me to leave them behind because they are too frivolous for the Massachusetts house to which we are headed.

Berlin, June 5, 1801

All my outings in Berlin have not been uplifting.

I lost what innocence remained to me here in this city. In some ways, I shall be glad to quit it.

My first shock took place in the very elegant and tastefully furnished rooms of the Dowager Empress, where I'd been included in the invitation she sent to Mr. Adams. What a contrast those exquisite rooms offered to the disgusting "tavern" where we started our diplomatic mission! We took a common hired carriage to the great portal marking the Dowager's Empress's imperial residence. Ushered in by a trio of liveried footmen, we were offered gilded French armchairs dating from the time of Louis the Fourteenth, upholstered in cut velvet. That upholstery seemed too warm for this hot June temperature. Whilst waiting, I smiled at one of the footmen, but Mr. Adams cracked an elbow at me to remonstrate, his frown signaling he considered that I was demeaning him because the footman could construe my smile as a bid for a flirtation. Good heavens, where does Mr. Adams dream up such ideas?

When the Dowager Empress entered this ornate sitting room, we stood. Mr. Adams made the Court bow, and I curtsied correctly. At that point all that was worrying me grew from my breasts beginning to fill with milk as I was approaching the hour to nurse baby George. I was nervous because only the day before during another outing, I soiled my gown when milk spurted from both nipples. We shared the waiting room with a very flamboyant lady, dressed in rows of costly lace with ostrich feathers in her hair, although we were not waiting to enter a ballroom, but simply share the tea hour.

The Dowager Empress entered all smiles. She embraced me, and again I felt terrified that milk would spill out. She also embraced the flamboyant lady.

We conversed in French. Both the Dowager Empress and her other guest were not particularly fluent in that language. When the flamboyant lady took her leave, almost tearing her laces with an overly extravagant curtsey, the Dowager Empress surprised us by switching to passable English.

"Yah, dat vas de famous Madame de Harburg. Very pretty, you t'ink?

Diplomatically Mr. Adams smothered a sneer and repeated: "Very pretty."

"Yah, very pretty, nein? Very clever too, she separate from husband. She has very handsome lover, Herr Graves. Yah, I very happy she and Herr Graves so well together. Yah, I hope their liaison will last."

On this comment Mr. Adams signaled it was time for us, too, to take our leave. We hadn't advised an early departure to her lady-in-waiting and had to wait until the Dowager Empress—put out that we hadn't praised Mme. de Harberg—stood up in a forbidding manner and signaled our audience had terminated.

Mr. Adams kept on with his frowns all the way to our lodgings. I said nothing more. I hate playing the hypocrite. In my own way, I admire Mme. de Harberg's independence. But then, there is such a spectrum of behavior here.

Due to my amazing popularity, I've met a polyglot assortment of people at Court. Being fluent in the French language has helped me there because most of the people I meet speak it, and I have easily picked up basic German. Mr. Adams's command of the German language is on a different level. He has translated Schiller and other great Germans' works. Mr. Adams delights in showing of his expertise in its finer points. To hone his speaking ability, he constantly goes to see plays. One night he announced he would go alone to the theater because the play's story was too of -color for a nursing mother.

No sooner had he left than a luxurious carriage came to our door and disgorged a ribald Countess with whom I have recently become acquainted.

She insisted I go with her to meet a certain Princess X, said to be most amusing. "She has been exiled from her own Court due to being very naughty. But I hear her levees are fun. You must come see," the Countess whispered. Feeling rebellious,

I called for my cloak and climbed into the Countess's superior carriage.

Princess X turned out to be far beyond "naughty." Her Highness should be termed Her Lowness. She lived in a huge palace, hung with portraits of licentious scenes. There were three halls, strung like the diamonds on a lavaliere. As we entered the first, we were pressed to enjoy the contents of a lavish display of sweetmeats. I deferred, thinking there could be something in them injurious to my health. Opium in the croquettes? I did accept a flute of pink champagne.

After being presented to Princess X, the Countess and I were given seats in throne-like chairs. A roll of drums and a trumpet's blast announced the entertainment in this hall. It consisted of a rather disgusting show put on by a male monkey coupling with a cat in heat. From that hall we progressed to the next, where again a roll of drums and a trumpet prepared us for an act. This one starred a naked man with a large member. When a naked woman joined him, his manhood became erect, and he was able to position three flutes of champagne on his organ and then proceeded to walk amongst us. In the third hall the show was beyond anything I could have imagined. Once more a roll of drums and a trumpet's call sounded, but could not have prepared me for what followed. An oriental man and woman proceeded to couple on the floor in various positions.

I thought I would be ill, so I had to ask the Countess to call for her carriage. We two left together, both of us pale and speechless. The ribald Countess enjoys a naughty joke, but not what we witnessed this night.

When Mr. Adams returned from his evening at the so-called lascivious play I was seated demurely next to baby George's empty crib, nursing the child. Mr. Adams smiled curtly, and said, "You would not have enjoyed this evening's drama work. It was in poor taste. I did not understand most of the dialogue; it did not make sense. I should have left the theater;

I did not as the ticket had been costly. What went on up on the stage was unacceptable for a man with Massachusetts morals. I am surprised at what King Frederick permits in this country. In future I will inquire in advance as to the subject of any entertainment—certainly, before I consider taking you to a play."

As he turned on his worn heels to go to bed, I thought, "What a temper tantrum he would blaze out should I be so stupid as to describe any part of what I had seen this evening!"

I resolve two things: I will be circumspect in what I told Mr. Adams, and I will also pick my entertainments carefully. But I will speak out when I so choose, and I will go out as I so choose.

My new resolutions were terminated abruptly when Mr. Adams announced we might be taking ship for the United States. He gave a series of orders which I was obliged to obey. What with three miscarriages and the recent agonizing birth pains I had suffered, I was not in peak condition to travel. But to travel on cue was one of the rules to which I had agreed when Mr. Adams finally made his offer of marriage.

On the AMERICA, August 12, 1801

One month we have been on these rolling waters, and still nearly a month left for our transit remains. Berlin seems so long ago.

I had my little George Washington Adams vaccinated against small pox, which I have heard is a raging plague in the United States. We packed up what we could take with us, and again subjected ourselves to bumping along the Prussian roads. Reaching Hamburg on June 21, we looked for the AMERICA, the ship scheduled to bring us to Philadelphia. It was firmly docked, and its Captain Wells had no intention of sailing before July 12. We consoled each other over the loss of all the lovely parties to which we had been invited between the last days of June and early July, but had forgone in vain.

In addition to another miscarriage on board, and being immensely seasick, I have suffered emotionally from learning a secret which Mr. Adams has kept from me to now. On the one fine afternoon when I was able to stand beside him on the AMERICA's deck, Mr. Adams told me his secret.

What I had not known was the fact that he was earlier deeply in love with a beautiful girl from Braintree in Massachusetts—well-bred and from a prominent local family. Her name is Mary Frazier. She reciprocated fully, declaring her love for him. He dreamed of having her for his wife and gave her the idea that once he was established as a lawyer, they could be married. But his mother, Abigail, and Mary's parents had conspired to thwart their plans. Mary Frazier bowed to her parents' wishes, and Mr. Adams obeyed his mother.

Again I peeked into his diary. Mr. Adams had written to his mother on the subject of Mary Frazier one week before he became reacquainted with me, complaining he had relinquished "an ardent affection" to the shrine of "the world's prudence," claiming he "suffered a widowed heart," and that "his love had been torn from him through voluntary violence." And that was not all! He wrote on that should he ever find another lover, it would be romance kindled by spontaneity, not from "the will."

GOODNESS GRACIOUS! Mr. Adams must have suspected that his mother planned to push him into an arranged marriage. He warned her that in novels such marriages required "a pistol" and that he would be "five and forty" before he would enter into a "marriage of convenience." Oh, my! And Mr. Adams was only twenty-eight years old when he wrote that letter to his mother!

Already extremely nervous at the prospect of meeting former President and Abigail Adams, the news that John Quincy was once in love and that his love had been snuffed out by his parents, I have become subject to shivering attacks. I fear his secret's sad ending bodes ill for my own appearance in their family.

Philadelphia, September 7, 1801

After my first long crossing of the stormy Atlantic, I had my first cultural shock when arriving in Philadelphia at the sleazy dock where our ship finally docked on September 3.

"Oh my, Mr. Adams!" I had exclaimed, whilst viewing rats scurrying unhindered on the neighboring docks. I stared, very disappointed at the unswept streets beyond. I had expected to see a real city, with proper boulevards and parks. Philadelphia fell short in that respect in my opinion as a Londoner.

Have I really arrived in that much-vaunted America? It doesn't look at all like I assumed it would. In Father's Tower Hill house, there had been sketches of famous houses in America: Mr. Jefferson's, and Mr. Washington's. I thought there would be numerous plantations with many-pillared homes. In the cities, I had expected imposing buildings of great taste.

I have since learned that Philadelphia has no more than ten lamplighters and only two men to call out the hours. Most of its touted grandeur is to be found only in the streets near the Liberty Bell. I always enjoyed London's "Tis five o'clock, and all is well!" that was called outside my father's Tower Hill home in time for the main meal of each day. There are too few such refinements here! Philadelphia lost its position as the capital of America when the President's House, the Congress, and all foreign embassies were moved to Washington D.C. It has since been in decline.

The voyage took fifty-eight days so now we are in summer. Mosquitoes dive at us like kites in heavy winds. But I am to find some measure of happiness in being reunited with my parents and sisters during a two months' stay with them, surprisingly permitted by Mr. Adams. He will leave me with them in Washington D.C., while he goes ahead to Quincy, to see his parents.

Mr. Adams was recalled to America with the excuse that his father, now no longer President, did not want him away from the United States now there was a new administration coming to the capital. At least, that's what he told me, failing to mention the fact that his mother wanted him back. I bowed to whatever reason he decided to give because what else could I do? Where could I go? My parents have left Maryland for Washington D.C., with my sisters, and I know they cannot afford to offer a roof to a divorced daughter, with or without an infant. My brother has enrolled at Harvard, and his fees there are a burden. I cannot write for help to my school friends, some of whom have four children or more and are struggling to make ends meet.

I am at the mercy of Mr. Adams' good will, and that is fickle at best.

Washington, D.C., October 31, 1801

The memory I have of elegance in 1801 will always be due to our forthcoming two-day visit to the widow of George Washington, Martha Custis Washington. Mr. Adams and I are invited to stay with her at Mount Vernon when he returns to collect me and baby George before the trip to Quincy.

Mr. Adams is NOT going to miss out on being a guest of Martha Washington's! His earnest desire to meet with her has me feeling anxious. Will I be sick at Martha Washington's? Oh, I do want to make a good impression on her! I was seasick on the voyage to Philadelphia. I know the smell of vomit displeased Mr. Adams. I wasn't able to do anything about that.

I became seasick. I became ill when I was pregnant. I'd been unable to hold down food from both on route to America. I lost another baby on the voyage. Lost, meaning I had another miscarriage. I cannot be suffering from pregnancy quite yet, because Mr. Adams went to Quincy without me. I wasn't pregnant, just nervous, but my anxiety was strong enough to make me fear similar results as morning sickness.

Mr. Adams has put of our trip to Quincy for two months, but it wasn't my fault we've postponed the visit to Martha Washington. Mr. Adams lengthened his reunion with the ex-President and Abigail, whilst I remained with my parents in their cramped little rooms near Washington, D.C. Mr. Adams had bolted for his family home, which suited me very well. I didn't want any more thrusting where I was still so sore from my recent miscarriage, and I didn't want another pregnancy either. What I did want desperately was to spend time with my own parents, my sisters remaining at home, and my dear brother. That last didn't happen due to his enrollment at university.

Father's situation is terrible. He has been pushed out of his partnership due to allegations that he harmed its name. That is totally unfair! Father MADE money for the partnership, thanks to his knowledge of France's incredible changes! For instance, he recognized that a bellicose new leader like Napoleon Bonaparte would alter the probability—or even the possibility—of importing French wine and had suggested switching to Portugal's Madeira wines. Didn't he give the example in our own London home of serving Madeiras at our dinners? All to no avail. It has been only thanks to the kind old gentleman, John Adams, while he was still U.S. President, that Father was given the position of Postmaster for the District of Columbia with a salary of $2,500 a year.

Maman has faced an enormous struggle to marry off my sisters. In their unfashionable Frenchstyle dresses—now very worn—our mother still managed to find husbands among our relations for Nancy and Mary Ann. For twenty-four-year-old Nancy, she angled for wealthy Walter Hellen, who owned a large house on the outskirts of Washington, D.C. But for unlucky Mary Ann, Maman was only able to get a struggling dreamer who whisked Mary Ann to the Middle West to make his fortune there and saddled her with squabbling children in semi-poverty. No fortune made in the Middle West! Mary Ann has always been unlucky. Nancy and I were given proper schooling until I was fourteen, when Father's crumbling business no longer permitted him to pay our school fees. There was a gap of four years between Mary Ann and me because Maman had given birth to another daughter in Nantes, who died there as an infant. Then Mary Ann had come along. So Mary Ann had little schooling. She was even too young to have enjoyed the lavish dinner parties and socializing in which we participated during our years in Maman's London house.

None of that marred my happiness when I had the utter joy of hugging my sisters and parents in Washington, D.C. Even my shy brother, before he left to continue his studies at Harvard, allowed me to kiss him.

My son, George, was cuddled and made much of in the boisterous way in which all of us had always reacted on the appearance of a new member of the family.

Oh, how I have dreaded the termination of my two months with my Johnsons! But letters from Mr. Adams demand that I prepare to travel to Quincy. Meanwhile we've received the letter from Mrs. George Washington reminding us she is expecting us at Mount Vernon for a visit. It means another few hours in a rumbling coach, but I look forward to the trip.

Mr. Adams wrote that he would return shortly from Quincy to collect me and little George.

That is what he wrote, but it was not what he did. First, Mr. Adams remained with literary friends in Philadelphia, and with his sister, Nabby, in New York. Then he returned to Quincy on September 21 for another reunion with his parents and extended family. There, while I sojourned with my parents in Washington, D.C., he changed as surely as do the colors of a kaleidoscope.

After many evenings exchanging ideas with his many relations, Mr. Adams has decided to pursue a career as a lawyer in Boston. For that purpose he paid out $6,000 of our desperately-earned savings for a house that had belonged to a bankrupt cousin, Dr. Thomas Welsh.

But, by October 14, Mr. Adams had embarked from Quincy for Washington D.C., intent to deliver me up to the excruciating test of meeting his parents as soon as we had completed the visit to Mrs. George Washington. One surprising letter came from him for me before he arrived himself, He wrote he could hardly wait to be in the "arms of my beloved."

Beloved! Really? And would that mean yet another pregnancy?

By October 21, when I'd moved to the luxurious home belonging to my brother-in-law, Walter Hellen, I was back in bed with Mr. Adams. And there was a great deal of thrusting, for half the night. I ended feeling as soiled as a toilet cloth.

We didn't leave the Hellens in a hurry. Mr. Adams spent two weeks claiming expenses from the State department for his work abroad. Not easy to squeeze money out of the State Department! However, with winter only weeks away, Mr. Adams resolved we should prepare for the overland journey to Quincy, as soon as the visit to the home of George Washington's widow, Mount Vernon, was over. And at last, that happy journey is upon us!

Mount Vernon, November 2, 1801

Mr. Adams hired a carriage, and we set out from Washington, D.C. on a bright but cold day promising a hard winter. There were no birds singing in the trees, although I did see a few flocks whirling to practice for a Southland trip, like children warming up for a game.

Our arrival at stately Mount Vernon was propitious: Mrs. Washington was waiting for us on an impressively-long veranda, wearing a cordial smile. Martha is sixty-nine, a tiny woman under five feet tall, but dressed in a gown of finest silk in the latest fashion.

Her home was of classical proportions, crowned by a handsome Athenian pediment. Nearby there was an acre of rich land laid out for a kitchen garden and a fruit garden. Both of these combined to form the shape of a boat. Inside this "boat" were the sculptured plots for the various vegetables and fruit plants, all arranged as formally as if they were part of the grounds at King Freddy's Potsdam Palace, a true gentleman's garden. Beyond was a plantation of eight thousand acres, all tidily maintained by one hundred and fifty toiling Custis slaves Mrs. Washington had brought with her as a dowry on her marriage to General Washington. These slaves had come into Martha's possession when her first husband, Daniel Custis, died.

Her slaves outside the house, working in the formal gardens, looked properly cared-for, wearing sturdy clothes, hats, and shoes. Her field hands worked busily with spades and rakes, preparing for a winter crop. I recognized the hoes were of the latest types available. Did it follow that her slaves were happy people?

No, it did NOT!

One young slave girl's shy, woeful glance locked with mine. She was close to weeping and batted her wet lashes, signaling she had a miserable life and yearned for her freedom.

Feeling sympathy for this girl, I asked myself if I wasn't also a slave, in bondage to Mr. Adams? I've been housed, fed, clothed, and brought to beautiful cities, but will I be separated from my children as so many of America's slave mothers have been? Thoughts of slavery chased through my head.

During our stay as a couple in Washington, Mr. Adams was invited to dine by President Jefferson. The two had bonded many years ago in Paris after Mr. Jefferson was sent there by the Confederate Congress. Mr. Adams, no gossip, hasn't passed on to me his opinion of President Jefferson's amorata, his black slave girl Sally Hemings. He wouldn't.

Sally Hemings and I had something in common: She was illegitimate. Sally's mother was a black slave called Betty. Sally's white parent was Mr. Jefferson's father-in-law. Mr. Jefferson inherited Sally when first his father-in-law and then his wife, Martha, died. The talk in Washington D.C. was how closely illegitimate-Sally resembled her half-sister, Martha, Mr. Jefferson's late wife. When in Paris as a widower, Mr. Jefferson ordered then fourteen-year-old Sally to live with him, where she got pregnant with the first of several of his illegitimate children. As President, Mr. Jefferson moved "Dusky Sally" to Washington. But I'll wager he didn't permit their bastards to run freely in the President's House. He likely tore her babies from her and sent them to slave quarters in Virginia.

Forcing myself to concentrate on the coming encounter, I put on a diplomat's smile like a frog before his mating call and prepared to join Mrs. Washington on the portico. From there, we were led with great dignity into Mount Vernon's front hall.

Here, two liveried Negro slaves, wearing powdered wigs and livery, stood as silent and immobile as pillars, just as did white servants in London.

Inside the house we found Mrs. Washington's furniture to be superb, obviously imported from England. These were probably the pieces she had taken with her when leaving the President's House in Philadelphia, a fact much lamented in President John Adams' letters to my husband because my father-in-law found it totally stripped of any home comforts with not a chair nor a dish left there for his occupancy.

Mrs. Washington took trouble to point out the finest pieces of furniture as she showed us the main "parloure," the library, and a hall that led upstairs. The plan for the main house was basic. From the portico we entered a Passage Hall with stairs inviting to the bed-chambers above. We remained downstairs and were led to a Sitting Room on one side which gave on to the library. From there we progressed to the dining room. A light refreshment of mutton and preserved fruits was on a George II stiltlegs table waiting for us. I looked out a window and saw there was an arcade with slim columns leading from the dining room to a separate two-story house for the kitchen. It had a second arcade to match it, but I didn't see that one until later when we crossed the passage hall again to enter first the west "parloure" and then went on into a generous banqueting hall graced by a beautiful mantel piece surrounding a fireplace large enough to roast a hog. On the parallel side of this passage was a music room.

Finally Mrs. Washington personally conducted us upstairs to our bedroom. I was exceedingly glad to reach it and plumped myself on the nearest chair. I would've been grateful to lie down on the four poster curtained bed, but Mrs. Washington took us to the window to point out the excellent view of her property.

At three o'clock, when we had changed from our traveling clothes, Martha Washington appeared to lead us downstairs and present us with a sturdy meal. And why not? She had a "booke" of recipes with two hundred and five pages of recipes for meats and fish and three hundred and twenty six pages of recipes for sweetmeats.

When we came downstairs and left the passage hall for the library, Mrs. Washington showed us several pages of this book. She said, "It was passed down to me from my former husband's mother. These recipes date from half a century ago. They were collected by my mother-in-law, Frances Parke Custis and given to me in 1749 when I married my first husband, Daniel Custis. They were written in her own hand using the ancient spellings with which she had been educated in the late 1600s." She drew the book to her breasts and embraced it like a doting mother might cuddle her favorite child.

From the library we were led into the dining room by Mrs. Washington, who took a stance at the head of the table to carve a roast of beef. She sliced it daintily and then placed the slices on a plate for each of us, not permitting the man-servant in attendance to take over what she seemed to enjoy as her privilege.

Mr. Adams looked with astonishment at the pudding plates on her half-moon-shaped sideboard because he'd seen only two such plates anywhere else: one at his own father's home, and the other at Thomas Jefferson's Monticello. They were called plateaus de dessert.

Personally I was much more intrigued by a large, oval surtout de table with a pair of candelabra on top of it. This piece took up a surprising amount of space on the table, what with its center holding a huge plaster-of-Paris creation with images adorning it and more images of men and women at its farther ends.

Mrs. Washington noticed I was admiring it. She said quietly, "Gouverneur Morris picked that out in Paris for President Washington."

I liked the candelabra in particular. In fact, there was an abundance of lamps and chandeliers everywhere in the house. They were needed because there were charming paintings hanging on the walls and over the doorways. Without enough candle light, they could easily have been missed.

In her dulcet voice with its accent so reminiscent of my dear Maryland cousins, Mrs. Washington brought our notice to her favorite foods, placed tastefully around the oval centerpiece. "Many of our foods have been grown on the plantation. We have five farms. Such a lot of work for all of us! I do much of the cooking myself, although I have a good cook now. We had a struggle to find one when President Washington was alive."

Was that because he was like Mr. Adams and not fond of paying a hefty salary? I couldn't help but wonder! There's nothing like being a house guest to learn the frailties of a host or hostess.

I was glad when she left the subject of her farms and suggested we eat. Mrs. Washington prepared three neat slices for each of us. I could understand that she enjoyed being mistress of this table.

My beef was growing cold. I went at it with fork and knife. It smelled so delicious covered with herbs, for which Martha Washington was renowned. The beef was still warm enough and didn't disappoint. The homegrown vegetables were piled on our plates—again by Mrs. Washington's own hand—and then we had the sweetmeats. Her pickled peaches were particularly juicy and flavorful in our pudding, which was very rich with God knows how many egg yolks and a superfluous amount of rosewater.

The scarcely seen tablecloth was removed, and alcoholic drinks appeared. I preferred to accept a cup of tea from Mrs. Washington, who presided over an extraordinary silver samovar.

She began an embarrassingly long soliloquy about the late President Washington, tossing her head like a robin in full song. "The first and dearest wish of my heart was that we should be suffered to grow old together in solitude and tranquility. I will not, however, contemplate with too much regret disappointments that were inevitable though the General's feelings, and mine were in perfect unison with respect to our predilections for private life. I cannot blame him for having acted according to his ideas of loyalty in obeying the voice of duty to his country."

That was uttered in a tone of lament! Keeping a straight face, I wondered if those same words were repeated for every guest who came to this house.

But she wasn't finished with her top subject. "You may know that the General was very fond of rising with the sun. You are not obliged to do so on the morrow, Mr. and Mrs. Adams, but the General believed his custom of rising early gave a good example to our workmen. He wrote about his feelings.

'If any hirelings are not in their places at that time, I send them messages of sorrow for their indispositions that, having put these wheels in motion, I examine the state of things further.'"

I thought, "Ha! Even such a grand hero as General Washington has as many facets to his heart as a kaleidoscope!"

We were called to another meal at nine in the evening. For this supper we were joined by a couple who had the effrontery to invite themselves to the meal. Apparently Mrs. Washington is too-often besieged by uninvited guests who appear at mealtimes. She asked her favorite granddaughter to act as a buffer, and the dear girl charmed us with a series of pleasantries in the west "parloure" before we took our places in the dining room. Oh, if only the conversation at table had been as delightful!

At our nine o'clock supper meal, the conversation was awful, horrible, and woefully embarrassing. I wanted to hide under the mahogany boards of the dining table as

I had in my father's own elegant Tower Hill house when I was a child and frightened by guests' talk.

It was the female member of that unexpected couple who took over the conversation. She looked on critically when the half-moon side table was taken from its place next to the wall to add space at the table. After the initial pleasantries—skillfully channeled by Martha Washington's cohostess, her grand-daughter, Nellie—that female guest launched into the extremely un-politic subject of Alexander Hamilton's family history.

"Would you not agree, Mrs. Washington, that your late, great husband's tutoring of Alexander Hamilton added much to his meteoric rise?"

Tight-lipped, Martha Washington replied with good manners, "Yes, I suppose that could be said. But he won the Battle at Yorktown on his own merits."

Sotto voce, Mr. Adams whispered to me, "And the appearance on the horizon of a French fleet."

Then came the bomb.

The gauche guest asked, "Is it true that Alexander Hamilton was born illegitimate?"

I wished I could die, but no, that would have called attention to my distress and prompted questions of why I had perhaps suffered a heart attack.

I stole a glance at Mr. Adams' face. Had his lips twitched, revealing he knew my secret?

No lips-twitching from Mr. Adams. Martha Washington blushed, as would be proper for an old fashioned lady, even now, at the mention of illegitimacy. She has not been exposed to modern Berlin's tolerance of immorality and the gossip it engenders.

She replied in her gentlest tones, "I admire Alexander Hamilton's accomplishments. He wrote parts of the Declaration of Independence. He established our national currency. He founded our Coast Guard."

The rude guest wasn't finished. Like a cat filing its claws, she purred to Martha, "Is it not true that President Washington had a Mount Vernon slave's teeth pulled out so the President could use them for a set of false teeth?"

This time Martha Washington stood up and prepared to leave the table. Very quietly she said, "He paid his slave for those teeth. Now, shall we ladies go into the sitting room whilst the men stay here to enjoy brandy and cigars?"

What a diplomat Martha Washington proved to be at that meal! I blessed her, without mouthing words. But I was relieved to escape from Mount Vernon before I would be exposed again to the forked tongue of her guest.

On the drive back to the Capital this morning, Mr. Adams asked me, "Did you enjoy your stay?"

What could I say?

I decided to speak out and tell him the truth, even though I recognized it was an unusual compliment to me for him to launch a question. "Beautiful house. Lovely furnishings and great food, but the slaves! She actually crowed telling us how she'd brought one hundred and fifty slaves with her as a dowry. Disgraceful. I'm outraged we took the hospitality of someone with that many slaves."

"Mrs. Adams, you must learn to accept how Southern hospitality depends on slavery. How could Mrs. Washington cultivate eight hundred acres if she had no slaves? These plantations are not like our Massachusetts farms where we can afford to pay our laborers because most of the farms have small parcels." Now Mr. Adams went tight-lipped. I know why.

He, too, detests slavery. He felt offended that I'd put him in a position to defend it.

All I want to do is to cringe at my mother's side, back in the suburb where Father has found cheap lodgings in Washington D.C. after his escape from his creditors in London. Thank God that exPresident Adams procured for Papa the postmaster job, or they'd have had nowhere to live and nothing to eat! Sadly that job may not last very long, now that Thomas Jefferson has become Chief Executive. He wants to name one of his political friends to earn those $2,500. Papa's position has become perilous, to say the least. Whatever, I know the two months' respite Mr. Adams permitted me to enjoy with them is destined to be over.

This visit to Mount Vernon weighs heavy on my mind with the question of my illegitimacy and whether it will someday be my undoing. I have never blamed my parents for being tardy in marrying. Poor Maman was lucky to have been married at all, considering that neither her mother nor her grandmother had managed that feat.

I spent the remainder of our drive to the Capital caring for our son and reminding myself I must savor to the full this last of the coming time with my family. I know it will be many months before I see any family members again.

New York, November 11, 1801

Parting from Maman and Father was bitter and painful. Both are angry and resentful that Father didn't find the welcome he expected to receive on his return to America. Surprisingly, from their letters it seemed that ex-President and Abigail are bitter about their change of circumstances too.

Mr. Adams' diary also reflects his disillusionment with a nation that neglects to admire his father's patriotism, which has been ignored by voters not free of "intrigue and envy." My Mr. Adams wrote to his mother, "I will sooner turn scavenger and earn my living by cleaning away the filth of the streets than plunge into the bottomless filth of faction." In other words: He doesn't want to be a politician.

How will that attitude affect my oncoming meeting with his parents?

On the start of my trip to Quincy, I became ill in the stagecoach, because I had a fever. This time Mr. Adams couldn't make loud complaints about the odor. We interrupted our journey for me to see a physician in Philadelphia. His name was Dr. Benjamin Rush. He was very outspoken. He roared out to Mr. Adams that I am, "under great apprehension."

There, the doctor diagnosed me as being extremely nervous about meeting my in-laws. He specified that I am particularly anxious about meeting my mother-in-law. Then he poured oil on the fire adding I am, "still more depressed in spirits than really ill."

Oh, my! Did I really need a doctor to discover that? AND pay him a considerable fee.

The next delay was to take a short hiatus in New York with Mr. Adams's sister Nabby. She proved to be kind and gentle, and she has acted most civilly towards me. I don't mean she is loving. That would be too much of an accolade.

Then baby George came down with diarrhea, and again we put off starting our trip to Quincy until today.

Quincy, November 14, 1801

When we finally arrived in Quincy I had a nasty cold, and baby George was not at all his usual rosy color.

On arrival at the Adams' family home, I stared at it in disbelief. The Second President of the United States lives in a paltry farmhouse not fit for a steward on any English fair-sized estate! It does accommodate twenty family members by overcrowding, but I don't fancy the idea of being crowded in with more than a dozen relations I've never met before.

Ex-President John Adams carried a hoe with a clump of weeds in his spare hand when he came to greet our carriage. I tripped and almost fell in the mud, I was in such a quandary. How was I to address these people? They appeared to be like simple farmers. But old ex-President John Adams had been a leader in the American Revolution; he had helped write America's Declaration of Independence and its Constitution. He had served as Vice-President to the legendary George Washington, a name now known all over Europe. Then he had succeeded George Washington as the Second President.

And, Abigail? I had read reams of her letters that indicated she was highly intelligent and very erudite. But now my scary mother-in-law, Abigail, was struggling with laundry trying to hoist it onto racks against a powerful wind. When she heard the carriage's wheels, Abigail had folded the laundry and then met me at her door. She said, "Come out of the wind, my dear. You can help me shell the peas for dinner." Taking my seven-month-old son from my arms, she cackled like a laying hen.

I saw Thomas on the landing. He had the grace to blush. He well knew how many servants my father had employed in the kitchen in our London home. There had been the chef, the under-cook, the pastry chef, the kitchen maid, seven lesser staff as footmen, and the butler who uncorked the wine.

Old ex-President Adams kissed me on one cheek and showed me the way to his kitchen. It was very small. There was a nice aroma of apple pie from a scalloped tin on a shelf above the wood stove, so I made an effort to complement Abigail on her baking.

"Lovely pie! Apple?" I breathed shyly.

Nephews and nieces appeared to stare as if I was an animal in a zoo. They abhorred my British accent. They disliked my extravagant clothes, which I had personally sewn to go to Court in Berlin. They were appalled at the way I dressed my son, George, to look like a European prince or an English dandy in a velvet suit with a lace-trimmed collar and a wide silk sash. They resented it when old ex-President John Adams brought out a delicacy from the larder for me. A niece, who has obviously been much spoiled with delicacies prior to my arrival, now burst into tears and fled the room.

Quincy, February 26, 1802

With the Quincy dinners such a disaster, in the following weeks Mr. Adams and the old ex-president lurked alone in the parlor, scheming how to achieve the next advancement for my husband.

I am a quick learner. I decided to make use of some of these Yankee farm folks' ways. I "give as good, as I get" when Mr. Adams scolds, and I talk back. When we quarrel, I no longer give in every time. Early on I recalled the second rouge incident in Berlin, and so occasionally I hold my own and take myself to a concert in Boston.

Where I continue to be a loser is in the education of our son, George. Mr. Adams insists on being extremely strict with the toddler. Once, when it was raining hard, I suggested we put off George's playtime in what was called "the yard." I reminded Mr. Adams that George had the "sniffles" and warned he could get a cold in the chest if he got wet. Mr. Adams contradicted immediately and, grabbed little George's puny arm to march him outside into the rain, even though he was still learning to walk. George's "sniffles" went to his chest—as I'd predicted—and George developed a bad cough that has lasted all winter.

With Abigail, I finally "got on." By constantly complimenting her on the ghastly food and offering to trade recipes, she has warmed to me. I gave her my favorite Prussian recipes for pigs' knuckles and sauerkraut where the trick was to add nutmeg. I also taught her how to make a Christmas lebkuchen with plenty of cinnamon and ginger.

Boston, February 2, 1803

Another fast-moving year! After several months we moved to a house in Boston, taking baby George with us, thank God!

I have tried to like the Boston house. I installed a backgammon table to play at that game into the wee hours with Mr. Adams. Backgammon didn't help. He was perpetually in foul moods. He felt disappointed at his reception among the other lawyers in the city, who resented his European manners acquired in the Prussian Court.

Clients were also in short supply. I had to let go our two servants and do most of the household chores. Two of my unmarried sisters came to help. Mr. Adams did the marketing! That way he could save more money. He became so disgruntled that there was serious talk of our leaving Boston for a frontier life in western New York State. When Abigail heard about it, she squelched that in a trice.

Partly out of desperation and partly because he wanted to shine in some field, Mr. Adams damped his hatred of politics and listened attentively when his Massachusetts friends appealed to him to consider accepting a run for State Senator. Oh yes indeed he would. In his mind, Mr. Adams felt he was heading for a career as a statesman. Not as a politician. He believed he had been summoned to do his duty by his country. Goodness gracious! How could my sophisticated, learned husband have fallen for his lawyer friends' gibberish?

On April 5, 1802, he won his election by a sweeping 2,345 votes demolishing the opposition's 1,498. Like a virgin who blushes at being kissed, but really longs for more of the same, Mr. Adams attended two sessions of the Massachusetts Senate last year and another this past January. But the political waters that Mr. Adams once likened to a bath in ice water soon started to boil. Early on in politics he felt like a knight in shining armor, opposing corruption, but in the waters of politics he had been caught off guard and could have drowned due to the armor of "righteousness" he wore.

The "mammon of unrighteousness is too strongly befriended" he wrote. I peeked into his diary and read how disillusioned he has become. Nevertheless, after losing in a congressional race, Mr. Adams astounded his doubting brother, Thomas, by announcing he would accept an invitation to go to Washington to the national Senate. I think he craved the salary. He was deprived of a nice income as a commissioner of bankruptcy when that perk fell to the new President's discretion. Feeling needy, he accepted to at least make a try for the nation's Senate. Mr. Adams must have pleased the Massachusetts voters mightily because he was duly elected to serve them in the United States Senate. But I made myself hide my quiet laughter inspired by the hypocrisy of acting-out that he had accepted. Accepted, my foot; he had grabbed at the chance!

Boston is too close to Quincy to suit me. Practically every weekend Mr. Adams leaves us alone in Boston while he rides to Quincy to be with his parents. I could be feverish and little George with the croup; Mr. Adams still leaves us for Quincy.

Boston, September 5, 1803

Mr. Adams began his service to the United States Senate on March 4. Meanwhile we remained in Boston tying up loose ends. A few months passed, and I gave birth to another son.

He was born on the Fourth of July, which is a very big holiday in the United States. Mr. Adams was gone all day giving speeches while I pushed and perspired with agonizing birth pains. At 2:30 a.m., when I was alone with a midwife, the infant crowned, and by 3 a.m., the baby was birthed. The midwife announced the baby was stillborn. A boy. She cut the umbilical cord, dealt with the afterbirth, cleaned me, and left. With no Mr. Adams present, nor any other family member, I took my newborn in my arms to give him a parting caress. AND HE STIRRED! For an hour I breathed into his tiny mouth and massaged his chest until at last I heard a faint cry. His cries became louder. LOUDER! Barely managing to walk, I took a christening blanket from the cradle I'd prepared, wrapped him in it after a brief cleansing, and finally gave the baby my left breast. He suckled normally. Eventually we fell asleep together.

In the morning Mr. Adams returned from Quincy, looked in on us, saw nothing abnormal, and went to his books in his library.

The child was christened John. That was a good choice. The old ex-President was duly pleased.

Unfortunately, Abigail was ill. She had tried to "blister" herself to treat a minor complaint, which had blown up like a firecracker into a serious infection. Although Mr. Adams returned to join me for a few days to meet his new baby, he has gone off again for the entire month of August to hold his mother's hand, not mine.

Even when Mr. Adams stays at home, his mind was elsewhere—not in Boston, not thinking about me and our newborn son. No. His thoughts are tied to Washington D.C. He is obsessed with the Louisiana

Purchase and how it could affect our United States, even though the treaty has already been signed and announced to the American people. Thomas Jefferson chose the very day our John arrived, July 4. And yet, it is that other event—the treaty—that has Mr. Adams so enthralled.

In Washington with other senators, Mr. Adams has busily reviewed the pros and cons. He considers it a pro that our nation has expanded so enormously. But he worries that when Louisiana achieves statehood we will have another slave state to unbalance the fragile truce that exists between slave and non-slave states. He cares a great deal that the United States has acquired as much land as to practically double the size of the nation. Mr. Adams has already made plans for what should be done about all that land.

Very au courant with French politics, he is approached constantly for his opinion on the ongoing threats from Napoleon's burgeoning popularity in France and that Corsican's plans for expanding its territory by grabbing more from its neighbors. Mr. Adams is not asked what he thinks about expanding our nation's frontiers. And he is very aware that in America's Southland there are already on average three slaves to every owner. In our house, it is nigh on the reverse. I am a slave to his whims and the demands of our two boys.

Washington, D.C., January 12, 1804

Back we have come to the Capital because here is where Mr. Adams earns our daily bread by serving in the Senate. He managed to speedily find a tenant for our Boston house. I packed up our belongings—forget that I was barely out of a difficult childbirth!—and after a few days of quiet leavetaking with the elder Adamses, we set off on September 29 with my sister Caroline, three maids, and my two infants for Washington, D.C.

Not an easy trip. This time Mr. Adams chose to go by water. But the waterways were in a terrible state from a series of succeeding storms.

On route I fell ill during a stopover in New York City, where there was an epidemic of yellow fever raging. Thank God, I didn't catch yellow fever. My Manhattan-based sister-in-law, Nabby, rescued the four of us and brought us to a refuge she had found due to her own desire to escape the epidemic.

When my health was restored we headed again for Washington D.C.

Oh, what a joy to settle in to my sister Nancy Hellen's home! Located at about three miles from the city, Walter Hellen's estate was comfortable, welcoming, and—best of all—fun! Her little girls adored my infant; he was a doll to play with and care for. George was enchanted with the ponies available for reckless riding. I could gossip with Nancy, Caroline, and my mother.

Maman had been widowed some months earlier. Father had succumbed to melancholy and uremia. I use the word "melancholy" carefully, because I refuse to believe he had a mental breakdown. Of course he felt sad, having lost all his wealth, but he was not a madman.

We Johnsons have had such great times together that our joy has overflowed into the realms of Washington society, which has embraced me as if I were a long-lost favorite. True, I mingled with the younger set when I first arrived, thanks to my Maryland cousins. This time I have been welcomed by a select group of important statesmen and their wives. We have even dined with such important figures as Thomas Jefferson and James and Dolley Madison!

Mr. Adams has holed up in an upstairs alcove in Walter Hellens's house, where he can read his favorite authors: Cicero, and probably Byron. I know he reads Byron's naughty Don Juan that he hides from me. He leaves early every day and comes back late, walking the entire three miles each way to save money.

When he mingles at parties in Washington, he often leaves my side to escape into a library to play chess or exchange views on the European situation. He certainly doesn't treat me as a person to be placed on a pedestal to receive compliments. But with my family and my children, I am finding some joy day by day.

Washington, D.C., December 9, 1806

After our first two years in the Capital, Mr. Adams decided to send our little sons to Quincy. How I hated that decision, and how I still wish I could contest it. No such possibility exists. I have been given no "say" in this matter or in any other. Mr. Adams insists I honor that horrible decision, invoking the marriage vows: "To honor and obey!"

My heart broke again, left without my two babies. The Old President and Abigail love the children, and Abigail means well when she insists the climate in Washington is bad for George. But there are concerns other than climate with George. He is moody, stand-offish, tending to pout and to lurk in corners.

When we lived in Berlin, Mr. Adams would take him about the city, pointing to the Prussian children. He often said, "Remember George, you are not like these children. They are Prussians, you are an American." Mr. Adams would not permit him to play with the Prussian children, even though he was yet a babe and could not possibly be influenced by them greatly. When we arrived in Massachusetts, George in his Prussian Court clothes and long curls looked and then acted different from his cousins. He frowned at them, wouldn't enter into games with them, and stood aside from them, and they seemed just as reluctant to approach him. I knew he wanted to play. But the child recalled Mr. Adams' admonitions, thinking he was not meant to play with any children at all, not just the Prussian ones. He obeyed the Berlin rules, and in Massachusetts did what he still believed would earn him plaudits. He ended a lonely child.

I argue loud and long with Mr. Adams about his parenting of George. The quarrels are to no avail. Forbidden to keep him at Nancy's, where he had interacted well with her two affectionate little girls, I find myself missing him and little John immeasurably. I pour all my need for giving love into Nancy's children.

I cuddle them, kiss them, and play games with them. I like the feelings of togetherness with them.

Nancy noticed the contrast between how I lavish love on her children, but merely tolerate Mr. Adams. She can hear us quarreling at night. The walls of her house are so thin she learned there is no lovemaking in those endless penetrations of my body.

One afternoon in her kitchen, when I was showing her Abigail's recipe for apple pie, she asked, "Doesn't Mr. Adams ever kiss you?"

"Never. He never has."

"Louisa, that's not true. I saw him kiss you on the head when you two were engaged."

"I thought you meant if he kissed me after we were married. In bed, when he is thrusting inside of me." That was the first time I have ever discussed my intimacy with Mr. Adams.

"Poor Louisa! No wonder you always have a peaky look! It must be awful to have intimacy without kisses. My Walter, he kisses me all over. Always, before lovemaking."

"What do you man all over?"

"Louisa, my neck, my breasts, between my legs." "No! I can't imagine such a performance!"

"He enjoys doing it; I enjoy it being done. Sometimes he sucks my toes. I adore that."

"Well, I never!"

"Louisa, why don't you initiate the kissing? You believe that women should have their own way. Make kissing your way."

"I couldn't. He wears those tall collars."

"He doesn't when he's in his nightshirt. Try kissing him on the neck. My Walter loves that."

"Your Walter has a very different personality."

"That's true. Thank God. But Louisa, try kissing him on the neck the next time he says something nice to you or brings you chocolate from Washington. He does bring you chocolates."

"Because, I'm still so underweight. Otherwise, I doubt I'd get any chocolate."

I did make an effort to follow Nancy's advice. I cooked an apple pie according to Abigail's recipe. His mother's recipe! That night at dinner, after apple pie I received a surprisingly gentle look from Mr. Adams. I felt a rush of blood to my inner being. How to respond? Later, in the marital bed, I kissed his neck. In return, for the first time ever, he kissed me on the lips. The thrusting did not feel so bad after that kiss.

We have been with Nancy and Walter for three years now. I continue to kiss Mr. Adams on the neck, and even went so far as to kiss his chest. He kissed mine! All that kissing has resulted in another pregnancy.

Washington, D.C., August 21, 1807

Our son Charles was born under different circumstances from my last lying-in. On the evening of August 17, Mr. Adams and I had been for a walk on Boston Common when I felt the first birth pangs. We hurried home, and after a few very painful hours Charles emerged from my body.

Washington, D.C., June 8, 1808

Mr. Adams made himself unpopular in the Senate. I learned that from Walter Hellen as I am not permitted to join my husband on his forays there. Mr. Adams didn't even invite me to join him when he returned to Quincy to take vacations there from May to December. I didn't resent that exclusion. Although I missed seeing my other two sons, still captives of their paternal grandparents in Quincy, I swallowed my bile and concentrated on making baby Charles happy, especially on our excursions with the Hellens to my Maryland relations.

The reason for his unpopularity is that Mr. Adams took a stand—alone in the Senate—of supporting and voting for an embargo on all American shipping. Mr. Adams considered the plan a "noble experiment," but it cost him his Senate seat. He was reviled by the Massachusetts Federalists, who considered him no longer a member of their party.

His downfall came because of that and also because of his continuing efforts to stop the threat of war with England over the impressment of sailors. Mr. Adams became as unpopular in the Senate as a passenger in a carriage who continually passes gas or, like me, finds herself ill nearly every time she is shut in that cramped little box.

Pressures on both sides of the aisle grew steadily, until he felt he must resign, before he might be IMPEACHED! He has done so today, and he is unsure now what the future holds, as am I.

Oh, my. If only he would have sat down in my kitchen and talked over these challenges. But no, he wouldn't want to listen to me.

Boston, August 26, 1808

So we have returned to Massachusetts.

Never mind. I am back with my two older sons, who love me as much as if I had been with them all these endless years. We live in a passable Boston house, which Mr. Adams pays for by opening a law practice and by giving lectures on rhetoric and oratory at Harvard University. The position at Harvard pleased the old ex-President, who has written more letters to him than before, although we are only a few miles away at Quincy.

Abigail keeps worrying about the impression her eldest son gives regarding men's fashions. She wrote to him on that subject while he was still a Senator: "I do not wish a Senator to dress like a beau, but I want him to conform so far as to the fashion as not to incur the character of singularity, nor give occasion to the world to ask what kind of mother he had or to charge upon a wife negligence when she is guiltless."

Mr. Adams has returned to his lifelong negligence regarding dress. Now that he has that job at Harvard teaching oratory and rhetoric, he could pass for the classic image of "the absent-minded professor" when he neglects to button his buttons where it most matters: the fly of his trousers.

Nearing Norway aboard HORACE, October 9,1809

How I wish we could have remained in that Boston house. But again within months, our destiny was altered. President Madison, newly elected to succeed Jefferson, surprised Mr. Adams by appointing him Minister to Czar Alexander's Russia. He accepted without consulting me.

I made the required prendre congé to the in-laws. But much as I detested Quincy, I had doubts about my acceptance in St. Petersburg society. Czar Alexander and his Czarina had no children, and were mooted to be keen on balls. As I am always pregnant and bursting out of my clothes, I did not see myself to be an addition to their balls. Again I was to pack up our belongings and move to an unknown capital where I neither had any friends nor knew the language.

Worse, much worse, was the possibility that Mr. Adams would refuse to allow our two older sons to accompany us.

"George is showing signs of serious depression," he said, which was a red flag warning me of what awful decision could be coming.

"Just growing pains," I countered.

"He lost his temper with his grandmother last Sunday. I will not put up with such bad manners." "George was out of his familiar environment. He prefers Boston to their Quincy house."

"I don't give a damn what he prefers. The boy is impossible. There is a slight improvement when he is with young John. He needs his brother John to keep him on his good behavior. I have a mind to leave them both with my mother while we are gone to my post in St. Petersburg."

I had another miscarriage. But that neither gained me any sympathy nor saved me from being parted from my two older sons. Down came the proverbial boom. Just before our ship left the harbor for Russia, I learned that my two older boys would definitely not be traveling with us. I was only permitted to take baby Charles.

Now I am the one who suffers from depression, from that day forward, all during our long voyage, and until now, weeks before we arrive in St. Petersburg.

St. Petersburg, November 5, 1810

It is one year today since Mr. Adams was presented to the Czar, and what a miserable year it has been. Always economical where I am concerned, Mr. Adams took second-class lodgings in Hotel de Lourdes. There are rats scurrying around our rooms. Unlucky rats, they have not found much food of ours left over! We barely have enough in the larder to keep Charles in good health.

I am pregnant again, but not from kissing or even tolerable thrusting. It is so bitterly cold most of the year in St. Petersburg that I believe Mr. Adams couples with me so often simply to keep warm.

I have been "puking," as Abigail calls vomiting, for many weeks. Just the same, much as he can barely tolerate being near me, due to his distaste for the smell of sickness, Mr. Adams insists we go to all the St. Petersburg Court balls in order to familiarize ourselves with the country's notables. With my stomach ballooning, it is worse than embarrassing for me to appear in old gowns stretched beyond their limits—cords breaking and buttons flying.

My escape is to go to concerts and operas. As I cannot speak Russian, music is my outlet. I love the melodies of the Fomin operas. I have no harp so I use the hotel's tired pianoforte to reprise those tunes. Some evenings other hotel guests will gather around and sing excerpts from Fomin's opera, The Coachmen at the Relay. I still hum passages. A British friend translated parts of them. "Those were the days, my friend," came with the best melody.

My burgeoning stomach is less embarrassingly noticeable in theater seats. It barely shows when I am at the pianoforte. Thank God for Russian music! I have learned to call out "Otche Harasho," and applaud furiously for encores. Yevstigney Fomin, was almost passé when we arrived in 1809 in St. Petersburg. Russian folk songs were all the rage. The newest composers feed them into their orchestral symphonies. The avant-garde librettists weave in social reforms. All of that comes together for me when my fingers dance on the keys of the borrowed pianoforte. I have discovered a talent for retaining tunes I hear and feeding them on to the keys!

St. Petersburg, June 5, 1811

I have found two good books written in French about Catherine the Great, the Russian Empress about whom I wanted to know more. I do not admire all her treachery, adultery, and wiles, but her strength of purpose to rule as a woman in Russia: That I can admire and do!

Mr. Adams has also bought several books written in French. He managed to get a copy of The Stone Guest, another version of the sexual escapades of Don Juan. I knew about those escapades from reading the poem about him by Lord Byron. It worries me that Mr. Adams has an appetite for such books. In our last home in Washington, I found a copy of that filthy novel, Tom Jones. Mr. Adams hid it among volumes of the plays of William Shakespeare. Why does he read those books? Mr. Adams has always presented a facade of strict morality. I know that his appetite for marital intercourse is interminable. But, depravity? Lust for easy women? Mr. Adams!

I have had many occasions to meet Czar Alexander, a very handsome man. He is extremely erudite, and that adds to his fascination. As the wife of the United States Minister, I am invited to his palaces. The Hermitage is a vast depository of art—some good, some awful. I prefer his country homes, although his unusual sense of humor reigns at several. Once I was doused with water when hidden fountains began to play, purposefully drenching his guests.

The Czar had ordered all his nearest relations to build country palaces outside St. Petersburg, near the shores of the Bay of Finland. We have been invited to many of these. What I particularly have enjoyed were the musical evenings when we sat in gardens while musicians with balalaikas would stroll from table to table. Wonderful. I particularly admired the position on a hill of the palace belonging to Prince Galitzine.

Each Grand Duke vies to provide more extravagant entertainment. One gave us an evening where the music was accompanied by dancing bears from a circus!

Spring was best in May. That was when I would have been able to go to more of those parties in gardens. But my lying-in was approaching, and I didn't want another miscarriage. On the balmy, warm days I was forced to hide in my dingy hotel room. The heat has increased as May has become June. I can hardly believe how hot it has become in St. Petersburg. It is hotter than the hottest July day in Massachusetts!

St. Petersburg, February 13, 1812

On the most stifling hot day, I gave birth to our daughter in the summer of 1811.

From the first pangs of childbirth, she gave me an easy time. She slipped out, causing me hardly any more pain than a monthly period.

She was beautiful from the day of her birth.

Mr. Adams amazed me by announcing that she should be named Louisa Catherine. Louisa! And was the Catherine part a nod to flatter the Czar by invoking early Russian history? Taking off his cap to Catherine the Great? Who knew what Mr. Adams had in mind! But he had named our first born George Washington, pandering to the then President of the United States. With Mr. Adams politics are always paramount. His focus on politics never alters.

I certainly suspect the name Catherine had been added to have more of an "in" with the Czar. Oh yes, and it is my middle name.

Oh, how I wish I were a talented poet and could write an ode to the joy of having a daughter! From her first day, I have had visions of the wondrous times we will share together, Louisa Catherine and I. We will go shopping together, stroll in parks together, and go fishing together. She will not be shackled by a restrictive marriage when she grows up, as I have been. Like her Russian empress namesake, Catherine the Great, she will rule not be ruled. She will ride horses astride like a man, not sidesaddle to be modest. She will read the books of scholars to understand law and medicine and astronomy. No silly novels for Louisa Catherine! She can be a doctor, or an engineer, or a Senator.

Yes, I will teach her the pleasures of cooking. I will share my best recipes with her and pass on to her the tricks that turn ordinary food magical. But she will never be tied to a kitchen—never tied to anything!

She is the first American citizen to be born in Russia, and what a citizen she will grow to be! She will have a vote in the United States to elect the right man for the job. Her votes will help other women to gain freedom and happiness. Her friends will come from all walks of life and enrich hers with their ideas of fun and accomplishment. I don't want her to be a blue stocking. I don't want her to look down on women who are still shackled. She will be broadminded, fair, and excel in various fields, but not be a snob who thinks little of others less talented or elegant. She will be and is adorable.

Kisses have returned in our marital bed after Louisa Catherine's arrival. I had ceased giving Mr. Adams any show of affection after our two eldest sons were torn from my arms and banished to Quincy. No kisses from Mr. Adams unless I initiated them. Ergo no kisses. Oh, those first months in St. Petersburg he continued to do his thrusting between my legs with that dour expression of duty on his face. He never seemed to tire of that. Never.

Duty! I glanced inside the pages of his diary and learned that he tolerated our marital fights because he had promised to honor me. That, in spite of my suspicions that he still resents the non-payment of my promised dowry—and, far worse—may have learned of my illegitimacy. But all seems forgiven on both our parts since Louisa Catherine's birth. I have discovered a new depth of sensitivity in Mr. Adams that certainly surprised me. Apparently there does exist a Father/Daughter bond that supersedes all. Well, not all. Politics still came first with Mr. Adams.

To improve our position with his fellow diplomats, Mr. Adams upgraded our lodgings. We moved into a mansion and acquired a small army of servants.

We had brought with us from America a Black freeman called Nelson, who served as valet to attempt to improve Mr. Adams' interest in suitable clothing for Court appearances. Nelson was best at fighting of the rats that swarmed in our rooms. I had brought a "personal maid," poor woman, who had early on spent most of her worst days cleaning up after my miscarriages, sopping up the enormous amount of blood I lost, and then disposing of the remains.

In our new apartments Mr. Adams found we were living beyond our means due to having this small army of retainers. Meanwhile Czar Alexander asked Mr. Adams to relinquish Nelson to serve him, because the Czar likes to have a group of Black freemen at his beck and call. "Blackamoors" are all the rage in the homes of aristocrats in England and Italy, and Czar

Alexander intends to emulate this vogue.

Nelson was succeeded in our establishment by Waldstein, who named himself our Steward. Waldstein proceeded to rob us, first by disposing of almost four hundred bottles of Mr. Adams' wine and then by forging receipts from tradesmen pretending that goods had been delivered and paid for when such goods had never existed.

Waldstein, who had to be dragged from our premises, refusing to leave, was followed as Steward by another Black man, a sailor called Baker. His peccadilloes were mostly committed through sex. Apparently, he had sex orgies in his rooms, although town women were strictly prohibited from passing our threshold. Mr. Adams roared out against Baker's mixture of women and alcohol, which he insisted caused thievery. Oh? And has Mr. Adams not partaken of too much alcohol, and has he been tempted by women of the streets?

The cook was a small-scale thief. He bought more than what we needed and sold off the rest. What did Mr. Adams do? He decided to buy our household provisions himself. Mr. Adams fired the cook and the cook's helper and visited the marketplaces in person. Very time consuming, as I saw he had noted in his open diary.

Not funny, although I laughed about it at the time, was the experience Mr. Adams had when he needed to go to a jail to pay the bail for his coach-man who had been arrested for sashaying dressed as a woman around the famous boulevards of St. Petersburg. He was accused of corrupting Russia's soldiers. Poor man, he suffered for being a transvestite. He whispered to me that he wished with all his heart he could give up that game.

For me, the most valuable servant has proven to be my new lady's maid. This new girl was brought into the household to attend to my wardrobe, help me dress my hair, and clothe me. But the dear person is not only perfection in those regards. She is far more adept than the simple Massachusetts girl I first imported for the care of my baby. She became the most able nursemaid imaginable.

St. Petersburg, April 2, 1812

For ten months I have reveled in my status as the mother of a daughter. With toddler Charles acting as her Guardian Angel and the new maid helping me with the onerous jobs of changing diapers and bathing the baby, I am in the only heaven I have known since leaving my parents' home. I am lyrically happy. I don't need concerts or parties to pass my evenings. I prefer to stay near my Louisa Catherine's cradle to peer at her rosebud mouth as it opens and closes with her delicate breaths.

Mr. Adams, brought up on the Puritans' axioms "A penny saved is a penny earned," and "To be thrifty is next to Godliness," as embroidered with cross-stitch on many samplers framed in Massachusetts' homes, nevertheless cheerfully pays my extra maid's salary, which is a great boon to me. Now that Louisa Catherine has begun her teething problems, the dear woman is at hand to cradle and comfort her for the few brief hours I snatch for sleep.

I have abundant milk for nursing her, and Louisa Catherine gurgles away with an amazing appetite. To celebrate Easter this past Sunday, Mr. Adams hired a three-horse troika. Louisa Catherine was not frightened at all by its horses. As the sleigh slid along on the Neva River's ice, Louisa Catherine laughed at the horses' breath curling among the snowflakes. She crooned to the beasts, her dimples dancing when they neighed in response.

But while all was well with Louisa Catherine, Mr. Adams, and myself, my spinster sister, Kitty, was the family member who brought trouble to us in the early days of 1812. Kitty, who had always been a terrible flirt from the age of thirteen, came on too strong for the men she had met in America. A disgruntled spinster, seven years past débutante age and still without a husband, unmarried Kitty had an unwelcome pregnancy. With Kitty's bulging tummy announcing the coming of an illegitimate baby, I was distracted temporarily from Louisa Catherine's teething problems.

We had brought my twenty-four-year-old sister to St. Petersburg in response to her wish to extend her net to try to catch a husband in Russia. At first she had received the attentions of several of our legation's aides. Their attentions faded when they learned her father was bankrupt. The most serious prospect who persisted was a Francis Gray. Mr. Adams caught the couple embracing and read out in a loud voice a sermon on, "The Character of A Woman Who Is A Sinner." Soon Francis Gray was dispatched away from St. Petersburg. But my spinster sister was not to be thwarted. Kitty's womanly organs were crying out to reproduce. Her tentacles soon found their way into the heart of Mr. Adams' nephew and additional aide, Billy Smith.

Whilst we were sitting happily, having been celebrating New Year's Day 1812, Kitty confirmed to me that she was pregnant. Early that morning, I sat, rocking Louisa Catherin's cradle with a foot, whilst my hands were occupied adding a half meter of new lace to freshen up my old ballgown's neckline. Suddenly, our Massachusetts maid interrupted.

"Madam, your sister, Kitty, would like a word. Shall I tell her you are busy?"

"No. Ask her to bring me my other sewing basket, the one with the supply of ribbons."

I kept my voice down, not wishing to wake my baby. I looked up, smiling, at the sound of Kitty's footsteps. That smile had a very short shift. When Kitty came through the doorway, I saw that her eyes looked as streaked with scarlet as a tropical sunset.

"Kitty, dear, whatever is the matter?"

I put down my sewing basket and took her hands in mine. They were as cold as an arctic glacier. I exchanged my smile for an anxious frown.

My loving touch was too much. Within seconds, Kit y was gasping with wrenching tears.

I said, "Surely an invitation to tonight's ball isn't worth suffering so much. And it may yet arrive for you!" "Invitation to the ball? Who cares? I need to talk to you—"

"Go on. Ask away, dear."

Gulping, as if she were drowning, Kitty struggled to push out her words. "Did you ever miss your womanly courses due to Russia's freezing temperature? Does this Russian food make you ill?"

Immediately, I caught her drift. After an embarrassed pause, I asked, "Kitty, have you felt changes in your breasts? Are they tender or growing?" My throat went dry from stress.

"Maybe? I know my stomach isn't as flat as it was. Could it be from the awful food here?" Kitty hung her head to her chest the way my spaniel in Tower Hill had done when he'd made a mess on Maman's best carpet.

Firmly, neither shy nor evasive, I prodded, "Kitty, have you lain with a man?"

With a nod, followed by a series of rattling coughs, Kitty slid to her knees and grabbed mine with both arms, crying out, "Save me! Make Mr. Adams force Billy to marry me!"

Silently, I digested her plea. I, make Mr. Adams force anyone to do anything? Not very likely! And my old fear of an illegitimate baby in the Johnson family surfaced like a blow from an axe. How could I hope to deal with such a problem?

Ignore it! Send Kitty back to America to Maman! She knows what to do.

I didn't get that chance. Mr. Adams loomed in the doorway. He'd been on the landing and heard Kitty's confession. He was more furious than I've ever seen him. He sputtered like the wet fuse of a cannonball.

He shook his fist at Kitty as if he'd strike her, but he didn't. Instead, he tore downstairs to where Billy Smith was calmly sorting the mail from the diplomatic pouch. He fell on Billy Smith, demolishing him like a building hit by a tornado.

"You have dishonored my sister, Nabby, and your entire family! You are a useless, spineless, disgusting creature. I despise the thought that you will be my nephew twice over. But marry Kitty you must!"

He raised his fist again, but again he did not strike. Billy was to marry Kitty, and as soon as possible. By mid-February, Kitty and Billy had a quiet wedding in our mansion.

What had caused that tornado of fury on Mr. Adams's part? Was it due to the fact that Kitty had "caught" his nephew? As he himself had been somewhat "caught" by me, although under different circumstances? Or was that whiff of a prospective illegitimate baby staining relations of the Adams family too much to bear on top of having learned of my illegitimacy? Had he learned of it?

St. Petersburg, November 19, 1813

Such dreadful, sad times have befallen us all, so many I have been loathe to write of any of these tragedies, even in this secret space where I keep myself company. A year and a half of constant sorrow. I feel it best to start with the hard news closest to me, then work my way to the troubles between great and new nations. How else am I to make sense of the whole world coming apart?

Life seemed fine enough late in the spring of

1812. When the cherry trees came into bloom in a nearby park, I took Louisa Catherine to toddle among the blossoms as they fell to the ground from the Neva's winds. She was engulfed in their petals and tried to catch them with her pudgy fingers.

Her health problems came with the arrival of her first tooth. Teething did not come easily, and her sparkling bright eyes often filled with tears. Of course I never abandoned the care of my teething child, but my good maid was so helpful, cradling my adored daughter, that I could leave those two cuddling together while I helped Kitty out of her distress.

Louisa Catherine's first tooth was through and she had a shining second one by the end of spring. By late June, seven additional teeth were trying to emerge, all at the same time. Then, on July 13, oh wicked day, Louisa Catherine had her first bout with dysentery. The Russian doctor we called in suggested we shave away her bouncing curls in order to permit bodily poisons to escape through her brain! We shaved her scalp. That did nothing to alleviate the dysentery. But it did bring out blisters on her poor head. Yet I couldn't complain about the doctor because baby Louisa Catherine seemed better for a few weeks.

In mid-summer, Mr. Adams decreed we should go touring around the Russian countryside. A trip of twenty-five miles to the Czar's Oranienbaum Palace was next. He decided we could travel in a public stagecoach. I had been nursing Louisa Catherine those early, joyful months of her life. It seemed perfectly natural to me to give her my breast in the stagecoach.

Fury on Mr. Adams' part! His shouts erupted like the lava from a volcano. I was not to show my breast to other passengers! At the first stop we made, he insisted I buy milk from a peasant's farm, and when Louisa Catherine balked at it, Mr. Adams suggested we buy water from the peasant. Mr. Adams ordered that Louisa Catherine must be weaned.

By the time we reached our destination, Louisa Catherine was suffering from acute diarrhea. To my horror, I soon noticed she had difficulty with her breathing. A local doctor prescribed bleeding her with leeches. Horrible! Those slimy black creatures dug into her rosy flesh to suck her precious blood, leaving hideous marks when removed. Another local doctor tried burning her with lighted sticks. In addition, unbelievable, primitive attempts were offered by ignorant midwives brought on to the desperate scene.

I hurried to return to St. Petersburg with Louisa Catherine. There, the air had been salubrious. That did no good. I ventured bringing her to the shore at the Bay of Finland and catered to her every gasp. Nothing helped. I tried cold compresses, hot baths, and herbal medicines.

Mr. Adams relied on the medical knowledge of two of his friends: Dr. Galloway, and Dr. Simpson. With Dr. Galloway out of town, he called for Dr. Simpson. When that good soul declined to assist us, Mr. Adams drove in a troika at two in the morning to rouse him from his bed and force him to attend to Louisa Catherine. No good. He prescribed an emetic. Why? Wasn't my darling baby empty enough? On Simpson's advice, I took to the road again with Catherine Louisa. With my maid and my sister we hired a small dacha in Octa. No good. She was totally dehydrated by the time of our final return to St. Petersburg, where she went into convulsions. Tortured beyond anything I could do!

Louisa Catherine died in mid-September. She breathed her last in my arms.

Mr. Adams blamed me as an unfit mother who had not done her duty by her child. I blamed Mr. Adams for bringing me to Russia where unsanitary conditions were beyond appalling.

Therefore no more kisses were exchanged in the marital bed. No more conversations in or out of bed. Total silence reigned between us.

I can write no more of this tonight. I am spent.

St. Petersburg, November 20, 1813

I retained the little nursemaid after Louisa Catherine's death. How could I blame her for our sorrows? Never! It was this world that I really blamed. Filthy Russia, with its veneer of gold and the flashy diamonds flaunted by the Czar's Court, while beyond St. Petersburg lurked dire poverty that bred diseases of the type that had killed my little angel. Typhoid, cholera, dysentery!

Rats and fleas and ticks and those terrible leeches are what still spring to mind when I think of the Russia I witnessed during our stay in Octa.

I grew to detest my comfortable room in the fancy mansion Mr. Adams leased in St. Petersburg. He had latterly felt obsessed with an urge to make some show of equality with the other diplomats at court. But how could he? The French Ambassador employed over three hundred servants. Britain's Ambassador owned a collection of fabulous Goya paintings. Our jewel had been Louisa Catherine, and she was gone. Never again would she romp in the Czar's Hermitage Palace, rollicking between his knees. The Czar had certainly enjoyed that!

The Czar and Czarina had no children to inherit his crown. It was known that the Czar had several illegitimate children. He would marry off his mistresses to army officers or diplomats once mistresses got pregnant and dispatch them to far distant locations. I was always very careful not to mention his illegitimate children, being so ultra-sensitive on that subject.

The Czarina had really adored my Louisa Catherine and had showered her with gifts. There were embroidered dresses or French dolls with eyes that opened and closed.

All those happy days are over now. Louisa Catherine has been committed to Russia's frozen earth in the Lutheran Cemetery where foreigner Protestants are interred. There is an empty space next to her little grave, and I sorely hope to be placed there as soon as God wills it. And I pray that will happen soon.

Late September brought ice and storms. The scenery, when seen from my St. Petersburg mansion's window, was as bleak as my heart. I stood at the panes of glass, streaked with snowflakes and pelted with hail, thinking how all happiness had vanished as surely as the cherry blossoms of the past spring.

Daily my heart bled for Louisa Catherine.

Winter's bite invaded our overly-furnished rooms, which had many ornaments sent from the Czar, but no decent fireplace. The house rent did include a supply of firewood, but it was far from sufficient for our needs. Parsimonious Mr. Adams certainly never bought any extra firewood. I could see the knuckles of my fingers expanding as a precursor to arthritis.

Mr. Adams kept warm by his nightly use of my flesh. No more kisses. But thrusting? Oh yes, he never stopped relishing that even without one word spoken to me. Thrusting was his right as a husband. He was never one to waste what was his right to have and enjoy. Did he know about the fact I was illegitimate? Did it count?

As my heart broke, the rest of the world unraveled simultaneously. We remained in St. Petersburg while avalanched with bad news from America. The war with Britain, which Mr. Adams had attempted to prevent when a Senator by voting against the embargo act, had duly erupted. In June 1812, when I was still so happy as to turn a blind eye to tragedy, the United States had declared war on Britain, unwilling to permit further impressments of American sailors. The involuntary naval conscriptions of over ten thousand sailors were an outrage, practically equal to kidnapping these men! Mr. Adams fumed over the situation, snubbing the British Ambassador.

For many long months, Mr. Adams had to pretend to the Russian Court that all was well with the war in America. He even had to bite his tongue when he learned of the Battle of Lake Erie just this past September, near where Mr. Adams had planned for the Erie Canal to be built.

Fighting raged from the border with Canada all the way to Louisiana. America purchased Louisiana from the French in 1803. Western Florida was acquired in 1810. Now there was so much additional territory to protect, neither the United States nor Britain seemed to be able to declare victory. Mr. Adams curbed his furies and played out his role as a diplomat.

Oh, 1812 was truly a terrible year! Napoleon, who had conquered most of Western Europe, had decided to invade Russia in that same awful June in which America declared war on Britain. Yes, Russia where we were posted. But he aimed for Moscow, not for St. Petersburg where we are ensconced. Moscow, the legendary ancient capital, had been the jewel in Russia's crown before Czar Peter the First had decided to create his new capital, St. Petersburg, alongside the Bay of Finland.

America against Britain, France invading Russia, those wars were additional reasons for me to fall into deep depression. In my official diary, I wrote, "I read, I work. I endeavor to occupy myself usefully, but it is all in vain."

St. Petersburg, November 21, 1813

The bitter harshness of 1812 gave way to the deep malaise of this year wherein little cheered me. Mr. Adams insisted I go to balls at Court, but to relieve my brown moods during the daylight hours, I took the little nursemaid to see the churches in St. Petersburg. Mr. Adams had declared them off limits because they were full of "icons" which he considered idolatrous. I believe the icons we saw were magnificent pieces of real art. The older ones included tiny miniatures of country folk in processions or adoring the saints. I could appreciate the costumes and hairstyles of those far-gone days. I loved the tranquility captured in many saints' expressions, particularly the Madonnas. The "Mother of God" icons sometimes showed a mourning mother after the crucifixion of Jesus. I certainly understood what a mother felt on losing a precious child.

The music I heard in these churches was sublime. In America it seems we have few male voices that can descend to such low notes as the choirs do in Russia. I loved the Our Father sung in these ancient churches with superb acoustics. I never heard better anywhere.

The worshipers themselves intrigued me. There were many Babushkas, which is what Russians call some peasant women. They not only went down on their knees, they would often press their heads to the floor in paroxysms of prayer. They seemed to be raging at past sins. What sins could these pathetically deprived women possibly have committed to induce such shame?

Even on bitterly cold winter days, when the canals of St. Petersburg were frozen over and carts could be trundled over the ice, I visited the churches with the little nursemaid. As women, we were forbidden to pass the elaborate wooden screen that separated the women in the congregation from a dusky, hidden altar behind it. Men could go beyond its elaborate facade. Not us.

There were not many peasant men praying. I had seen enough of them cleaning streets, driving carts, and carrying loads on their backs like pack animals. Occasionally one of these workmen would slip into the church I was visiting. He would light another of the multitude of candles, cross himself from right to left, and with an embarrassed expression, then vanish.

I brought Charles with me on the least bitter days, but cold weather meant nothing to my healthy son. He loved snow and showed no signs of grippe or catarrh no matter how far down one of Gabriel Fahrenheit's mercury thermometers plunged. Fahrenheit had invented them in 1724, and we found ours second-hand even in Moscow!

I taught Charles the melody to a peasant song, "The White Nights of Novgorod," and he whistled it going from one of our nasty cold rooms to the others.

I can't whistle. I've never learned how to pucker up my lips so they would do the job.

Dear, loyal Charles, who comforted me with small gifts he had made himself of waste paper or torn cloth. He tried so hard to lighten my dark moods and to bring me closer to Mr. Adams. But Charles couldn't help me reach out to his father. The chasm was too deep and ever-widening.

I read fifty-three volumes during the endless winter. Rudely, Mr. Adams had presented one of them to me as a gift, a book titled Diseases of the Mind. Was he about to have me committed for insanity? Tear me from Charles as he had torn me from our older sons?

Although Mr. Adams deferred from dwelling on the subject of my never-produced dowry, he did speak incessantly now about my father's reputed mental problems. Unfortunately, it was true that Father had been in his dotage. His mind had no longer functioned as it had when he was at the peak of his earlier successful business career. In letters to me in St. Petersburg, my sister Nancy had described some of the aberrations of his last days, even though his death was a decade ago. For instance, he had walked outside his Washington house in his nightshirt.

But surely, dotage happens to many very elderly people. Insanity does not run in my family. depression, on a seriously-sick scale, and alcoholism do run in the Smith side of the Adams family. Abigail's brothers had suffered from both.

Driving from our apartments to yet another engagement at the Czar's Hermitage Palace, our carriage passed one of the most glorious examples of Russian ecclesiastical art. Mr. Adams attacked me when he saw my eyes light up. This particular church had one of the most dramatic onion-shaped domes of the many in St. Petersburg. I truly felt my spirits rise whenever I passed the sky-blue dome with its sprinkling of painted stars. It inspired me to feel I was rising into the heavens to soar through the universe passing un-named planets.

Mr. Adams frowned, whilst grumping that I had no right to expose his son to Russia's orthodox churches. "Priests in cloaks embroidered with gold thread and studded with precious gems! What a sight for a boy from Quincy! Don't try to hide from me that you have been taking Charles to Russian churches."

"I wanted Charles to have a glimpse of Russia's peasant women," I countered, pulling my far hip from touching his, although the carriage's rear seat was narrow. "I never see the real Russian peasant women except in the churches. Not at the farmer market, certainly not at Court. Not even as servants. Russian aristocrats tap the middle class for their servants, and so have we."

"Idols and icons—it is an outrage that you drag Charles to these churches. They are filled with gems and gold, which, according to Christ should go to the poor."

"They are Protestant churches, with the same creed that Quincy churches have. They have Christmas and Easter, those same wonderful feasts we celebrate. The Russian people and priests just have a different way of expressing their love for Christ. Since when have you, Mr. Adams, taken offense when someone is different? For instance, if the color of a person's skin is different?"

That shut him up. He blustered and blew wind through his nose to make the snuffling noise, but Mr. Adams knows I share his views on the wicked way that Black slaves are treated in the United States. And by France! Had I not seen the human cargo from France's slave ships in Nantes?

Having gained the advantage, I pressed home. "Russian women aren't permitted to approach the altar; they're barred by a huge screen. Believe me, if the women had more say about their churches, I feel sure they would strip away the gold trappings to give their worth to educate and feed the poor."

We had arrived at the Hermitage. We were stuck in a long queue of elaborate carriages. We were too close to their passengers to quarrel further. We could have been overheard. I nodded, smiling at the neighbor party-goers. Mr. Adams wore a grim expression, with lips tightened, but so did men in other carriages.

There were officers in white uniforms prior to leaving for the Front, and with them were ladies in extravagant gowns who were trying to control tears. Guests of Czar Alexander were not permitted miserable expressions when arriving for his parties. All invited were bound to come, even if a mother had just learned that her only son had been killed in a battle at the Front. Or even if disease and barbaric medicine had claimed her infant girl.

News of Napoleon's advance was not good; he was reaching Moscow. Mr. Adams had been kept up to date on the French positions. As Minister from the United States, he had a conduit to the Czar's spies. With my baby Louisa Catherine dying, I hadn't followed the progress of that war. How could I? My eyes had been too flooded with tears to read reports.

I don't criticize Mr. Adams for doing his job. He needed to know what was happening on the Niemen River. More than that, he ached to know who was winning this war. But he hated war. He'd ruined his career in the Senate by battling against the embargo bill, hoping to avoid the war with Britain.

For months in 1812 it looked as if Napoleon had pulled off another outstanding victory. His Grande Armée of two hundred and seventy thousand French veterans had swollen to six hundred and fifty thousand with his allies' forces who followed him across Russia to gain Moscow. But fat, one-eyed General Kutuzov, as ugly as Czar Alexander was handsome, had assumed the defense of that area.

When alerted that Napoleon had entered Moscow in June, Kutuzov ordered its people to abandon Moscow, leaving it as empty as a graveyard. They left it with no wood for fires or food to eat. Napoleon's soldiers deserted in great numbers out of starvation and from the cold. They rushed away into the countryside to eat whatever was not hidden by the astute peasants. There, they were picked off by those same peasants, armed by guerrillas, while their Grande Armée colleagues froze to death from the cruel winter and hunger.

And then brilliant General Kutuzov gave the order to burn Moscow. Its last stores of wheat, its remaining piles of kindling wood, and the very homes of its inhabitants went up in flames.

"General Winter is winning the war," Mr. Adams learned. With food and fuel gone, the French troops couldn't survive in Russia's freezing climate.

By October 12, Napoleon gave the order to abandon Moscow.

After constant harassing by Russian guerrillas his straggling troops finally arrived at the Berezina River, the point at which his Russian campaign finally ended.

Napoleon's army had shrunk to twenty-seven thousand able men. With it he traveled west to defeat and plunder easier enemies. He left behind in Russia three hundred and eighty thousand dead, plus one hundred thousand who had been taken prisoner.

But the only death in Russia that matters to me still is that of my own little girl.

St. Petersburg, January 21, 1815

While Napoleon quit Russia last year, the troubles of war did not quit the world. While Mr. Adams had bitten his tongue over the battle at Lake Erie, he had a much harder time stifling his fury over the burning of Washington by the British with the partial destruction of the President's House. Had not his parents been its first occupants? Distant though we were, posted to Russia, we both felt deeply the devastation. That architectural jewel that we'd called The President's House, had been torched and scorched. There is a rumor that the place is now called the White House after it had been painted white to hide the soot from the conflagration, but that is a farce. Many have already called it the White House informally for a few years now.

Elsewhere, Napoleon's Russian campaign's failure did not dampen his immense ego. He fought on in Germany and in Denmark. And my fear was that he would reach Ghent.

Why was I concerned for Ghent? Because without a word of warning, Mr. Adams had suddenly left me in order to travel to Ghent. I felt as defeated as Napoleon had been in Russia.

Mr. Adams, having had an index finger cocked his way by President Madison, with orders to go to Ghent representing the United States to sign a treaty there with the British which would end the War of 1812, walked out on Charles and me. He has left us stranded in St. Petersburg with a vague promise to let me know when to meet him elsewhere.

In addition he left me a note saying he would send money for me to pay our bills and hire a carriage to join him wherever he would go next. Meanwhile, he suggested, "Sell our St. Petersburg furniture to have money for the trip." Oh, I knew very well that any money from Mr. Adams would be a long time coming. If at all!

His orders to sell our furnishings were not that easy with which to comply. There I was, a single mother of a seven-year-old boy, deserted by the husband who had been my entry card to the Czar's Court. Oh yes, a woman who now had even less money to pay our enormous bills.

Letting go most of our household staff, I kept on a personal maid and two footmen whom I needed for protection. I went to work selling our possessions, feeling cheap to have to haggle, but determined to get the best prices possible for our furnishings.

Amazingly, the invitations from Czar Alexander kept coming. I had to at end his parties. I had to go to the Dowager Czarina's levees, or I would be blackballed in this mad country. War or no war, their parties creaked on.

On one bleak evening I found myself alone with Czar Alexander in the Hermitage's grand salon. The walls echoed as he said, "I heard that you once spoke sharply to the then French Ambassador, who told you, 'When in Rome do as the Romans do.' And you answered him with, 'If I should go to Rome, perhaps I might.' Dear Louisa, surely you would not speak in such a manner to me."

I tried to laugh off this provocation. But the Czar remained tight-lipped. So I told him in an outspoken way what I felt as the daughter-in-law of a revolutionary, "Your Imperial Majesty, I am a Republican." And guess what? The Czar's face wreathed with smiles, and he gave a huge guffaw.

Several ladies at Court murmured behind my back that Mr. Adams had left me for another woman. They said he had a mistress in Ghent. I countered my qualms by writing a letter to Mr. Adams with a tongue-in-cheek suggestion that he get a mistress! However, I read in his pages on Ghent that he found the ladies there badly-dressed and ugly. Lucky me? What he did find was a valet, Antoine Guista, who stayed very close to him indeed.

Meanwhile, I had a challenging experience at the last of the Czar's balls I was obliged to attend. A member of the Czar's Inner Circle asked me to dance the minuet. I accepted, knowing it would be bad manners to refuse, but also thinking he could be aware that my husband was absent from Court. He was brilliantly outfitted in a Hussar's white uniform, adorned with many medals. That seemed strange because I'd heard that this particular "officer" had never fired a gun in battle.

We lined up with the other dancers, and suddenly he grabbed my right hand and kissed it. I wasn't wearing gloves! When his lips grazed my exposed flesh I felt a startling rush of blood below my stomach in an area totally un-used to a feeling of that kind. I hadn't sensed any such rush of blood there since that distant day in Hyde Park when I hid behind a tree to be caressed by the suitor who subsequently left me to return to America.

Oh no! I believed I mustn't have such feelings! I withdrew my hand, and would have spun away but the minuet music had begun.

Was I about to commit ADULTERY? Blushing like a girl in her teens, I danced correctly to the end. Then, without a word I fled out of the palace and waited alone for my hired carriage.

What a flood of sensations came! Whilst freezing cold snowflakes swirled around my bared head, my lower regions were on fire.

From the corner of an eye I noticed that the fake officer had followed me to the waiting carriages! I rushed to ask another departing lady guest if I could share her carriage.

My request granted, I tore into the back seat and cringed there whilst her footmen secured the carriage's door.

All the way home, attempting to make polite conversation with my Good Samaritan, I secretly pondered if it wasn't a good thing that I could still have such sensual feelings.

Oh, if only those feelings could be inflamed by Mr. Adams!

Paris, March 27, 1815

It turned 1815 before I quit St. Petersburg. I left on February 12, my birthday. Mr. Adams summoned me to make the trip to Paris immediately, although we were in the depths of winter. Yes, I was ordered to cross most of Europe struggling against snow and ice.

My maid stayed loyal and offered to accompany me. I hired two French coachmen and a manservant, and had the coach fitted with runners to make it slide like a sleigh over Russia's ice-frosted roads.

Charles, now almost eight and a studious schoolboy, said he was man enough to protect me no matter what ruffians might attack the carriage.

Suf ice it to add that before I left Russia I learned that Mr. Adams had finally signed the treaty ending the War of 1812, which warmed my Londoner heart because the treaty released Britain's forces tied up in America to continue the fight in Europe against Napoleon. Typically for Mr. Adams, the date he signed the treaty in Ghent was Christmas Eve. He never had the slightest sensitivity about such things. Never.

The trip from St. Petersburg to Paris was ghastly. The manservant I'd hired to accompany us in our carriage stole a silver cup belonging to Charles and most of my money. But on hiring him, he had seemed promising; he spoke the languages of countries we were to cross on our way. I had mastered some Hochdeutsch in Berlin, but nothing else. The coachmen knew only French. I couldn't risk traveling without these two coachmen, and so they remained in my employ.

Our first challenge was the Vistula River, where my coachmen removed the runners and fitted wheels on our carriage. It was perilous-decision-time for me because I had to give the order to cross the river although its ice was beginning to split into floes. We made it to the other side, but my maid had hysterics.

In all, I endured almost two months of traveling. In addition to crossing perilous rivers, I was threatened by bands of army deserters who had no salaries and no way to pay for food. For those soldiers it was steal, or starve.

We passed gangs of dogs foraging on battlefields for the bones of soldiers who had died fighting for their respective countries. It was a horrible sight to see.

Nor was it only dogs that foraged in those tragic fields. Peasants robbed the bodies of the recently dead, whose watches might still be ticking and the powder still dry for their expensive pistols.

Approaching France, my two French coachmen deserted me, terrified they would be pressed into Napoleon's re-assembled army. To replace them, I had to find two peasants who could drive a team of horses. Not easy, when you are nowhere near a major town or city.

I learned that Napoleon had escaped from his Elba Island imprisonment and was heading for Paris to reassemble an army. Napoleon had the same destination as I did! Worse, it was too late for me to return to St. Petersburg.

Several times my Russian-built carriage was stopped by crowds of French survivors of the failed Moscow Campaign, screaming I was a Russian who deserved to die. I stopped that by standing tall outside my carriage and calling out "Vive Napoleon!" That, although I am the British-born daughter and wife of an American. I resolved to continue on our way, in spite of continued threats made by bellicose French peasants.

Not the greatest of my decisions! By March 20, Napoleon was within a few miles of Paris with a new army having recharged the immense loyalty of what remained of France's able-bodied men.

I was also but a few miles from the same destination when a furious mob congregated in front of our carriage to block any further progress. Listening to the crowd screaming at me, I trembled violently remembering the stories I had heard of the French Revolution and how mobs literally tore people to pieces before the guillotine took over to do the killing.

Protection? I no longer had my trusty French coachmen. I didn't possess a set of dueling pistols. But, as so often has happened in my jumbled life, a "knight-in-shining-armor" appeared just in time to save us. He was a French officer in command of some reservists, and he inquired if I carried a passport. I showed him my American papers.

The officer, who had been courteous to me, yelled to the raging mob, "This is an American lady on her way to join her husband."

Unbelievably, those ragged peasants lifted off their shabby hats and yelled, "Vive les Américains." The Republic of America is still popular in France!

My "knight in shining armor" disbanded the desperados, and I backed up his judgment by permitting him to start a rumor that I was a niece of Napoleon's. What would ex-President Adams have thought of that?

Forewarned by that experience, I delayed three days to give Paris a chance to settle down after Emperor Napoleon's disastrous return.

It was eleven at night on March 23, when my worn-out carriage delivered Charles and me to the door of Mr. Adams' hotel. And where was Mr. Adams? At some theater enjoying a play! As if there wasn't enough drama going on right under his nose in Paris, plus his wife and son arriving after many months of separation.

When he returned to his room Mr. Adams was perfectly astonished to hear of my adventures. Everything in Paris was quiet, and it had never occurred to him that it would have been otherwise in any other part of the country.

Quiet! With Napoleon back in town?

Mr. Adams welcomed Charles with a hug, showed him to his bedroom, and then marched me to the marital bed. Stripping off his clothes and mine, he wasn't amorous; he was positively lewd. I imagine he had been re-reading those books based on the naughty adventures of Don Juan. At least he hadn't learned any Parisian tricks to inflict on me since last we had lain together. Oh, he didn't fail to get in where he wanted to go, unlike when he pissed in an unfamiliar chamber pot, when he often missed the bowl.

Paris, April 26, 1815

In Paris, the city of lovemaking, I was starved of it again. He used my body, certainly, but I don't equate that with lovemaking. There had been no kissing, no fondling. On either part. But as weeks wore on his seed was deposited nightly, just as thoughtlessly as ever.

How I would have appreciated being given a new dress! Doesn't any woman new to Paris want a dress from there and in the latest fashion? No dress for me. Mr. Adams growled that money spent on any clothes for me would be a waste because I would probably soon be pregnant again, and the figure of a woman changed so markedly when she was with child.

He never invited me to go to the theater, especially the same theater that he attended nightly.

Why? Were the plays so lascivious they were unfit for a lady, even a pregnant lady? I went on my own to concerts, or took Charles with me if it was a vespers performance. Charles and I heard blissful music.

One night, I dared take Charles to a comic opera at Versailles. A Bourbon, Louis XVIII, had been placed on the throne of France and re-opened the exquisite small theater inside the Palace of Versailles. The theater was decorated in red velvet with gold leaf trimming-carved woodwork. The decor was better than the acting, which I found stiff and unrealistic, not portraying real living characters.

That little theater had been used by Queen Marie Antoinette to perform in "masques." I thought how lively she must have been and how delightful it must have been for her audiences to view her in her favorite role of shepherdess before the terrible onslaught of the bloody guillotine. That perfect neck, with its Austrian pearl skin, had been severed by the mobs, which, within several more years, shouted with fervor to welcome Napoleon as an emperor and eventually welcomed Louis XVIII.

On the evening following our expedition to the Palace of Versailles' theater, Mr. Adams faced me down with one of his temper tantrums. I was removing my cloak in our rooms when Mr. Adams heard Charles whistle tunes that were unfamiliar to him. With his face turning purple and veins on his forehead bulging like worms, he demanded I tell where I had taken Charles for him to learn such tunes. I spoke up truthfully. I was in a mood to "talk back."

"Versailles."

"You paid for a carriage to and from Versailles? A veritable fortune! I could have bought a new pair of boots for that money. Good ones."

I peered at his boots. Yes, they were shabby. He did need new ones. He could have bought several pairs if he had foregone the theaters he attended. Oh, I wasn't going to have an argument over shoes. I retreated from our room, rushing to help Charles prepare for bed in his room.

I was well aware that Mr. Adams wore clothes that were almost always shabby and well past when they should have reached retirement. Mr. Adams rarely refreshed his wardrobe with the excuse that he had no time for frivolities. He wore one of his hats for ten years! Too bad Mr. Adams had no love for clothes. Paris at that time was such a center for dandies, who had been hiding out during the French Revolution keeping their heads on their necks until Napoleon founded his empire. When I'd arrived in Paris, Napoleon's Marshals were among the best dressed men in France.

Speaking of elegant Marshals, the gossip in Paris concerned ex-Maréchal Bernadotte who had been created King of Sweden by Napoleon. There were snickers behind fans from the ladies and guffaws from even the lowest coachmen. The former Maréchal Bernadotte, who for years had been one of Napoleon's best generals, had been sent by Napoleon to reign in Stockholm as King of Sweden because—as rumor had it—Napoleon wanted Berndaotte's wife to be a queen. Earlier, Bernadotte had surprised Napoleon by marrying Napoleon's first love, Désirée Clary, the daughter of a silk merchant in Marseille. Napoleon had romanced Désirée during his earliest time as a commissioned officer. More surprises when gossips predicted Queen Désirée would walk out on the King, which would leave Sweden with the excuse that it was too cold and ruining her health.

How I wish I could walk out on Mr. Adams. Another night in our bedroom when Mr. Adams railed on about how immoral the French were, I reminded him about all the gossip concerning Thomas Jefferson and his slave girl, Sally Hemings. It was common knowledge that Jefferson had brought "Dusky Sally" with him to Paris during the days when the French Revolution was hotting up. When Jefferson returned to Virginia with her, Sally Hemings gave birth to several illegitimate mulattos. They were reputedly either Mr. Jefferson's or the children of one of Mr. Jefferson's nephews.

A strange tale, to say the least. Particularly when you consider that Sally was the illegitimate daughter of Mr. Jefferson's wife's father, Mr. Wayles. So, Jefferson's wife and Jefferson's "dusky" mistress were half-sisters! Oh, I never dwelt on that subject, because I always become nervous when that word "illegitimate" enters a conversation. But I certainly recalled being filled in about "Dusky Sally" before Mr. Adams and I went to visit Mrs. Martha Washington with her army of unhappy slaves.

That night I would have far preferred to discuss the immorality of dueling—a subject close to Mr. Adams' heart—if he'd been willing to discuss anything at all. Not that he often talked to me about dueling, because WE were still not speaking to each other. But he did rail on about that evil, reminding anyone—me—who was listening as to how many fine and talented men had been downed in a duel.

When he seemed shocked by all the duels fought in Paris, I dared to add, "And how about that duel when America's Vice-President Aaron Burr shot and killed Founding-Father Alexander Hamilton?"

That was the end of any conversation for the night. It meant bed with him for me and a return to being used as a piss-pot.

London, June 7, 1815

Spring in Paris was bearable. I could walk in the Tuilleries, take Charles for pony-rides, and then let him graduate to horses in the Bois de Boulogne. But I was not looking forward to summer in that city because I'd heard it was so stifling hot that most people of means—that meant who could afford to—escaped to the countryside. According to Mr. Adams, who was hoarding our moneys like a squirrel gathers nuts, we couldn't afford to lease a country house, nor even to stay at a coachman's inn.

However, I needn't have worried about Paris in the summer. By May, Mr. Adams received notice that he'd been appointed the United States Minister to the Court of St. James. We were going to move to London! My birthplace. Best of all, Mr. Adams relented about leaving our two eldest boys with their grandparents in Quincy, and had them embark for London to join us there!

Crossing the Channel gave us no difficulties. We were fortunate to sail from France when the sea was calm. No illness! I felt I could have swum across, I was so happy. Within weeks I would see my two elder sons and have them live with me!

Mr. Adams paid a scurrilous Danish captain a hugely inflated price to get us to England, and when we arrived in London, he wasn't disappointed that he'd broken his lifelong penny-pinching to get quickly to the Court of St. James.

London is fun, and gloriously frivolous! Sickly old King George has been relegated to a mere figurehead, whilst his naughty, eldest son, George, runs the country as Prince Regent. What parties we have attended! What palaces we have visited!

Prince George's fantasy pavilion at Brighton was by far the most erotic. I have never been in a Turkish seraglio, but I'll wager that even the most sophisticated Pasha was out-done by Prince George. He had erotic furniture, such as comfortable chaise longues that in Paris were made for ladies to lounge in, but in Prince George's Brighton palace were for sexual intercourse.

I had the privilege to watch the artist Rowlandson draw a pencil sketch of the Prince with his lady, Mrs. Fitzherbert. He created good likenesses of both.

And yes, Mrs. Fitzherbert was exceedingly pretty. It made me get depressed again when I learned that under the rules of Britain's ruling family, no Roman Catholic could enter it, nor could the children of a Roman Catholic succeed to the throne. So Mrs. Fitzherbert, a Roman Catholic, was unable to admit that she had been married secretly to Prince George. She couldn't acknowledge they had children. Women are wronged in so many ways.

Also because of the rules laid down for the British Royals, Prince George was pushed into marriage with a Protestant first cousin, Caroline of Brunswick, who was so vulgar that she munched on raw onions in his presence! He was so revolted by her that on their wedding night he got drunk, fainted, and fell into the fireplace. Unhappy Prince

George! And unhappy wife!

King George sent a carriage for the two of us to come to St. James's Palace for Mr. Adams to present his credentials as the new Minister Plenipotentiary from the United States of America. For this occasion it was not I who had a surprise on that day.

In the carriage on our return journey from the palace, Mr. Adams gloated, "Yes, Mrs. Adams, I had a most extraordinary happening after I presented my credentials. King George suddenly rose from his throne and asked me, 'Are you related to that first Minister from the United States, also called Mr. Adams?'"

"'Sir,' I responded with the utmost pleasure, 'indeed I am. He is my father.'"

London, May 20, 1817

We have been in England for these past two years, and every bit of it has been bliss! My sons love it here. They have enjoyed learning to fish and to ride horses, both of which are sports I share with them. I LOVE that sharing! We took a house in Ealing, eight miles outside London. Its name was Little Boston.

From the outset, Mr. Adams did bring me along to some of the main social events. I've seen a side of London denied to me when I was a girl. All the parties I attended then were in my own parents' home. I suppose that was because the society's matrons knew I was illegitimate.

With Mr. Adams as Minister Plenipotentiary to the Court of St. James, I have been included at literary evenings. There, superior conversations are the rule. I particularly took note of manners and dress when we went to Lord Holland's house. What magnificence I found in that great house, and what culture! Ladies declaimed poetry and joined with some of the men to participate in a game to strike poses as statues to suggest the titles of the newest books. I love that!

Some of the participants use stilted words and phrases. One evening, Mrs. Mellones said to me, "I quite dote on you. I knew I would adore you the first moment I laid eyes on you." Never! I hoped she wasn't one of those who play the flat game.

One of the grandest features of Holland House is its long interior walkway, created in order that the ladies of the household can have necessary exercise when inclement weather determines that the ladies must remain indoors. Part of this long walkway cum-hall was lined with the most intriguing books. On every visit, I want desperately to find a chair to sit down and look through one of the volumes. Not possible. Manners do not permit.

I content myself by peering at the sumptuous jewels and gowns the ladies wear. Their noble husbands don't lag far behind in the matter of clothing or jewelry. The men sport embroidered waistcoats sparkling with diamonds, in the tradition of the Duke of Buckingham who'd so entranced Louis XIV's mother that it was rumored he had been the King's "natural" father.

Many of the foreign ambassadors wear the wide ribbons of decorations across their chests, accompanied by the medals awarded. Some of their Ladies show off hillocks of hair wrapped in turbans, Turkish style. Their dresses are copies of Napoleon's first wife's style; Empress Josephine had favored narrow skirts of the most gossamer materials which revealed naked bodies underneath the silk. At one literary evening, I heard that Empress Josephine had died due to catching pneumonia caused when she had her gown made wet to create a transparent look. Nobody blushed when that rumor was repeated. The ladies at the party had heard many more startling tales. I felt tempted to tell them of my visit to Princess X in Berlin, but I still felt too disgusted at having viewed the events to regale anyone with a recount.

Another evening Mr. Adams declaimed on politics to the Duke of St. Albans, a descendant of King Charles II and the apple seller Nell Gwynn. He stated, "I am not sad that a part of Massachusetts has been taken to create the new state, Maine. I wish to be a man of the whole Union, not to restrict myself to be known as a man of Massachusetts only."

The Duke replied, "My dear chap, do not give the matter much thought. Money is what matters, not one's birthplace. Will you make any money on this event?"

"No. And I do not behoove it right to do what is useful if it goes against the laws of justice."

The Duke turned away, busying himself with his snuff box. He took a pinch of snuff and applied it to each nostril, holding his head high.

A Mrs. Beacham took the Duke's place. She walked very bent with her body almost doubled. It had shrunk in her late years. Before opening her mouth to speak she hid her missing teeth by raising a fan of peacock feathers and fluttering its ribs in front of her pus-marked gums. "Fancy turning away like that!" she muttered. "The Duke need not have scorned you because you believe in justice, my American friend. The Duke of St. Albans is always pleading for justice be given to his ancestor, the Earl of Oxford, whom he believes wrote most of Shakespeare's plays."

Mr. Adams bowed politely. "Indeed? I have heard that is so."

"This Duke is one who is proud to have been descended from an illegitimate son of King Charles. In fact, he would have none of the money he so worships if King Charles had not married his bastard son St. Albans to the very rich daughter of the last Earl of Oxford. In the days of the Restoration, it paid to be illegitimate if the child's father was the King or a royal Duke."

Now I did blush. Oh, why do I always have to feel faint every time I hear the word "illegitimate?" But Mr. Adams seemed not to notice. He drained his glass of a favorite brand of Madeira and offered his free arm to Mrs. Beachem to proceed into the dining hall.

I was offered the arm of Prussia's refugee Ambassador-in-exile, who had been a great favorite of ours when we lived in Berlin. Napoleon's earlier victory over Prussia had robbed him of his estates and fortune. He felt relieved to be in London as a displaced diplomat because the Court of St. James often welcomed exiles, particularly those who had tasted ruin due to Napoleon. Although that false emperor had lost the Battle of Waterloo and been sent to die in St. Helena, there were still many displaced and impoverished exiles in London who moved in society like the flotsam a swollen river leaves behind after a storm subsides.

Another pleasant afternoon was spent in the dining hall of the House of Lords. We sat at first in a small salon opposite the entrance to the Lords' Dining Hall. We were offered an introductory drink whilst we could overlook the Thames River. Pulsating with life, the river offered amazing contrasts. Although a dull gray color, tiny darts of sunshine sparkled like stars in the wakes of the many varieties of ships. There were imposing seaworthy brigantines. There were fragile canoes. There were turtle-backed tugs pulling rafts loaded with local goods.

The sight of ships brought out a rare smile from Mr. Adams and an endearing phrase to me. He said to our host, Sir Edmund Burke, "This scene reminds me of Boston harbor, although there we would see whaling ships. My dearest friend, Mrs. Adams is a poor sailor, but I believe she could manage a day on the Thames."

"Hear, hear!" our host encouraged my husband to say on.

He did. "I expect to see more roads, canals, and bridges to be built under the new administration in Washington. I would like to see improvements to river communications. I hear there are plans to sail the ORLEANS, a steamboat, down river from Pittsburgh."

I ventured a comment. "Do not those steamboats explode on occasion?"

Mr. Adams changed the tone of his voice. In a disparaging way he looked down his ample nose, quivered those nostrils, and declaimed, "Balderdash! As my country grows larger, so will our ships, and they will be perfectly safe—on average, ninety percent of the time."

I murmured, "I wouldn't want to be aboard one for the other ten percent of the time."

Sir Edmund brought out his snuff box and busied his hands with it. He said nothing.

Mr. Adams kept on his subject. "It is the object of government to improve the condition of the people.

I believe more roads and river traffic are essential to my Nation's further expansion. My only worry is that the United States will expand too rapidly and change our traditional way of life. The almighty dollar will reign, instead of justice and propriety. My hope is that expansion will include the building of universities and astronomical observatories."

Sir Edmund belched. I believe his stomach was crying out for dinner.

Mr. Adams plowed on, "I personally welcomed the entrance of Louisiana into the United States. Bought in

1803, it had already become a sovereign state by 1812. Fast enough for any one's taste. We Americans thought it great when Massachusetts exported 2 million dollars of goods. Louisiana exports twelve million a year! Now I am looking to Eastern Florida as the next great venture. I profoundly disapprove of the way Spaniards, and—sadly I must admit—some British behaved, rounding up hundreds of the native Indians, and sailing them of to Cuba to be sold as slaves. These native peoples have been in their areas for many thousands of years and have a right to remain on those lands. I am very concerned for them."

Sir Edmund had finished with his snuff box. "But they are savages, my dear fellow, are they not?" "Many tribes have superb skills. I have witnessed how they can make amazing utensils out of local materials. A ship's captain brought me a sword made from a strong wood studded with razor-sharp shark's teeth. They make drinking cups out of conch shells, and even a hammer was shown to me made of a conch shell notched into a sturdy pole. They build swift canoes. They build mounds to bury their chiefs, not unlike those of Britain in the days of Druids."

A liveried servant came to announce that our first course was on a table inside the Dining Hall. Only his dutiful manner could have interrupted my Mr. Adams!

Another memorable event was the evening we spent at Sotheby's, the Auctioneers. Due to my having sold most of our possessions before leaving St. Petersburg, we have very little to remind ourselves of the eight years we had spent abroad. Surprising me that evening, Mr. Adams declared he intended to buy several paintings to bring back to Massachusetts. He chose to go to an auction specializing in Sporting Art. What a lark!

My stingy husband suggested we walk to Sotheby's to save on hackney fare to apply it to what we would spend on paintings. On arrival at the luxurious premises of these auctioneers, carpeted with Turkey rugs and with ceilings hung with magnificent crystal chandeliers, I felt embarrassed to be so simply dressed. My hair was messed and my hat askew.

There were a number of extravagantly-gowned ladies, not only wearing layers of silks trimmed with furs worthy of the Silk Routes of Asia, but strutting with the aid of the newest fashion: five-foot-high canes. I slithered close to one of these ladies, whose eagle eyes were scanning each new painting that was brought out to be exhibited on a large easel.

To Mr. Adams' fury, this lady proceeded to bid over any price he offered.

"Six guineas," Mr. Adams roared when a portrait by Sir Joshua Reynolds of Sir Edmund Burke took its place on the auctioneer's easel. It was a dark picture, showing the parliamentarian's face and shoulders against a black background. "Sir Edmund Burke was the only parliamentarian to speak out for the Colonies. I could get a high price for that in America," Mr. Adams said in an aside to me.

"Seven guineas," contested this brazen lady. I thought she must have enormous strength of character to take on Mr. Adams and attempt to outbid him. But of course she could not know that he is very careful with a sixpence, let alone six guineas. She let that painting go to another bidder who topped all offers.

My wily husband let her bid first when a charming portrait of a partridge arrived. This painting was by John Nost Sartorious, noted for his works catching the individuality of a bird, thanks to giving flecks of light to the one eye that showed in profile.

I whispered, "I like the way every quill is portrayed in such a way you could feel how delicate a feather is."

The arrogant lady bidder, the ostrich plumes in her huge hat fluttering, called out, “Five guineas.”

“Five-fifty,” choked out Mr. Adams.

“Sold!” announced Mr. Sotheby, and to Mr. Adams’s chagrin, he had bought that picture!

He growled, “I really came here to acquire a painting of a horse. I could double my money if I resell it in Maryland to my horsemen cousins. All they care to do is go to horse races, or race in point-to points.” He did buy one—by a Henry Alken, showing a chestnut-brown colt with a wild eye. The arrogant lady had not attempted to bid against him. Why?

I asked Mr. Adams, “I don’t understand why that lady has seemed to have lost interest in buying any painting on which you bid.”

“Simple. She must work for the auctioneer and gets foolish bidders to compete with her. But when she saw I was not in that league, because I only went up half a guinea. She did her job properly and waited for the next fool.”

I found that information very interesting. Glancing across the salon to observe the lady more closely, I could see her eyes glint when a foppish peer showed off his full purse. A woman at work! What an amazing revelation! I love it. Here is a lady who has discovered a new way to earn her living. I can but admire her ingenuity.

Mr. Adams had to wait until the end of the auction to collect his two purchases. They proved to be too bulky to carry. He had to hire a hackney to drive us. Lucky me! I’d dreaded the prospect of another eight mile walk to go home to Little Boston.

We hung the Alken portrait of the horse above our main mantelpiece and found an empty wall opposite a window for the Sartorious partridge where the evening’s pink sunset rays gives it a glow. I like the partridge picture best, and eventually Mr. Adams grudgingly admitted to liking it too.

"It will remind me of that day of shooting I had at the Duke of Marlborough's estate, Blenheim."

A typical comment, reminding me of his having gained social stature among the London elite. I have had to keep silent and hope he will not sell the painting for a profit.

Contrasting with that auction evening and the parties in London were my glorious days going fishing with my three sons. Stingy as he was, Mr. Adams still bought proper rods for all four of us and hired a ghillie to give us lessons in fly-casting. He provided us with hooks hidden in hand-made lures prettied with bits of feathers.

It turned out that in Surrey, near where we lived, most fishing is done at private rivers where the beats cost in the hundreds of guineas. But Mr. Adams, ever thrifty, used his friendship with Lord Bellows to arrange for a few afternoons of casting for free on his water.

On one such afternoon we four were spaced a few yards apart, so as not to get our lines entangled.

I waited long minutes with no action along my beat except for the swaying of rushes that seemed like ballet dancers pirouetting. Suddenly, something moved. What had appeared to be a group of pebbles now revealed itself to be a sizable trout. With the dignity of a Spanish grandee, the trout meandered into the center of the stream. I cast right into his territory. Treating me as if I was an interloper—as he knew full well I didn't belong on the shore of his river—he playfully took my hook. Away he went, my line spinning, while my friendly trout headed for a clump of rushes. There, he spit out my hook and jauntily returned to his own territory.

Charles, my youngest, now went into action. Skillfully he cast his line dropping its hook precisely in front of my friendly trout. Again the trout took the hook, but this time Charles gave it no chance to run with his line and jerked up his pole to hold it high until the hook was firmly planted in the trout's cheek. Letting out the line and then hauling it in a few yards, he tired the old trout until finally our ghillie could net the fellow.

"We'll cook this prize here and now," the ghillie announced, not chancing foregoing his share should we take it back to our kitchen. He erected a tent of twigs, lit it, and grilled our trout. My sons collected large leaves to use as plates, but our fingers had to do for forks.

"Delicious!" I exclaimed, wishing I could prepare fish like that at home.

George, always the fussy eater, complained, "It is good enough this way, but needs salt. And some sauce."

We had squatted in a circle around the fire, like so many Indians around a tepee. Taking advantage of the cozy closeness of this arrangement, I initiated the resulting talk with a subject I had waited too long to broach.

"Dear boys, I know you want to learn about love and lovemaking. I will let your father deal with the latter, but I truly believe a mother's tender words are best where love is concerned. I am not a great authority on all kinds of love, but a mother's love I can speak about. In my opinion, that love should be weighed as carefully as the ingredients for a perfect recipe: not too much and not too little of the essential ingredients."

"And what are those?" My always-inquisitive Charles demanded.
"Caring, and doing."

Charles raised his eyebrows; he had a query: "I want to know about sexual intercourse. Tell me, Ma. Did you have sexual intercourse with Pa before you were married? Is that the way to go? Should I try out a fiancée to be sure we will be a good match for coupling?"

I stared at Charles in disbelief. I knew he had grown impudent during the past year, but never in my wildest dreams could I have imagined he—or any one of my sons—could ask such a question! I debated whether to answer him, slap him, or gather my skirts and call for the cart that was waiting to take us home. I decided to answer him, to the best of my ability.

"Shame on you Charles! I will have Pa reprimand you, or worse, when we go back to the house, maybe he will take a rod to you. I will not. But I will tell you, never, never, NEVER again speak to me without courtesy! However, I will answer the question. I went to your father a virgin. Subject closed."

The cart was called, and we put out the embers of our fire—doused with river water the surrounding area to prevent any possibility of a conflagration—collected our rods, and went back to Little Boston.

In spite of that rude interruption from Charles, I reveled in the togetherness of that afternoon. It was one of my very rare times alone with my three sons. I treasure it. Does not every rose have at least one thorn?

On the whole, here in England I have felt happier than I have managed to be ever since Louisa Catherine's terrible death. I even have warmed towards Mr. Adams and began the kissing again. He responded avidly, thanks perhaps to all those Don Juan books he read.

As of this spring, I am pregnant again.

This time, Mr. Adams doesn't chide me if I wanted to go to a play. He accompanies me to whatever I want to see. I went into town to Drury Lane and watched Shakespeare's The Taming Of The Shrew.

I can't say that it was a play I would recommend. Starve a wife into submission? Revile her in public? With that play Shakespeare showed how ambivalent he felt towards women. In The Taming of the Shrew, poor Katherine had to submit to her husband. In other plays, Twelfth Night and The Merry Wives of Windsor, he wrote about powerful women who tamed men.

He could never have been inspired by Mr. Adams' early treatment of me. In Shakespeare's Warwickshire hometown, Stratford-on-Avon, there could have been no Massachusetts puritans, although Queen Elizabeth's Protestants had ousted the Catholics loyal to her elder sister Queen Mary. Shakespeare had most certainly agreed with Mr. Adams' belief in the rights of a husband upon marriage.

Our contemporary playwright, Richard Brinsley Sheridan, is kinder to women. Since Sheridan recently died, his name is on every society person's lips. There have been many kudos about him in the newspapers, and it is difficult to get tickets for any of his works. We went to see his play, The School for Scandal, which made me gasp, causing people in the audience to hush me.

Richard Brinsley Sheridan certainly understood women. He created roles for them where they were smart, dangerous, and cunning. The women in this play knew who they were. They didn't worry about viability or pretense, or even acceptable manners. They went after what they wanted and got it. Like Mr. Adams does. Oh, but he is a man!

Quincy, August 26, 1817

After May, my London idyll ended. The United States' newly-elected President Monroe invited Mr. Adams to return to America to assume the position of Secretary of State. Would he accept? Of course he would. Mr. Adams knows only too well every step he needs to take on his climb toward the Presidency. His ambitious parents schooled him from childhood to emulate his father and become President. And how to go about that! The position of Secretary of State was the major step to a United States Presidency.

His parents learned that Mr. Adams had accepted to be Secretary of State only by a letter from New York, sent after we had arrived there.

We had another tragedy that delayed him writing to his parents. I lost another baby aboard ship when I was four months into my pregnancy. I had a terrible time crossing the Atlantic. Waves hurled at the ship accompanied by crashing winds that howled like a hurricane. That surely caused this miscarriage.

I made such a mess of our stateroom with not enough towels to sop up all the blood. It shamed me to learn that my three sons—all old enough to understand where babies came from—had to watch while the pathetic little bundle—their lost sibling—was consigned to the raging seas.

My pregnancies have NEVER been easy. Of my many pregnancies, I have brought only four to full term. My poor body has tried too many times to bring babies into the world.

When the two old people in Quincy learned we had docked in New York, they sent a flood of letters to urge us to come to Massachusetts. But I wanted so desperately to see my brother and sisters, who had managed to stay in Washington. I was pushing Mr. Adams to permit me to visit with them. Not a popular request. He turned it down.

By return post Mr. Adams received from the old exPresident a jubilant letter saying, "Yesterday was one of the most uniformly happy days of my whole long life."

He left no doubt as why he felt so happy. It was because his eldest son was returning after eight years in foreign lands. And the old gentleman duly expected that both of us would be on the next coach north to Quincy.

After my years of exposure to European ladies who danced until dawn nightly—when they were not dallying with lovers—I was changing from the docile supplicant I had been when I left my parental home. I was in no hurry to see those two old people. I dreaded the reunion. In the back of my head was lurking the fear that somehow they had learned I was illegitimate and would turn me out.

No, that didn't happen.

As for Abigail, she penned, "God be thankful. Come then all of you."

All? There were only the two of us and the three boys. The old people seemed to have forgotten that we had once been a couple with a daughter!

They'd never seen our little Louisa Catherine. Dead, out of sight, out of mind.

True, Abigail had penned a note to me, during my mourning Louisa Catherine in St. Petersburg, reminding me that she too had lost a child. Oh no, I cannot accept that Abigail had suffered as I did. Massachusetts did not have the same filthy conditions as had killed my Louisa Catherine!

We traveled from New York to Quincy by coach. On arrival at their grandparents' home, my two eldest sons bounded out of our coach-and-four.

"Oh, Grandmother!" both yelled and succumbed to huge embraces from Abigail after bowing to the ex-President.

Charles, at nine years of age and not remembering them, stayed close to me, for which I felt grateful for a long time.

I went up to the ex-President and saluted him, then brought forward Charles. Old ex-President Adams looked him over carefully and must have sensed that Charles was also prime political material. Those two—like conspirators—waited together for me to go ahead of them into the house. The old exPresident and my Charles had immediately bonded.

Same old place, same terrible food. I was not asked to shell peas as on my first arrival, having garnered some measure of prestige during my travels as a Resident Minister's wife. I was accorded a very thin slice of acceptance.

That was NOT what my husband received! Certainly not. He couldn't have been more kowtowed to if he'd been a pasha arriving at his harem.

The best new addition to this household is an affectionate dog. I love dogs and have not had any since I had left my childhood home. Now, I made great friends with this dog. This special friendship mitigates the loneliness I feel, surrounded as I am by people who merely tolerate me as the mother of Adamses, who—like the moon—have only the gold which is reflected from the sun, the center of the universe, THEIR JOHNNY!

Washington, D.C., February 2, 1818

With the position of Secretary of State looming for him, my husband spoke even less to me, if at all. During those balmy days of a warm, late September I occupied myself going fishing with my three sons. Those times together would soon become merely special memories.

A few days before we left for Washington, down came the boom again. They sidelined my boys from me. My husband delegated his brother, Thomas, to inform me that all three of my sons would not be accompanying us. The boys were enrolled at the Boston Latin School as a preparation to eventually attend Harvard, and they would be living with Abigail and the old ex-President. So my hopes for a family with children evaporated again. Agony! Now I was not to have even my youngest son to live with us.

All my three boys are special to me. George, I had almost lost to dysentery on arrival in the United States, when Mr. Adams insisted I stop nursing him. At that time Mr. Adams was outraged by me suckling my firstborn in the public stagecoach, exactly as he had been later in Russia in another public stagecoach when I nursed my darling Louisa Catherine.

As for John, I nearly lost him to Scarlet Fever, the ravage of Massachusetts nurseries.

Charles had also almost been cheated of his chance to live. He had very early contracted Scarlet Fever, same as his brother. Although for his birth there had been both a doctor and a nurse present, there had been no one to stop him when as a toddler he'd run into a room where a child was dying of Scarlet Fever. I'd been consoling the dying child's mother, who had been about to warn me of the high incidence of contagion, when naughty Charles had rushed from my knee to plough into the sick child's bedroom looking for toys.

I nursed him as best I knew how, but the soups I prepared he could not swallow. What kept him alive was applesauce. Eventually the day came when Charles could sit up and play with a favorite plush dog. Weak as he was, he cuddled it as if it were a live puppy.

He not only lived, but grew healthy and handsome. Some months later, on a dark dock, he was wrenched from my arms by a strange man who went tearing off with my little son. I chased the thief and beat at him until he released baby Charles. The wretch said, "He is such a beautiful child. I wanted to show him to my wife." Some excuse! As my father would have said, "A bad excuse is no excuse!" There are several other possible explanations for his act, all too disgusting to write about.

Faced with losing my boys, I once again reviewed my opinion of Abigail. Beloved in Massachusetts, admired in London when her husband was Minister to the Court of St. James, and well thought of in Washington both when he'd served there as Vice-President and then as President, Abigail had seemed to have taken more kindly to me.

I'd written in my official diary, "She herself told me she was sorry she had not better understood my character."

I hesitate to write this, but I think her actions belied those words when twice she had collaborated with my husband to defraud me of the company of my sons. And she was very critical of my mother during those heady days when Papa still had money and the senior Adamses were in London. I saw how she had written that my mother gave extravagant parties and insinuated my mother was careless about money and overdid playing the bountiful hostess. My poor mother! She died in poverty, a poor relation living off her wealthy son–in-law to whom she married two of my sisters. Walter Hellen had wed Amy after my darling Nancy died in childbirth.

Oh! Those letters from Abigail, controlling my husband as if he was still a toddler who might run out into the street and be run over by horses. How desperately she had attempted to hold on to him when he felt the first stirrings of his romantic urges. With what desperation she had broken up his lyrical romance with that Mary Frazier. But Abigail lost at that same game when she criticized me too much without having met me, and that caused her Johnny to marry me before she could again stop a wedding.

I was not cheerful during our move to Washington. Neither of us spoke during the long hours of the trip there. I knew that the exalted position of Secretary of State could almost certainly assure that Mr. Adams would become President! And what would that mean to our shaky marriage?

I had not been permitted to state my wishes as to having one or more of our sons in Washington with us. I was not permitted to choose the house there which I was expected to transform into not only a home, but as a platform for entertaining members of the government. Mr. Adams did speak to me about polishing my job as a hostess to please politicians who might eventually vote for him to become the next President.

Now we have become fixtures on the Washington social scene, but it took some doing. Mr. Adams quickly leased a house on Four and a Half Street. I was prepared to turn our home into a free restaurant, but he wanted to invite people whom I didn't know. There has been a considerable turnover since I was last in Washington. Long gone are the few real friends left from when Mr. Adams was in the Senate.

I decided to practice giving dinner parties. To these parties I invited my Maryland cousins. Out came my collection of recipes. I made friends with the best green grocer and butcher in our neighborhood and selected the ripe fruits and prime cuts of meat by going very early in the morning to make my purchases. My cousins were willing to be used as guinea pigs. They praised my unusual European recipes.

However, there was a price to pay for their praise. The eldest wanted to know how Mr. Adams had wrangled the position of Secretary of State.

“Tell us dear cous-Louisa, how did he get this cotton-gin of a job?”

“Oh, dearest cous, Mr. Adams is quite the astute fellow, you must know that by now.”

But, alone later that night seated in the small living room, which was too hot near the fire and freezing away from it, I began to think I should give a thorough review to my answer to that cousin’s question.

Secretary of State! Why Mr. Adams? Was it due to his having helped negotiate the end of the War of

1812? Or was it that old ex-President Adams had somehow leaned on President Monroe? As far as I knew, my husband had never been a particular favorite of newly-elected President Monroe. Yes, a favorite of ex-Presidents Madison and Washington. But, Monroe?

My husband had been of two minds about the offer: flattered that his talents had been duly recognized by Monroe, but on the other hand concerned that his father had pulled strings to get him this offer in order to have his eldest son return to the United States. Mr. Adams hated any whif of nepotism. And that was the ugly word echoing in his wake. But nepotism or not, he had accepted this position.

Meanwhile, our lives have moved on, inside or outside of politics. And I am moving on, my character and aims not the same this year as last year. I’ve matured into a more thinking individual.

Washington, D.C., February 23, 1821

Over. It is finally over as of yesterday, but what a long preoccupation with Mr. Adams mind has this been! His first assignment was the regulation of Weights and Measures, a job which truly pleased him. He had already become interested in that study in St. Petersburg. But to accomplish this job and bring it to fruition in Washington has taken him nearly three years!

I wrote in my official Diary, "His whole mind is so intent on weights and measures that you would suppose his very existence depended on this subject." How I wish he would apply that much dedication to lovemaking!

My mother-in-law, Abigail, passed away with great dignity on October 28, 1818. She died from typhoid fever. Mr. Adams took her loss raging against her fate, furious that a mere illness had been able to slay her. Yet, even in direst mourning, he knew his new job had to be attended to.

He had to make a success of his new position as Secretary of State. And, NEVER had he had such challenges as awaited him in this position. Mr. Adams commented, "The path before me is beset with thorns." Eight years in European capitals had failed to prepare him for the pitfalls of being Secretary of State in Washington D.C. "At two distinct periods of my life heretofore my position has been perilous and full of atrocious forecasts," he wrote, "but never so critical and perilous as at this time."

One of his early mistakes was to keep in their jobs several employees of the former Secretary of State. Not a good idea! Of course such men would not prove loyal and would not work to help him make a success of the job. But when had Mr. Adams ever depended on others to build his fortunes? Unless that other had been his own father!

He approached this new position like a bricklayer by readying the "bricks" for a solid foundation. Once ready, he proceeded to build the edifice of his second career.

Alongside the Department of State-ordered report on Weights and Measures, the next great challenge for him was reviewing the possible repercussions if Missouri was admitted to be a State. We both feared that if it did become a State, this could further upset the delicate balance of Slave and Non-Slave States. Recording his feelings in his diary, he wrote, "Oh! if but one man could arise with the genius capable of comprehending, a heart capable of supporting, and an utterance capable of communicating those eternal truths that belong to this question." And, given the chance, Mr. Adams would expose slavery as "an outrage upon the goodness of God." However, with the Missouri Compromise behind us, it is likely Missouri will be admitted to the Union as a slave state within months.

Two events in this era of his life gave him some relief. He was named President of The Arts and Sciences Society. Then, later his writings on dogma harvested the other honor of being elected President of The American Bible Society. He wrote in his diary, "The arts and sciences have been the objects of my admiration through life. I would it were in my power to say they had been objects of my successful cultivation. Honors like these produce in my mind humiliation as well as pride."

Humiliation? Mr. Adams? Well, I NEVER! I re-read that word, "humiliation," twice sneaking a look again into his diary, but I don't believe for one minute that Mr. Adams has ever accepted feeling humiliated.

My husband certainly suffered deeply at the death of his mother. But his political future had a setback too, which distressed him. Of course not as much, but sorely.

He had been strutting around our house with the pride of a peacock. And are peacocks not said to bring bad luck? The reason for his strutting was that he had been delegated to bring about a formidable treaty. Oh, and Mr. Adams felt that treaties were his specialty and that he could astound all of Washington with the brilliant way this treaty would be constructed.

It became known as the Adams-Onís Treaty, but otherwise called the Transcontinental Treaty. Beginning negotiations on February 12, 1819, Mr. Adams had remained most nights closeted with Spain's Minister, Don Luis de Onís y González-Vara. Just before dawn February 20, he had signed what he believed to be a great leap forward for the United States, acquiring lands as far West as Oregon and acquiring Eastern Florida for five million dollars. It secured a favorable boundary between the Louisiana Purchase and Spanish Texas to the Continental Divide and west to the Pacific Ocean along the forty second parallel. Areas of Florida off the Gulf of Mexico surrounding Pensacola had already been acquired in 1803, but Spain still had ruled the long Florida peninsula along the Atlantic coast and inland. In 1818, Seminole Indians had been encouraged to make forays into Georgia, whereupon General Andrew Jackson invaded that area and punished two Brits for arming the Seminoles. He put the Britishers to death. The incident turned a spotlight on the need to acquire Eastern Florida.

Mr. Adams took enormous pride in his work on that treaty, improving his posture to stand taller among the Senators and Representatives he met socially and in government. He crowed that this treaty was "The most important incident in my life, and the most successful negotiation ever consummated by the Government of this Union."

Oh, Oh. Does not pride come before a fall? And DOWN went Mr. Adams. His so-called friend Henry Clay, hoping to be a candidate for the Presidency in the election of 1824 and wily as ever, spitefully discovered and PUBLICIZED an enormous error in the Adams-Onís Treaty.

He pointed out to Mr. Adams and President Monroe that according to a part of its Article VIII it permitted two huge tracts of Spanish grants of land made by Spain in Florida to remain AS VALID after the United States occupied the Eastern part.

Horrors! Mr. Adams's reputation dissolved like snow on an April morning. He became a laughing stock in the Senate, which had endorsed the treaty. During those interminable nights between

February 12 and 20, somehow that foxy Onís had slipped in a change of dates. Onís had written in the date 1818 unnoticed by Mr. Adams, who thought he had secured an agreement for the date to be 1802, after which land grants would have been null and void. Mr. Adams was so proud to have been the negotiator for the successful Treaty of Ghent, that he had let that very important change go unnoticed.

He said, "The treaty is doomed to be a magnificent abortion."

President Monroe deemed it international fraud. Mr. Adams bleated, "I thought it too great a blessing not to be followed shortly by something to alloy it."

And so it was. But Mr. Adams did not take this defeat without fighting back. Didn't I know he was a fighter? He went straight to his friend the French Ambassador, Baron Jean-Guillaume Hyde de Neuville, and with his long established diplomat's skill, he worked on him to somehow win the cooperation of a balking Onís to mend the treaty. They did. And Mr. Adams could soon face the Senators and President Monroe without shame.

It was a sobering experience for my cocky husband. He believed it was sent to cleanse him of "all vanity and self-conceit." Never! Vain he remained. His conceit hardly wavered. Did he not order portrait after portrait painted of himself?

He congratulated himself on the fact that now America had expanded from sea to shining sea with the part of his treaty, which stated that the Oregon area would be jointly occupied for ten years and which also fixed the northern boundary of the Louisiana Purchase.

Mr. Adams crowed in his diary, "The acquisition of the Floridas has long been an object of earnest desire to this country. The acknowledgment of a definite line of boundary to the South Seas forms a great epoch in our history. The first proposal of it in this negotiation was my own."

Oh, Oh. What next?

I gave my preoccupation with Mr. Adams a rest when the joyful Christmas season of 1820 brought all three sons to me in Washington. I felt as gleeful as a teen girl with her first successes with boys. But Mr. Adams made his usual mistakes with our sons. Instead of going fishing with our sons, he read Pope's Messiah to them. When they wanted parties filled with pretty debutantes, he insisted they stay with their books to prepare for exams. When Mr. Adams complained that none of our sons had any interest in literature, I sharpened my tongue and quoted from one of George's poems. When Mr. Adams scoffed at the poem, saying George should read the Bible instead of books of poetry, I tried quoting his much-esteemed father.

"Your father thinks George is a diamond. That is what he wrote in his last letter. And he told you in person that he considers John to be a thinking man."

None of my tactics worked to allay Mr. Adams' downhill-toboggan-slide-relations with our sons. I had to intervene when he wrote such a furious letter to George that I feared for my child's future!

But perhaps his mind was far too occupied with the completion of his work on Weights and Measures to be an understanding, proud father. Others, in Monroe's cabinet, thought he was too much interested in history and philosophy, and by dwelling on those subjects at too great length, he may have buried the true importance of Weights and Measures in his report. When it was finally finished, I commented, "Thank God we have no more of Weights and Measures!" I believe the cabinet members felt the same.

Washington, D.C., January 10, 1824

Our highs and lows continue in rapid succession. For many months following the submission of his Weights and Measures report, I gave myself leave to focus more on the running of our household than to listening to Mr. Adams' political pursuits. When I resumed caring about his career, he was embroiled in overseeing the outbreak of revolutions which had erupted all through Spain's colonies.

President Monroe had already asked Congress to formally recognize the United Provinces of the Río de la Plata, Colombia, Peru, Chile and Mexico. And Congress had duly recognized each of them. In Colombia and in Venezuela, a vibrant hero had emerged: Simón Bolívar. In Río de la Plata, Peru, and in Chile, another such character, José de San Martín, emerged. Mr. Adams exulted, "These men are heroes just like my father, leading revolutions to gain INDEPENDENCE from the mother country."

Being born a Britisher, I was not sure I concurred, especially when I learned that Señor Bolívar was known for having a hot adulterous affair with his Manuelita. I was at the age when longtime married women trembled at news of adulterous affairs.

I felt I couldn't live with Mr. Adams, but couldn't live without him.

Nevertheless a sort of truce had prevailed in our household for some time. Then, that period of tranquility between us was suddenly broken.

I was sitting in my kitchen one evening, sorting my recipes, when I heard the crunch of carriage wheels outside our front door. Was it a lady dropping one of those boring visiting cards? NO! I peeked out my window and saw Mr. Adams arguing with a hack driver over the fare. Mr. Adams, spending money for a hack when he ALWAYS walked to his office? Oh my, that boded ill. Was he sick? Or had the roof fallen in at his office?

I heard the front door slam. Then he strode like a gladiator into a Roman arena to face me with a thunderous look of fury. No doubt about it: he was seething, and heading for one of his worst temper tantrums. If he had been a dragon, there would have been flames jetting from his nostrils. If he had been Jupiter, it would have been lightning surging over his head. "Mrs. Adams," he roared and then stopped, obviously having difficulty with breathing.

I sat down, my knees knocking until they were too weak to support me. Good gracious, what had I done?

Spluttering like grease in a frying pan, he roared louder, "You are impossible. You are responsible for me having been summoned to the White House, by The Top, and Mrs. Top."

I whispered, "President and Mrs. Monroe!" "Exactly. Both of them insisted I make an immediate appearance to explain why you are not dropping visiting cards first as you are required to."

Silently, I gulped down my saliva. Of course, it was true. I do not drop off a card first, having been glued to the European custom of returning a card after one has been dropped on me.

Total silence reigned for two full minutes whilst Mr. Adams, glowering, condemning me, waited for a reply. He held on to the back of the cook's empty chair to try to control himself. From striking me?

Finally, I choked out, "I thought you had agreed I need not drop off a card to anyone who had not dropped off one to me first."

Not altering his furious demeanor, he spat a contentious phrase: "Now BLAME me. All right, I DID agree at that time. After all, you were following the European custom. But now I agree with Mrs. Top's opinion, 'When in Rome, do as the Romans do.'"

"You know what I said to Czar Alexander when he asked me if I had told the former French Ambassador that I MIGHT NOT?"

"That does not apply here in Washington. This is almost a village. Many of the ladies whose husbands are in government will not understand. It is THIS place's custom for the wife of the Secretary of State to drop off cards first. And you are NOT in Europe now. You MUST comply."

Recalling how I had stood up to Mr. Adams in Berlin when he insisted I remove rouge from my face, I straightened my shoulders. "I will NOT. I hear that General Andrew Jackson's wife, Rachel, smokes a corncob pipe. If THAT becomes the custom here, must I smoke one?"

That name, General Andrew Jackson, invariably caused his hackles to rise. Jackson was the main contender for the coming duel for the Presidency.

Mr. Adams swallowed his bile, and because he is a wily debater, changed the course of the conversation. "Mrs. Adams, you are constantly berating me for what I do to my sons to make them shape up. And now that George has succeeded in getting into the Massachusetts House of Representatives, would your obstinacy about dropping cards first destroy his chances for advancement?"

I blushed. He had hit where it hurts. Compromise was the only solution. "Give me the list of names of ladies and their addresses where I should drop cards," I moaned.

And the next morning I called on eleven ladies. Most of them had called on me first.

With the dropping cards problem partially resolved, Mr. Adams really took the bit in his teeth to help the emerging republics in Latin America. Having pushed Congress to recognize them, he proceeded to ask me to entertain in our home the newly credited Ministers from these Latin nations.

I started out with an intimate dinner for twelve in honor of the Colombian Minister. He had no Legation as yet and was living with his half-British wife in an uncomfortable hotel. Remembering how much I appreciated a home-cooked meal when Mr. Adams and I had been cramped into a second-class hotel both in Berlin and in St. Petersburg, I made every effort to accommodate these Colombians.

The Minister's wife was descended from one of the Scottish mercenaries who had been out of a job after Napoleon was defeated and had moved to Bogotá to get paid for fighting with Simón Bolívar. Due to the wife's British background, I had warmed to this couple and wanted to please them.

From a Colombian businessman who was selling quinine and chocolate to local purveyors, I gleaned that potato soup followed by arroz con coco would be favorites. He gave me a great recipe for the rice. He told me it was customary in Colombia to add shredded, roasted coconut and raisins to the rice. I soaked the raisins in Madeira wine to add my own special touch.

For the Peruvians, I asked my wines purveyor what was the favorite drink in Lima. He told me that it was called Pisco Sour, and it was a blend of their local brandy with fruit juice. I could not manage to provide the Peruvian brandy, but I experimented with our best French brandy by mixing it with various fruit juices until I got that right.

The Chileans were not completely satisfied with the French wines I served. "We have our own wonderful vineyards in Chile," they told me over my braised beef. But that dinner, too, was a success.

As for the Mexicans, Mr. Adams had not made up his mind about how to handle General López de Santa Anna. So we did not give them a dinner. Thank God! Where would I ever have been able to find hot chili in Washington?

Weeks later Mr. Adams furthered his goal with the

Latinos by talking with them about founding a Pan American Union with a Pan American Conference to start it. From that success Mr. Adams faced the grueling pre-election months of his challenge for the Presidency.

We needed to move to a more suitable house for entertaining. We didn't have to look far. Former President Madison and his wife Dolley told us we could get their former home. Hooray! That certainly suited me.

The move to our F Street house helped alter my hatred of myself. I began to feel I could accomplish something worthwhile in my own name. The Madisons seemed to bring good things into my life. What they had not envisioned was that their successors in these halls would give a party for three hundred people, as we did on January 8.

Mr. Adams and I had conjured up the idea we should honor Andrew Jackson with a party that would put my husband ahead of that braggart in the duel for the 1825-1829 Presidency. General Jackson had loomed as a fearsome opponent. He had gained a military reputation, always valuable for winning over voters. He was tall, handsome, and had a great shock of white hair. My husband had never been a soldier, and he had grown fat and balding. Oh, my!

The fact that I was still not dropping cards on the wives of members of congress who hadn't visited me first was an issue that would not be obliterated. Refusing to be dictated to by Mr. Adams—or even by President Monroe or Mrs. Monroe on this subject—I'd managed to calm their furies by calling on most of the ladies but preferring those who had dropped their cards on me first. I duly paid for my brazen behavior, because when I gave my first big party only three people attended.

I made this entry in my official diary, "It is understood that a man who is ambitious to become President of the United States must make his wife visit the Ladies of the members of Congress first. Otherwise, he is totally inefficient to fill so high an of ice." Oh my!

But Mr. Adams did develop the principles behind the Monroe Doctrine! Surely such a huge endeavor should equalize my not dropping cards!

Hoping to avoid a scene with him when next he brought up the subject of the visiting cards, I went to my collection of European recipes and used some of those to create fancy dishes for parties no one would want to miss no matter how low I had fallen in anybody's esteem. The food would be great, even if the hostess called herself a "nobody".

I began with a series of At Homes every Tuesday. They succeeded beyond my highest expectations. Even Mr. Adams complimented me on that success when all of Washington's most distinguished government people lined up to come to our home for my dinners.

Surely I should have foreseen that eventually Mr. Adams would dream up a way to capitalize on that success by plotting to have a bigger one. When all the devious manipulations that led to the Presidency had matured to the point where very few other candidates stood in his forward path except for General Andrew Jackson, Mr. Adams came up with that idea on how to trump that fabled general's grab for the White House. Oh, yes, it was Mr. Adams who invited three hundred important government people to a ball in General Jackson's honor, although I shared the credit.

Nicknamed the Hero of New Orleans, the general was famous because he had fought a battle there against the British. That, in spite of the fact the Ghent Peace Treaty had been signed some days earlier by Mr. Adams, making any battle there unnecessary. But most people didn't know that fact, and maybe even General Jackson hadn't known the peace treaty had been signed. Evil tongues babble that he did know, but I believe only God is privy to the truth.

In any case, General Jackson couldn't refuse to come to our home when the ball we'd give was in his honor. Oh, Mr. Adams really is a sly old diplomat!

And I was supposed to produce a ball for three hundred important government officials and their wives within three weeks! I didn't even have a nice new dress.

That, I dealt with in my own manner. Mr. Adams has a close friend in New York, Mr. Lewis Tappan, who is an Abolitionist but co-owns a huge business. He imports fine silks from France and good woolens from Britain. I wrote to Mr. Tappan and asked if he could make a contribution by sending me five yards of silk suitable for a ball gown. He did. He went far beyond friendship by dispatching a rider who came more swiftly than the Pony Express bearing five yards of a rare silk, shot through with steel threads. Beautiful! I had those five yards of silk run up in three days by my favorite cut-rate dressmaker. From a cut-rate jeweler I purchased a necklace and bracelet made of shimmering steel to match.

I have a superb recipe for dressed crab, and wrote to my Maryland cousins to ask them to provide the crabs. They did. To keep them absolutely fresh, I had the crabs packed alive in barrels filled with salt water from Chesapeake Bay. Those crabs were certainly alive when they arrived—their shells nicely packed in seaweed with fresh salt-water. I saw bubbles on the top of the water in their barrels. Bubbles meant they were alive and breathing happily. My cousins had made sure these crabs would not give my guests diarrhea.

Those same cousins descended on my F Street house to help cook and to provide flower arrangements. Mr. Adams, with foresight, hired workmen to build a large ballroom. I had several pillars added to the street level parlor to hold up the ceiling in case the second floor might collapse and come down on us from the weight of the three hundred guests we could expect, plus those who'd bring their wives.

But in the middle of these preparations, Mr. Adams ruined our 1823 Christmas, refusing to permit John to come home. John had been rowdy with a wild group of school fellows. Also, preferring sports to studies, he had come in forty-fifth in a class numbering eighty-five.

Our poor son John was berated by letters, when Mr. Adams did not do that in person. "I could feel nothing but sorrow and shame in your presence until you should not only have commenced but made progress in redeeming yourself from that disgraceful standing."

Charles, still very young, escaped his frowns and growls. Was Mr. Adams so proud of himself that he could not bend a little? I was aware that his position as Secretary of State was of real importance to getting to the Presidency. But did he have to be so hard on our boys? Even flowers wilt when they get burned by too much sun. If Mr. Adams thought our boys needed to measure up to being sons of The Secretary of State, I began to wish he had never accepted that position.

On the night of the ball, I felt glad to be wearing a warm gown because the weather had turned nasty. Holding my breath as I descended into the parlor, I wasn't smiling. And rightly so, as two events occurred that could have spoiled the ball.

But they didn't. What looked like the worst possible disaster was the fact that one hour after the time stipulated on our invitations, General Jackson had still not arrived. All the guests had appeared and the musicians were tiring from their uninterrupted fiddling when General Jackson finally "honored us with his presence" coming through the front door, more than an hour late! The wait had been agony for me because I feared he would not show up at all.

I suppose he wanted to make a grand entrance when all the guests were already assembled. I took his arm and paraded him around the rooms, and nobody thought he had erred in judgment.

I dealt with the second disaster with equal aplomb. While I was parading General Jackson, a wall lamp that was filled with oil fell from its perch and flaming oil cascaded down my dress. I kept calm, excused myself, rushed upstairs, changed into an old gown, and came back to General Jackson and my guests. That was when I began to smile and continued to smile until the last of our guests had left.

I can hardly believe it, but for weeks afterward I received notes complimenting me on the party. It made a huge difference to Mr. Adams' campaign plans. There were now three hundred government people favorably disposed to him. Oh, but I resolved that should Mr. Adams win the Presidency I would give tea parties in the White House and might never again attempt such a daunting ball.

I don't know why I did the next thing. People say it was out of the kindness of my heart. I decided to work as a secretary to Mr. Adams, write his letters, and correct any faulty spelling. He wouldn't permit me to shorten his too-long sentences, but that is a matter I hope to deal with at some future time.

I don't think it was due to the "kindness of my heart." I believe I was trying to prove that a woman could be involved in government work.

Mr. Adams didn't smell that rat. He's always been so adamant that women were unfit for anything to do with government. I foresee a day when there will be women lawyers, women legislators, and maybe even a woman president.

His plan for a ball had worked well, although scandalous allegations could have destroyed my husband's chances. For instance, I was termed a slut who had slept with my husband prior to our marriage during our extra-long engagement period. Oh, if they only knew how barren of love and lovemaking those times were for me!

But much as those newspaper-men dug to find out the worst dirt they could throw at me, they never unearthed the really BIG secret. Instead, they had to make do with crying out that my husband had made an insidious deal with Mr. Clay, Speaker of the House of Representatives, promising Clay his job of Secretary of State if Clay would use his influence in the House of Representatives to swing the electoral votes to him. My first opinion was, "Disgusting allegation!"

Having put behind me the complaint over the delivering of cards, our star began to rise in Washington society. Mr. Adams is an artful negotiator, as he had proved with the Ghent Treaty ending the War of 1812. In 1818 he'd delivered another coup by beating down the British negotiators over agreeing on a permanent border between the United States and Canada at the 49th parallel. Invitations to private homes came like flurries of snowflakes.

Mrs. Crawford, wife of the Secretary of the Treasury, gave a party for six hundred guests. How could I match that? But it didn't propel her husband into the White House; Mr. Crawford suffered a stroke!

Paralyzed, Crawford is out of the race for the Presidency.

For various reasons I took on the mantle of a leading Washington hostess, and, in addition to my ball for General Jackson, I now use tea parties to help my husband gain the White House. Perhaps my principal reason is because I am tired of feeling a Nobody. I truly want to achieve something.

Have I chosen the wrong aim? Is it frivolous? Am I secretly selfish?

Washington, D.C., September 30, 1824

Oh, it seems Mr. Adams could soon win the Presidency if he woos enough Southern voters and gets a substantial political party to choose him as its spearhead.

During my teenage schooling in London, I didn't read about the system by which Americans elect a president. I was forty years old before I learned that the freemen in each state vote for Electors in The Electoral College, not directly for the candidate of a person's choice. Each state gets a number of electors equal to the number of its members in the House of Representatives, but due to something called the Three-Fifths Clause, the slave states are allotted more votes. There, the voters consist of white males who, when they are slave-owners, get additional votes: three more for every five slaves they possessed. Mr. Adams, who depends primarily on voters from Massachusetts and the other northern states, will have to go to great lengths to get those Southern votes. If none of the candidates got enough Electoral College votes to win, it falls to the House of Representatives to select the next President.

Consequently, it has become imperative that I entertain non-stop the members of the House of Representatives! Add to their number the Senators, the members of the judiciary, and all the other members of the government whom I should also entertain, I see that I've been handed a daunting job.

Mr. Adams has gone into his Presidential campaign with intense fervor. I help in any way he suggested, although I would have preferred to be able to just VOTE. No chance of that. Women are on a lower rung politically than male slaves, whose numbers are counted giving their owners more votes. No extra votes if they have women in their households: wives, daughters, spinster sisters, widowed sisters.

I have been trotted out for display or to entertain guests when it is deemed valuable. Otherwise I am kept in the shadows. Why? Does Mr.

Adams know my secret and fear the story would explode in newspaper accounts just on the eve of the election?

Washington, D.C., April 17, 1825

Oh, how I long to be able to vote! On one of my trips to the Visitors' Gallery in the Congressional Building, I heard one legislator bellow, "Why would I give the women a vote? Next, I could be asked to give a vote to the cow on my farm!"

General Jackson, didn't need any votes from women, had we been permitted that privilege. He was a frontiersman of great charm and a renowned battle-hardened hero. He garnered ninety-nine electoral votes. Mr. Adams got eighty-four. Any candidate needed one hundred and thirty-one electoral votes to become President.

On the evening of that final tally, Mr. Adams deigned to speak to me about his awkward position, "Difficult for a non-military man to win. The title of 'General' has a clarion call that 'Secretary of State' does not."

I feared I might get the brunt of his temper if he lost. Each day he seemed to be suffering more and more from some sort of depression I couldn't fathom. His dour expression and quarreling voice could hardly endear him to even those Massachusetts constituents who had been so loyal so long. Yet the votes for these two main candidates seemed close enough that Congress was required to make the selection. Early in 1825, Mr. Clay's manipulating in the House of Representatives gave Mr. Adams the Presidency.

Awful for me! I'd become fond of the home on F Street. I liked my neighbors and was in walking distance of everywhere I wanted to go. Having helped Mr. Adams gain it, I dreaded the move to what was now called the White House. I did not even go to his inauguration.

The atmosphere was worse for Mr. Adams. There were scurrilous claims from Jackson supporters and others saying that Mr. Adams had made that ignominious deal with Henry Clay. They alleged Mr. Adams had promised him the stepping-stone job of Secretary of State if Clay would get the House of Representatives to declare Mr. Adams as the winner. And, although Andrew Jackson had the most electoral votes, the House of Representatives duly named my husband the next President of the United States. Oh my, which meant we moved into this unpleasant White House under a cloud of gossip and innuendo.

At this point in our lives, Mr. Adams has become a semi-recluse. There was no doubt he'd got fewer votes than Andrew Jackson. Could my wily husband have made a deal to get the House of Representatives to declare him President? Oh yes, Mr. Adams became the sixth president of the United States under those conditions. Is that why he's become a hermit?

Perhaps that is why he was so reluctant to meet with journalist Mrs. Anne Royall. Or maybe it is just because she is a woman.

Mrs. Royall came to Washington, D.C. to claim the pension money owed to her as the widow of a veteran. While in town, she decided she wanted to become the first female to ever interview a President, and she requested an interview. Oh, she referred to him as Mr. President, and that was unfortunate. Mr. President denied her request. The exact truth of what happened next remains unclear, but there is a popular story circulating that she found out that Mr. President, even at his advanced age, still goes swimming in the Potomac, NUDE. It is said she followed him for his five a.m. swim to where Mr. President had shed his clothes to go naked into the icy water. And then she sat on his clothes until he agreed to be interviewed.

Hooray for Anne Royall! Hers is a spirit I admire, and wish to emulate. When Mr. President arrived home that same morning—after the story had arrived to my ears—his body blue with cold and his eyes afire, I asked him, "Why didn't you agree to be interviewed earlier? Here, in your library?"

Mr. President did the snuffle thing through his nostrils—that north Massachusetts snuffle noise. "I don't give interviews to women," he choked out through his snuffles.

“There has to be a first time, as the old whore told the young whore.”

“Louisa, really! You must watch your language. Someone from the press could hear you make such remarks! I don’t generally grant interviews in any case, but I was most certainly not going to be the first sitting United States President to fall for a woman journalist’s pleadings.”

“And why not, listen to Royall’s pleadings? She must be a very strong individual to have dared sit on your clothes and study your nakedness. By the way, did she comment on the wrinkles over your stomach?”

“Certainly not. There were no indiscreet words out of her mouth. She did not want to do the talking. She asked me questions about the life I envision after retirement as President, and I answered them. I told her I am not a man who savors retirement. When I retired before, I embraced the offer to be Chancellor of Harvard University, but after I had two years of that, I realized that academia is not my chosen world. I told her I would likely pursue something more in politics, such as being a Representative.”

“Did she ask you how you would manage to be elected a Representative when you had fallen out of favor with your party?”

“No, Anne Royall may be tough, but she drew the line at asking that.”

“What about asking why the Massachusetts voters, those privileged men, would send you back to Congress after they dropped you following your one term earlier as a senator?”

“I volunteered that information. I explained that most of the high emotions were spent on electing a new President, and the less competitive job of Representative did not bring about any animosity. I am a man from Massachusetts, after all. Many of my fellows know me there and believe I am honest.”

And in truth, he is perhaps more honest than I as First Lady—the first “First Lady”—to be born illegitimate and to be born on foreign soil, the latter being problematic but not as catastrophic as the former, should it become widely-known.

Washington D.C., November 2, 1826

Mr. Adams hasn't been happy during his first year and a half in the White House. He could not get any of his measures passed either in the House of Representatives or the Senate. He was accused openly of having made a corrupt bargain with Clay. He was jeered after his opening speech as President. He received assassination threats. The worst came from a nasty piece of work called Dr. George Todson. His was considered so serious that Mr. President was advised not to venture outside the White House.

My husband soldiers on, but he is suffering from serious bouts of depression. He cannot comprehend why his most ardent projects are subjects of ridicule. He wanted to found a National University. TURNED DOWN. He hoped to start a series of Observatories to forward Astronomy; he believed that men could go to the moon, if only they knew more about the universe. LAUGHED AT, Mr. President has turned his attention to the construction of more railways.

Socially, as President and First Lady, we have received fewer invitations from Senators or Representatives than when we first arrived in Washington. Some members of Congress and their wives refuse to accept our invitations. Simply stated, they have boycotted us.

I have had a few good days. And, nights. Although I was instructed by him to use the title Mr. President when addressing him, towards the end of 1825 he said I may call him "dearest" when we are alone and being intimate. Dearest?

Now, after all those years of diplomats' parties and government receptions, he wants merely to sit by a fire in his bedroom slippers. It doesn't help that his favorite fireplace is one in the White House. Realizing how depressed he is, I don't complain. I am inured to his moods and have accepted living without evenings of theater or parties. It seems so strange, however, that after reaching his lifelong ambition to become President of the United States, Mr. Adams would fall into this deep depression. But it does mean that I am not to give or go to parties.

I packed away my box of recipes, although we still have to give the occasional event for national holidays, Christmas, New Year's, or upon the arrival of a foreign dignitary. Those events do cause me to bring out my recipes, particularly if we have a foreign visitor for whom I can present the specialty dish of his home country.

The White House has helped my marriage in ONE way. In winter, for the most part we stayed close to the bedroom fireplace and then went on to the marital couch. There, Mr. President wasn't up to a nightly performance of sexual congress; he was too tired and disgusted by the US Congress! One bout of sexual intercourse a week is now enough.

I tried to get Mr. President to write a biography of his father. He balked like a mule who wanted to stay in a field where there was hay. I wrote him a letter although we were sharing a bedroom, and I scolded him. YES, I SCOLDED HIM for not working on that biography. I knew I could "get away" with that scolding because he was always so tied to memories of his parents. His adored Mamma and Pappa. And I was right. Instead of giving me a scolding in return, Mr. President astounded me by agreeing it was "Good advice." Amazing. Wonders never cease.

On early summer days both last year and this one, Mr. President went swimming in the Potomac River as long as he remained in Washington. But by mid-summer he didn't stay in the Capital. He took a vacation to return to Quincy and live with his relatives in the old Adams house.

In the summer I remained in Washington or spent time with my relations in Maryland. I heard rumors that our absences in Massachusetts were not popular with Washingtonians, so I tried to allay those criticisms by having at least one of us in the capital during its hot summers, although that could be a danger due to its Yellow Fever epidemics.

Mr. President feels proud of two accomplishments to date. First, he slowed the entry of additional slave states into the Union. He's always hated slavery, ever since he witnessed the horrible conditions of slaves in Poland as Secretary to Mr. Dana. Already at the age of fourteen he wrote, "The farm workers are in the most abject slavery. They are bought and sold like so many beasts and sometimes even changed for dogs or horses." Yes, he's hated slavery—whether the slaves were white or black—all his life.

Second, he bought Eastern Florida from the Spaniards. It will become a productive state. I've always loved adding orange juice and zest to many recipes. After Florida was purchased, I added avocado and guava to my favorite list of edibles. And I'd never eaten either of them before Eastern Florida was purchased by the United States.

Washington D.C., October 23, 1827

He refuses to write my name as Mrs. John Quincy Adams when addressing an envelope to me, substituting his altered version of my correct mode of address. Mr. President addresses those envelopes to Mrs. Louisa Johnson Adams, as if we were legally divorced.

During these years in the White House my sole compensation has been that I was allowed to invite two of our sons to live with us, as well as some of my nieces.

George and young John duly arrived, and began to compete for Mary Hellen's favors. Dear Mary Hellen: my favorite sister Nancy's daughter! Within a short time, George convinced Mary to become his fiancée, but he failed to come up with a firm wedding date. Instead, George set off to start a law practice in Boston. Maybe he felt he needed money to support a wife. When he didn't write so much as a note to Mary during the following weeks, she broke off that engagement and settled for my second son, John.

Washington D.C., December 2, 1828

What joy this year has brought, and what sorrow, culminating today in the pinnacle of each!

Mary and John had a superlative wedding on February 25, the only one ever to be held for a son in the White House. If anyone doubted that John loves his Mary, it was sufficient to see his face alight as she walked into the ceremony looking so beautiful in her white satin gown. With Maryland flowers I transformed the place into a house of beauty.

Mary became pregnant quickly, and I had the joy of looking forward to a grandchild whose mother loved me and would never keep me from seeing the baby. My second son bloomed with her love. Now young John felt more important than his elder brother George! Oh my, what impending fatherhood can do for a young man!

Meanwhile Mr. President took little notice that he would become a grandfather. Perhaps it was the tragedies of his own family that had robbed him of looking forward to even more familial ties. His adored sister Nabby succumbed to breast cancer in 1813 after a horrible operation without anesthetic. And my revered father-in-law died on the Fourth of July in

1826. He'd always loved that national holiday and had been known to encourage all Americans to celebrate it with fireworks. He had reached ninety. Too bad he didn't make it to one hundred! I wrote in my official Diary how he had "always treated me with the utmost tenderness." On that day, July 4,

1826 he even forgave his lifelong opponent, Thomas Jefferson. Coincidentally Thomas Jefferson also passed away on that Fourth of July.

I particularly admired my father-in-law for his stance on ending slavery. I followed with great interest his correspondence on the subject. He embraced the anti-slavery issue in his old age when writing on the subject of admitting Missouri into the Union as a slave state. He wrote that the issue might "follow the other waves under the ship and do no harm." I thought he expressed that beautifully. But he'd been quite savage when he wrote, "I know it is high treason to express a doubt of the perpetual duration of our vast American empire." He predicted that a struggle over slavery "might rend this mighty fabric in twain." How I hope he is wrong on that measure!

His father's views had most certainly caught on with my husband. He worried as more territories asked to be granted statehood because some of them would enter the Union as slave states. No doubt there was an essential need for enough manpower to develop the expanding territories. The Southern states' answer to that need oft-times meant the importing of slaves from states where they were "manufactured" by slave owners having sexual intercourse with the females they owned. Horrible!

What became very worrying for Mr. President was that he might not be re-elected to a second term due to his championing the anti-slavers. One night in front of the bedroom fireplace, roasting like the marshmallows we enjoyed in Paris, he muttered to me, "I cannot win without the Southern votes. Slave states, but if I want a second term, I will have to woo them."

Frankly, I could foresee that he wasn't going to get a second term no matter what he did. Not only had he grown charmless, but he had become such a scold.

Worse, there were amazing calumnies spread about the two of us. Most incredible was how reporters were still beating that old tattoo that Mr. President and I had been lovers before we married—a huge sin among the many religious sects that had sprouted around the nation. Reporters still got it wrong—how we had a miserable honeymoon, followed by three decades of loveless coupling. Nor do they know that I had a romance in my late teens, and its flame burned for years after.

I do know that several of those badgers have gone to London to scour through church records. So far, I have been fortunate in that these sloppy researchers have looked at the wrong dates, thinking that perhaps my parents had wed a year or two after my birth. They haven't thought of visiting Soho's St. Anne Church in Westminster and thumbing through the registry for 1785, nine years after I was born!

Of course after Mr. President's much-disputed election, there had been bound to arise some accusations of nepotism—that he reached the heights he attained on his father's record, not on one of his own. I knew for a fact that it was General George Washington who had started him on his upward move, not my father-in-law.

Closer to the bone, had there been some truth in that old jibe that he'd got the presidency due to a deal with Henry Clay? I hated to believe that. Many people did. Voters! They hadn't forgotten the deal whereby if Mr. Adams got the Presidency thanks to Mr. Clay throwing House of Representatives votes his way, as Mr. President he would and, in fact, did give Mr. Clay the powerful cabinet post of Secretary of State. Memories of "the corrupt bargain" effectively drowned any hope of Mr. President staying in the White House for a second term, whether or not he could lure the Southern voters, somehow blindfolded to his hatred of slavery. His personality, with its facile explosions of temper, lack of sociability, and obvious lack of affection for his wife were other deterrents to victory.

There had also been angry murmurs because he chose John Calhoun as his Vice-President. Again, there were heinous accusations of under-the-table bargaining. Could he also be criticized for naming Robert Rush as Secretary of the Treasury in his administration? Mr. Adams was honor-bound to give such positions to the best man for the job, and how could he be sure they would be the best if they weren't part of his former circle where he could weigh their accomplishments through the years? But scurrilous tongues always pretended there had been under-the-table deals with each appointment he made. Gossip also shadowed the Adams and Clay National Republican Party, alleging all kinds of skulduggery.

There were other reasons why he was unpopular with the voters. One criticism was that he took the Oath of Office on a book of laws rather than in the traditional manner: on the Bible. That angered many Protestants, who failed to understand that he was actually making a statement to separate church and state.

There had been angry shouts when he had furthered the interests of Native Americans. To many Americans, our Indians are a danger, deserving to be annihilated. The Sovereign State of Georgia was so incensed by President Adams' stance that it waged a war of its own against the Cherokees. My husband, to his credit, foresaw that the Indians would be sent off their lands and that there would be terrible forced marches West, killing women and children on such a long and arduous journey.

Meanwhile, he had a falling out with Calhoun. As is said in Massachusetts, he smelled a rat. Mr. President guessed that Calhoun was sparring to go for the next Presidency. Jackson had been miserable while aiming to become President in 1829, alleging that the cruel campaign had shortened his wife Rachel's life.

Rachel Jackson's bigamist marriage to General Jackson was blazoned from many newspapers when it was learned that she'd had to marry Andrew Jackson a second time after her divorce went through. Columnists even made fun of her, reviling her as a primitive frontiers woman, who smoked a corn cob pipe. So, I believed that Jackson might not want to win. But Calhoun realized that Jackson might succeed in the 1829 election and be pressured now by his followers to accept to run. After all, why should Jackson's fans be sycophants unless there was a chance for plum jobs? The Jackson hangers-on would not be easily stopped from pushing him into the White House.

Calhoun is another wily politician. He saw that Jackson had

vacillated and jumped on that weakness, quietly urging journalists to play upon Jackson's heartbreak at losing his wife to the cruelty of politics. Calhoun intended to win the Presidency at any cost. No wonder Mr. President referred to this mess as the electioneering cauldron!

What I thought was particularly unfair was when Mr. Adams was attacked for not signing more Treaties. Hadn't he always been the gladiator who arranged nearly-impossible Treaties? He didn't further certain commercial treaties because he guessed they could harm his bid for the Presidency. That had backfired, infuriating many Southern states. The South, formerly basically agricultural, aspired to pursue industry in addition to its fortunes made in the fields. A different wind is sweeping across the whole country, where the railroads and canals have opened up areas for giant factories that were spouting out smoke and changing the look and smell of the land. Money is the end-all for many parts of our nation. Commerce, commerce, commerce. Commerce is the big new thing. Ideals are passé. That certainly puts me down in the dumps.

All of this is too bad for him, because as President he did accomplish various worthwhile aims that I applauded. He worked towards getting Federal support for the Arts and Sciences, although that success was not politically valuable.

But most of all, he took his responsibility deep into his heart. Years before all this juggling for the Presidency I almost felt a twinge of pride in my unloving husband on an Independence Day, July 4, that date which was so dear to his father's heart. He addressed Congress with a warning against foreign entanglements. And in that, he echoed President George Washington. Mr. Adams spoke of the United States as if the nation was the woman closest to his heart—which didn't surprise ME! "But she goes not abroad, in search of monsters to destroy. She is the well-wisher to the freedom and independence of all. She is the champion and vindicator only of her own." Could the people not see that Mr. President was doing his best? Politics! How I hate them.

To counter the attacks on my husband, I resolve to try in my own way to offset them. I recalled the success of my party for three hundred government officials and their wives honoring General Jackson. Oh I knew my husband would not agree to another ball for that candidate! He'd grown to detest Andrew Jackson. And he resisted any late-night party-giving, although we did offer afternoon levees for the public to enjoy our hospitality in the White House. Forget spontaneous formal dinners! They would compete with his preferred nightly relaxation with his Turkish slippers in front of his bedroom fire.

So, I gave tea parties to keep in the "social swim." There were important preparations to be made. It was only a little more than a decade since the White House had been burned by British troops during our War of 1812. What china and linens available for tea parties had been sadly diminished at that time and not been replenished in full. During Mr. President's tenure as Secretary of State, I acquired satisfactory Irish linen tablecloths. These had been shipped at government expense, and we'd used them for our famous General Jackson ball. After Mr. President's Inauguration we installed them in the White House in proper linen presses. In London, I happily managed to buy second-hand tea sets of Aynsley China for forty-eight guests, foreseeing we might entertain upon our return to Washington D.C.

Again I implored my Maryland cousins to provide specialty foods to tempt our party-weary politicians. We made marrons glacés from the nuts of local chestnut trees and cradled them in maple syrup. I concocted pastries such as raspberry tarts with Grand Marnier liqueur. I also resurrected Martha Washington's tea-time recipes that I collected during our visit to Mount Vernon.

Mrs. Washington hadn't had the opportunity to give tea parties in the White House because it was not built during her husband's two administrations when they presided in the President's House in New

York and then in Philadelphia. Lucky me, I could copy her tea goodies and serve them here. Of course I gave Mrs. Washington full credit, and the politicos applauded. They also ate everything.

Martha Washington's recipes celebrate the harvest of each season. Following her example, I made cherry tartlets in spring, peach tea cakes in July, and miniature apple pies in autumn. In winter I frosted my cakes with sugar tinted pink using candied cranberries. Delicious? I hope so. Whatever, all my trays went back empty to the kitchen for refills.

My own specialty was from a recipe I learned from Maman. She spiked afternoon tea with the best Jamaica rum. RUM? Rum! Even the Prohibitionists drank their rum-spiked tea with pleasure, chez moi, perhaps not recognizing what produced the great flavor. Politicians enjoy a treat as much as the next person!

Unfortunately, much as my drawing room tea parties filled up with senators and congressmen, I didn't see much improvement in the tongue-lashings against President Adams! His new policy of turning a cold shoulder to Calhoun didn't sit well with many of our lawmakers. Personally, I've lost any regard for Jackson after he was so cruel about our Native Americans, fighting the Seminoles and calling the Cherokees an inferior race with inferior minds. Horrible!

Why do politicians crave reaching the White House? I never wanted to move there for my own, most private reasons. In the White House, I wasn't pleased that I must sleep in the same bed as my husband. By Mr. President's inauguration, we had insisted for years on separate bedrooms. From mid-1825 to now, I've had three miserable years in that double bed in the White House.

The other furnishings hold little hope of comfort. They are dismal. They suit the house because the entire place is dismal—from the kitchen to the bedrooms to the salons. Worse, there is no plumbing in the White House! No running water of any kind. I have been reduced to squatting on a chamber pot, much as I did as a little girl when my father took us to live in France. I blame the bad piles I've suffered here on the squatting and pushing. Eventually I followed my brother's example and went to his doctor in Baltimore to endure a terrible operation to remove the piles that were crowding inside my colon. The operation took place with no pain-killer of any sort, not even a tumbler of brandy! It was beyond excruciating. I've endured eight miscarriages and undergone the pains of giving birth to four live babes, but those experiences were nothing compared to the removal of my piles.

Mr. President had piles too, but he left them where they were and sneered when doctors told him they came from too much sitting. "Sitting?" He'd roared back. "I am a man who swims at least a mile every day and takes a walk for two to three hours daily."

Mr. Adams was not immune to causing me domestic embarrassment. Twice earlier I've located copies of the racy novel Tom Jones hidden among his dirty shirts when I collected his laundry. A third volume of Tom Jones surfaced in late 1828. Why does he read this book? Over, and over? I asked the White House's main housekeeper what she thought about this, because I knew she'd seen that book too, and her comment was to the point, "He must want it to excite his libido."

Libido? When he hadn't lifted MY nightgown with any emotion other than primal mating urges?

My eldest son has become a worry. Several years earlier, our fears for George had abated when he was elected to the Massachusetts legislature. When he wasn't re-elected, he'd tried hard to build up his law practice with negative results. Nobody in Boston wanted to be a client of George Washington Adams, even when he was the son of a sitting President. More recently, I've become concerned by George's letters; every single one details serious problems. He needs money, has fallen into debt, has no friends, and feels a failure. God knows he IS a failure. Mr. President has pressed George from his earliest childhood to excel. When George had to take an exam at Harvard, he was so nervous he became ill. I fear Mr. President will lose all interest in George. Mr. Adams hasn't given up on John. He made him his secretary, as HE had been HIS father's secretary. But George hasn't measured up. Accounts have been sent out months late or lost and not sent at all. Broke, he sold his books to Mr. President for $2000, but it took him six months to mail off a list of them to the White House to his far-busier father.

If not through his progeny, Mr. President has been doing his best to leave a good political legacy. But oh my, he, too, didn't measure up to HIS father. Even his Massachusetts constituents have to admit that he isn't the man that John Adams, the second President, was.

Now I urge him to greater things. In his four years as President, struggling, he has managed to order much road-building to go ahead. He was instrumental in bringing forward the opening of the Erie Canal. He signed the Tariff Act of 1828, which made him hated even more by the Southerners, who called it the "Tariff of Abominations," because it harmed their industry, even as it helped the United States as a whole. He became interested in the nations south of the border. He sent a Minister to Mexico, the touchy Mr. Joel Poinsett. He was our one diplomat who had a flower named after him, the poinsettia. And, Mr. President promoted the founding of the Pan American Conference by nominating two delegates to its initial meeting in Panama. That unfortunately didn't end too well. Our delegates arrived too late when the conference had ended.

Other international relations have better results. Mr. President gritted his teeth and studied how to placate Mexico's fury at the many new American pioneers who are settling south of the Border. He worked out a treaty with Mexico that he hoped would avert a war. I recalled how he had been the envoy to sign the Treaty of Ghent to end our War of 1812 and felt compassion for what he was enduring: humiliation from the knowledge that his endeavors were not appreciated. Mr. President could have been a Quaker; he was so opposed to war anywhere, any time.

With all that on his schedules, on one occasion at least Mr. Adams did take off for Boston to help George in person. He found George living in a filthy mess. In squalor! George hadn't bathed or had a haircut. Our eldest son looked, smelled, and behaved like a wild man.

On his return to the White House, this time Mr. President didn't blame me. That was ominous. It reeked of the old yelp that insanity ran in the Johnson side of my family.

With that scare strangling me, I took one of the new trains to Boston. I discovered George was indeed living like a mentally ill person, too sick to shave or empty his chamber pot. I should have called in a specialist in mental aberrations. I didn't. I was loath to have my son's condition reported and have it noised about to be fodder for Mr. President's enemies. And mine.

There are women in this great nation who have petty criticisms of me mainly because Mr. President hadn't favored their husbands or sons by getting them government jobs. The same criticisms have surfaced again. I am accused of being a snob, that I spend too much money on clothes. I have even been reviled because we bought a billiard table for our resident sons to enjoy in the White House and have sought to be reimbursed, as we intend to leave it behind when we quit the domicile.

Never mind. I am not going to let those harpies add to my worries. I have plenty to keep me worried due to the men in my life.

My dear brother-in-law Walter Hellen, when he lost Nancy, had married another of my sisters, Amy. Instead of bringing joy into my life, that marriage has caused trouble. In my girlhood I was never very close to Amy due to the difference in our ages, and because I had already chosen Nancy as my bosom buddy. So when Amy arrived at the Hellen home as Walter's new bride, I felt closer to Nancy's children and invited them to live with us. Amy wants children of her own and isn't disposed to being a stepmother to Nancy's brood.

My Hellen nephew, Nancy's son, whom I'd invited to live in the White House, promptly got a female member of the staff pregnant. When he thought we'd learned the news, he decamped and has yet to be heard from again.

The brother-in-law on whom I'd leaned during the early days of my marriage, Thomas Adams, had sunk into a loathsome state of alcoholism. He and his wife lived in the old Adams mansion without contributing a cent to its upkeep. Thomas hardly leaves his bed except to scour for another bottle of wine. Very distressing!

With all of this chaos swirling around us, I am little surprised that Mr. President has lost his run for a second term today, December 2, 1828. My only consolation on that score is that all Calhoun's rotten, underhanded political swordplay didn't help him a bit; Andrew Jackson went ahead and won the race. But this loss is well-tempered by an even greater boon in our lives, one which I am hoping will cheer Mr. President-no-more as we move forward. Our son John's wife has delivered a baby girl this very day. She is named Mary Louisa, and she makes me merry Louisa!

Washington D.C., January 11, 1829

It is a relief for both of us that the dreadful four years in the White House have come to an end. During our stay, I wrote in my official diary, "There is something in this great, unsocial house that depresses my spirits beyond expression." In other writings I became more specific, grumbling that a husband expects a wife to, "Cook dinner, wash his clothes. Gratify his sexual appetites." Oh, I wrote further that a wife must then, "Thank him and love him for permission to drudge through life at the mercy of his caprices."

But just as he had tried to please the American people, Mr. President tried a little to please me. During our final days in the White House Mr. President surprised me with some sweet words. He even wrote secret notes to me that are quite erotic, speaking of my pubic hair as a "diadem" leading to ecstasy! I have kept these notes for posterity. Ha!

But then we have been hit again with the troubles of our eldest son, George. This month, George was upset by the malicious gossip that was spread during his father's campaign to be re-elected. His fragile mental state was worsened after he borrowed

$1000 from a tomb maker and then wasn't able to repay him. George appealed to his father to cover this debt, but only got more outraged letters from Mr. President.

George, beset by so many worries, babbled to himself when a letter from his father arrived ordering him to Washington. He told a neighbor he "heard voices." Birds in trees outside were talking to him.

Charles was in Boston to start a law practice of his own, and went to call on his elder brother. Deeply distressed at the pathetic condition in which he found George, Charles could think of nothing better to do than to help George pack for the trip to Washington. Charles couldn't calm him when George wildly accused a neighbor of stealing his books.

Washington D.C., May 27, 1829

George committed suicide on April 30. He'd gone aboard a spanking new steamboat that was to journey to New York City. Mr. President and I learned part of the story on May 2, two days after the tragedy. We were seated at our very long dining table in a rented home on Meridian Hill—where we came after departing The White House—being served breakfast by a member of staff. We heard a furious clatter of horse's hooves, and then my brother-in-law, Nathaniel Frye, tore wildly into the dining room. He brought us a copy of the Baltimore American, with a notice of George's having disappeared under the wake of the steamboat.

Our kinsman, Judge Cranch, also asked for admittance to the dining room. He listened as Nathaniel told us the details. Adding to the horror was a note from a firm of undertakers, Davis and Brooks, notifying us they had charge of George's baggage. Attached, was a bill for storage.

His hair in a mess, his cloak untidily around his waist, Nathaniel had tears streaming down his face. I think I knew what he was going to tell us before he croaked out a word. "Suicide!"

Had George put a pistol to his temple, or had George thrown himself under the wheels of a train? Looking as ashamed to have to give us this news as if he had murdered George, Nathaniel whispered out a few details. "Your son, Mr. George Washington Adams, Mr. President and Louisa, boarded the BENJAMIN FRANKLIN, at Providence. It's one of our newest and best interstate ships. It really is a fine ship, captained by Mr. Bunker. George boarded on the morning of April 29, in fair weather. He seemed cheerful enough and conversed with Captain Bunker. Came evening, he told the captain he had a bad headache. He requested the ship put to shore and let him get off. Meanwhile, he sought out a missionary who had some Indians on board and gave him a charity donation."

I began to weep. Choking on his saliva, Nathaniel interrupted this horror tale until President Adams insisted he continue the story.

"Very much later, at about three a.m., he told a fellow passenger that the ship's engines were talking to him, saying, 'Let it be, let it be.' Then he found a candle and went to various berths to wake up passengers asking if a rumor had been circulating against him. That's when he asked Captain Bunker to be set ashore. But the BENJAMIN FRANKLIN was in Long Island Sound making sixteen knots. Captain Bunker asked, 'Why do you wish to be set ashore?' George said, 'There is a combination among the passengers against me. I heard them talking and laughing at me.' When the captain explained he could not stop the engines there, and then, George went up to Mr. John Stevens, a Jackson supporter going to Washington for a job with the new administration. They talked about your loss in the election process. A few minutes later Mr. Stevens heard a splash. He saw your son's body hit the waves. Mr. Stevens called out, 'Man overboard.' It was sunrise, Monday, April 30. Sailors took a skiff. They searched. Mr. Stevens saw his hat and his cloak. Nothing else has been found of George." Lamely, he added, "The shore has been combed."

My husband, shaking as if he had an awesome fever, managed to stand up to thank Nathaniel and Judge Cranch for coming. They shook hands; Nathaniel patted his back.

When they had left the dining room Mr. President walked the length of the room. He helped me up, took me in his arms, and groaned. Murmuring into my hair, he whispered in agony the most remarkable words I've ever heard from him, "Louisa, dearest. My fault. My fault. All my fault."

What to say? Nothing.

For a moment, I couldn't speak. As if I was at the feet of God, I finally whispered back in the same loving way, "Dearest, my fault. Only mine. I should have brought him a specialist to help his condition." I blamed myself. I've become a thinking woman, a feeling woman. I was no longer like that spoiled girl from the brick house on Tower Hill.

Mr. President blamed himself. "I pushed him to exertion beyond his nature."

"My first-born son, my first-born, only twenty eight," I moaned. I couldn't help myself. But at least I did know I should have kept silent.

"He was... all goodness and affection. He loved his books, novels, poetry."

"He was happy in England. On horseback, or in libraries. Going to theaters!" I was half out of my senses. I kept ranting on, when I should have been soothing him.

I gasped, reminded of George's sweetness. I had to bite my tongue to stop myself from reproaching Mr. President. Or even to whisper the tiniest sting of reproach. I was afraid that either of us would lose our minds completely from such awful grief.

And then Mr. Adams gave me a very great gift. Holding me tenderly he said, "Please, dearest, call me Johnny. I need to hear that name from you!"

I found a narrow bed and collapsed on it. I stayed there for days, or was it weeks? I couldn't bear the pain of this loss. Terrible as had been Louisa Catherine's death in St. Petersburg, I had been able to survive the passing of an infant. George, at twenty-eight, was a fully grown man. This pain was too terrible.

Weeks later George's peccadilloes began to surface. George's dissipated life—hours hanging around taverns and flirting with available companions—had resulted in a girl getting pregnant. At least, he thought her baby could be his. Oh God, an illegitimate baby!

The girl's name was Eliza Dolph, and she was employed as a housemaid by Mr. President's relation, Mr. Welch, with whom George had lived as a boarder. This was the first we learned of that story. In George's will he gave any monies left from the inheritance granted to him by his grandfather to sustain the young woman, Eliza, unless she went off with another man. Sordid as that sounded, it didn't ease my grieving. The story made me suffer worse because it showed that George could have married and raised a family.

Charles went through George's papers and found specific instructions regarding the poor girl. From the tome, among fifty-six pages of an autobiography George had begun in 1826, Charles read, "The debts to my father were so large that the balance will amount to little, and that would not be much to put into the hands of a weak young girl, to say the least of it. It should be secured from her and forfeited in case of ill conduct."

George wrote about Eliza Dolph three years ago! That meant her infant could be three years old, and we've known nothing! My husband was too busy being Mr. President. And where was I when I was sorely needed by George? I'd been doing what I'd always been doing, hiding my own illegitimacy!

As time went by, it was still too painful to look out for the girl, Eliza, or her child. We were advised she'd kept her employment with Mr. and Mrs. Welch and that they would help her with the infant. I learned that Johnny had studied our legal responsibility and determined to give Eliza the minimum recommended by law. I could say nothing. I wanted to give her much more than the bare minimum, but where could I find the money? Poor misguided girl! And, as always before, my terror of having my illegitimacy revealed smothered any initial desire to help Eliza.

In St. Petersburg when my sister Kitty became pregnant, Mr. Adams had quickly arranged for her to marry his nephew, her paramour. When Kitty's child was born it had been legitimized by her husband. With his father officiating as President of the United States, George hadn't felt he could marry a servant girl. Hence, Eliza's infant was illegitimate.

George, dead, could not legitimize the child. As Mr. Adams would give Eliza nothing more than the minimum demanded by decency, I used grieving for my eldest son as the excuse not to search out Eliza or her child to offer my help.

I descended into the deepest hell of my life. Johnny decided to go to Massachusetts for his annual holiday, needing it as never before. I couldn't go with him. I was too bedridden at that point. I felt as if I'd fallen into a pond full of glue. I could move my body at first, but only just. But after three weeks, I couldn't move at all. I asked my daughter-in-law to care for me, and the darling woman brought along my Hellen grandchild to cheer me. Cheer? Would I ever be cheered again?

Yes, on May 21, I did experience a first flutter of cheer when I opened THE NEW BEDFORD MERCURY and read a poem published by that newspaper written by GEORGE! He'd sent it in to the editor some weeks before he committed suicide. I copied it out. The words clutched at my heart from beyond the grave.

There is a little spark of sea
Which grows 'mid darkness brilliantly,
But when the moon looks clear and bright,
Emits a pale and feeble light,
And when the tempest shakes the wave
It glimmers o'er the seaman's grave
Such friendship's beaming light appears
Through the long list of coming years
In sorrow's cloud it shines afar
A feeble but a constant star
And like that little spark at sea
Burns brightest in adversity

When Johnny returned from Quincy, I showed him George's poem. On reading it together, again Johnny and I held each other in one another's arms. We wept, but we found our torn voices to quote George's line, "In sorrow's cloud it shines afar." That little light of which he wrote saved our sanity.

Johnny had an epiphany. It happened during a walk when he was caught by a cloudburst accompanied by lightning and thunder. He'd taken refuge under a tree.

All around him growled the thunder. Above him lances of lightning struck out to hit him. There ahead was a huge oak. He crouched beneath it. Not a great idea, considering that lightning often strikes trees! But instead of any more horror, Johnny suddenly found himself at the foot of a glorious rainbow.

There, he felt a presence, an ecstasy, which somehow he related to George. I have read that in ancient Sanskrit Hindu records there are descriptions of such moments of spiritual ecstasy. The Buddhists describe them too. I believe it's what they call Nirvana, which is a beatitude attained by the extinction of individuality. My Roman Catholic friends in Maryland had spoken of their saints who had such experiences: St. Paul on the road to Damascus, St. Teresa of Avila, and St. Anthony of Padua.

Washington D.C., September 21, 1829

Johnny's letters helped me too. After he left Meridian Hill for his annual sojourn in Quincy, I received the first of Johnny's new-style letters, now addressed to "Dearest Louisa." Those brought some measure of cheer until I received one with the horror story of Johnny AND John having been stopped in New York with a request to officially identify George's remains. The remains had been washed up on June 13 with the tide on City Island above the East River at the Sound's western end.

Amid the ghoulish sounds of foghorns on the East River they traveled to East Chester. The inquest on George's body had been taken care of, but there was an internment to endure. Johnny and John went into the crypt where George's body lay. There, they had been revolted by a fetid smell. They ordered George's body to be removed. Within weeks his sodden remains were moved again. This time to Quincy, where it arrived in the autumn, shortly before Johnny was scheduled to return to Washington.

Finally, his remains found peace in the family mausoleum.

What a summer.

I got sick of feeling sick. I'm no invalid and detest being treated like one. That's true, although my detractors like to pretend that I enjoy being sick.

More importantly, it was time for me to put love into lovemaking to ease Johnny's pain. A natural benefit I received during the past winter was that I reached the age for what some ladies call "the change," menopause. It means that I can have intercourse with Johnny without the fear of getting pregnant again. That certainly brings added pleasure to our new-style of completely satisfying couplings. Now, when Johnny approaches me with his organ erect, I needn't cringe and pull away from him, obsessed with loathing to be pregnant again, when pregnant for me not only means a swollen, heavy belly, but nausea followed by constant bouts of vomiting. My last few pregnancies added an occasional fainting spell where I lose consciousness completely and cease being me.

I have to admit to one consolation: Johnny became more loving in his attitude towards me. In fact, together in bed he was ARDENT. He felt so sorry for my suffering that he had re-initiated kissing. I had suffered so much. I'd been tortured even worse than heretics under the Spanish Inquisition. I have heard stories—possibly untrue—of how those Spanish zealots refined the Iron Maiden wherein a victim was placed inside a life-sized cabinet studded inside with knives that cut up a body when its lids were closed. The Inquisitors refined the "supplice"—torture whereby a man had a red hot poker shoved up his anus and a woman would have a fiery rod jabbed up her vagina. My fiery rod had been to lose George, whilst knowing that I should have sought a doctor who could control his periods of madness.

Somehow, there is an even deeper agony over the death of a mature child. When Johnny, holding me with his naked body and kissing, kissing, kissing me, murmured words of endearment my agony melted into that sweet sensation that flooded my body in exaltation.

"Dearest," he repeated again and again with other words even stronger.

More kissing, kissing, and kissing. The feeling took me out of myself, as though I'd reached into outer space, soaring like a meteor, luminous as I entered a new atmosphere.

After another surprisingly and delightful thrusting, which caused me to have a series of exquisite rippling sensations in my female organ, sensations totally new to me, and enchanting me, Johnny said, "Perhaps we should not kiss so much. We are in mourning."

I retorted gently, "Speak for yourself, I know I won't run out of kisses."

After that night, neither of us have run out of kisses. I need them. The very thought of having lost George is such a terrible nail in my heart, that the pain can only be lessened by Johnny's new style of lovemaking. My beloved George having jumped overboard from a steamboat, a suicide, God, how could I have survived such tidings without Johnny's kissing and caressing?

I cannot give Johnny's newly ardent advances total credit for my return into the land of normality. But they certainly have helped me go on living. After months of continuous weeping, the feel of his body next to mine and an important part of his body entering mine while kissing and fondling, gives me a measure of solace that nothing else can. Moreover, he finally has taken heed of my brother-in-law Walter's advice on the subject of lovemaking and began to kiss me "all over," exactly as Nancy had described Walter's style. More, he often used endearing words, calling me his "Dearest friend."

What a difference his new manner of lovemaking made to our marriage! But earlier I had been made to endure those thirty-two years of abject misery in all the beds in which we lay together from England, to Berlin, to Massachusetts, to St. Petersburg, to Paris, to London, and to Washington D.C. Those years of misery are what I detail in the book I've started to write: A Story of My Life. Again I detail the misery I'd hinted at in my 1827 opus The Metropolitan Kaleidoscope.

What a pity that Johnny chose to add caressing and kisses to sexual intercourse at such a tragic time in our lives! How much sweeter the tasty preludes to his new style of lovemaking would have felt, if only he had begun them on our miserable "honeymoon."

One night, weeks later, Johnny came into my alcove to chat. Johnny ended the talking and poured a large amount of wine from his special decanter. It is one which I keep upstairs in my alcove for just such an eventuality now, hoping that he will join me there, next to my BEDROOM! Pulling up a spare chair that is usually tucked next to my drapes, I provided a blanket. It was one I keep in the cupboard for his knees on the winter nights when even a man from Massachusetts would feel the polar temperature in spite of our many fireplaces.

I'm rather spoiled for comfort, having a fireplace both in my bedroom and in my alcove. I needed them, even now in September. Dolley Madison must have felt the cold even more than I do. When we first moved into this house before Johnny's Presidency, I had grown fond of it immediately. We now live permanently in it. Johnny bought it when F Street was not so expensive, partly choosing it for our home because it had been well-provided with fireplaces by former President and Mrs. Madison.

Johnny threw off the blanket and stripped to be nude. Thank you, dear ex-President and Dolley Madison for those comforting fireplaces! In that delicious warmth Johnny rapidly undressed me with my help, and when I was naked he began that wonderful caressing and kissing me all over. Then with his remaining strength he carried me in his arms to our bed. At last, I received that much wanted "being carried over the threshold" to what should have been our honeymoon bed!

Washington D.C., July 7, 1832

I thank God Johnny also got a new horizon to explore: the House of Representatives. Never a person to enjoy being idle, he had no doubt used his time in Quincy in 1830 to sound out the Federalist Party for a new job. His speculations in the interview with Mrs. Anne Royall must have been correct. He must still have had loyal supporters in the party's midst because they speedily made an offer he didn't intend to refuse. Yes, although he had the rank of an exPresident, his party didn't delay in asking him to represent it in the lower branch of Congress. And Johnny, needing the salary, never hesitated to accept the chance to be elected to that office. It was our youngest son, Charles, who took umbrage.

"What? Father! You cannot humble yourself in such a Manner!" Charles had his own ambitions to have a successful career in politics. He believed that Johnny accepting to be a Congressman could damage his own advancement in politics. Charles used his proximity to Johnny, summering in Massachusetts, to argue for hours in the small library.

Finally, Johnny had told Charles, "I must fulfill my destiny."

Oh, Oh. That wasn't at all what Charles wanted to hear. Charles, biting the tip of his perpetually pale tongue, replied bitterly, "I cannot help thinking success would be far more certain if you rejected the idea of DESTINY altogether."

Reverend Joseph Richardson came to Johnny's Quincy home with a suggestion. In the now too crowded library he said, "If you will serve, I believe the election can be carried by a large majority. I think that the presence of an ex-President of the United States in the House of Representatives would elevate the representative character instead of degrading it."

Johnny replied, "In that respect I have no scruple whatever. No person would be degraded by serving the people as a Representative in Congress, nor would an ex-President be degraded by serving as a Selectman of his town, if elected thereto by the people."

Later, describing this encounter with Richardson, Johnny wrote, "I do not know how the election will turn, and, if chosen it might depend upon circumstances whether I should deem it my duty to accept or decline. The state of my health, and the degree of opposition to the choice, and the character of the candidate in opposition, might each or all contribute to my determination."

Oh? I was reminded of how I felt when he accepted to go to the Senate. Of course, he would go. He had never had any intention of turning down a salary-paying job. Had I not compared him then to a virgin who'd been kissed and complained but really wanted more of the same?

Back in our F Street house, in front of our living room's fireplace, Johnny had sipped his Madeira wine and commented, "Charles will never be President. Maybe he should try for the Vice-Presidency one day. But I will wager he does not even get THAT."

Johnny had put aside his glass without finishing his drink. He did not drunk much wine while deliberating on the subject of accepting the offer of being a Representative to Congress. Maybe because he'd endured such struggles when pushing forward any of his projects as a Minority President, Johnny had thought a lot about accepting the candidacy. He didn't want to be in a Minority position ever again. He would only enter the fray if he could be assured of a huge majority.

He need not have worried. In 1830 he garnered 1,817 votes as against 373 for one and 279 for the other candidate. Those were the totals from the thirteen townships involved. Very different from when he first tried to be in Congress in 1802 when he only carried Medford! It meant that we would be back in the Capital's swim. Did I want that? I felt tremulous about taking on the Washington politicians again.

After George's death, Charles had chosen to wed a rich Massachusetts girl from Medford, Abby Brooks. Perhaps he read his father's Harvard paper on the importance of choosing a bride who had a fortune! Too bad for Johnny that he'd not managed to do the same! He'd married the daughter of a bankrupt man who never paid her dowry. Abby's father was Charles Brooks, an insurance broker of considerable wealth.

I couldn't attend the wedding because when Charles came to New York to help me continue my journey to Massachusetts for the nuptials, he'd booked me on that same BENJAMIN FRANKLIN vessel that had brought such sorrow into my heart. I simply hadn't the strength to go aboard that distasteful ship from which George had jumped. I returned to Washington, and Charles had to rely on his father as a back-up at his wedding.

Abby fitted nicely into our family. She was of strong puritan stock and brooked no quarter. I learned to stand up and be myself from that skinny girl. She took Charles in hand and stopped him from being a poodle for his father. Charles, who of all my sons was the one who had spent most time with us, had developed superbly. He thought so. Much as I love him, I do have to admit that my youngest is a man after his own heart.

Whatever Charles put his hand to, flourished. If it was a seedling that grew into a handsome tree or a horse that outran all his competitors or a legal contract that needed skill, Charles was the best gardener, jockey, lawyer, etc. He was too much the best at everything. That could prove a bit trying at times. He was a good son, but not a simpering leech. He'd lived in the White House, graduated with honors from Harvard, applied himself to law, and built up a decent practice in Boston. It was only on that one occasion that Charles took a negative stance: when he scorned the suggestion that Johnny should return to politics as a Congressman in the House of Representatives.

At the time that this suggestion first emerged, my husband had stayed too long in Massachusetts. He caught a cold swimming from his adored Greenleaf wharf. The cold persisted and threatened to go down into his lungs. I didn't like what I was hearing in letters from his Adams relations: that Johnny had been spied wandering around outdoors in his nightcap to protect his head from draughts, acting eccentric, and being snubbed by former friends in Boston who neglected to invite him to their balls or suppers. Even Charles continued to be downright difficult in some of his notes.

As for me, I found solace in work. I began my lugubrious book Adventures of a Nobody. Simultaneously, I penned a description of my perilous trip from St. Petersburg to Paris.

Washington, D.C., November 8, 1833

As was still our way, Johnny wrote from Quincy he was ending his summer vacation. Alone in our F Street house, I was advised he would return shortly. I had been sitting in the hall one evening when finally

I heard a hack arrive, I opened the front door to find Johnny with totally unkempt hair, his cravat askew, and wearing only one mud-and-blood stained shoe.

"Good heavens! What... " I gasped and helped him to the only chair in our hall.

"Train wreck," he supplied, his voice rasping like a child's with whooping cough.

"Your train? Anyone... killed?"

He nodded, not attempting to speak. He craned his head toward the library where he kept a bottle of Madeira near his bookshelves. It wasn't difficult to guess what he wanted. But I brought two glasses, one for the Madeira and a snifter for the brandy. Both of the bottles were carried by hand; I didn't bother to be fancy with a tray. Johnny sidelined the Madeira and took my hint by serving himself a huge amount of brandy. He followed that with a disgusted frown, because, of course I'd brought him the brandy

I use in the kitchen for my Christmas plum puddings. He was accustomed to the finest brandies. Still, he poured out another huge snifter with the golden liquid almost to the lip. He removed his one shoe, plus the damp soggy sock, and finally told me what had happened.

"On the Hightstown train, I was reading from my favorite volume of Cicero's works, completely oblivious of my surroundings. I could have been on my porch in Quincy, I was so comfortable. It was a woman's constant high screams that alerted me to pull myself out of my book. The woman who was screaming had lost a leg; it had been severed at the hip as the wall of our coach sliced inward. Almost silently, our coach continued to tilt, a deadly ballet. As I watched in horror, another woman was crunched by the oncoming wall as our coach met with trees and rocks. Her screams ceased. She was dead! Next to her an elderly gentleman had his white hair and sideburns coated with blood so that now he seemed a redhead. A clever old gentleman, he used the woman's dead body to cushion the impact that hit him, and therefore was thrown across the aisle. There, a middle-aged woman, probably a grandmother, badly injured, gave me the child on her lap to be rescued. I grabbed the child and, since our train had stopped, I pushed my way out its side door, now almost our roof. Two women followed me, but one didn't take the step properly and tumbled down on the track. Finally assistance appeared, we were told of the train's broken axle, and I was relieved of the nameless child. I was put on a steamer for Baltimore. Then a hack was summoned for me, and I was driven all the way here. Very expensive."

I ran upstairs for a cloth to clean his face, pulled his dressing gown and slippers from their perch beside our bed, and hastened back to the hall.

Johnny was asleep there, snoring. I shrugged, took the cloth to the kitchen, covered him with his dressing gown, and thought how this accident had ended differently from the time when we were together in a hack that turned on its side on a muddy lane and we were both thrown onto cobblestones. That time neither of us had been hurt, or bloodied. But after we'd returned safely to our home Mr. Adams had soothed his nerves by rushing me to the marital bed for more thrusting. That time I took myself to the single bed in our guest room and asked myself: what did I feel? A salad of emotions! Relief, yes; that my husband whose salary paid for the food, clothing, servants, and taxes was still in one piece. But there had been other ingredients: prickly thoughts of wishing him dead and that I'd been out of an unhappy marriage, with no more couplings engendering fears of getting pregnant. Those thoughts were followed by remorse that I could even imagine that ending.

But this time? I pulled up a chair next to him and held his hand while he slept. He had been there for me in the grief of losing our George, and now, I would be here for him when he awoke.

Washington D.C., October 26, 1834

Young John, a confirmed alcoholic, has made a widow of Mary only four years after George's awful end. Our son John has tried so hard to make ends meet and provide for his growing family, but he just didn't have a knack for making money. Johnny had landed him with a too-challenging job at the mill in which he had a share and which had belonged to my cousin. John did his best, but while he was managing the Columbia Mill, it was during years of either too much grain—left to rot—or too little grain to make the mill profitable. Our struggling son wore himself out. And alcohol—cheap tavern liquor—had become his bulwark against criticism for mismanagement.

My husband came down from Quincy on October 23, 1834 to find John in a coma from which he never recovered. Never. Dear John, who had offered me his home when the house on Meridian Hill was taken back by its owner! Dear John, who had been an arm to lean on during the George tragedy! Dear John had gone to Heaven to join George, as so often during their lives he had offered himself for George to lean upon.

Washington D.C., November 3, 1837

We lately found ourselves bordering on financial ruin! I did not think the May 10 financial crash would affect us, but we have suffered from another of those amazing twists of fate that periodically hit our lives.

I did not suspect anything of the kind until one evening when Johnny strode into the kitchen and removed the plate from a table next to the stove where the butter was melting like snow in sunshine. Carefully, he repositioned the plate on a shelf in our cold larder.

"We have to be mindful not to waste food," he said grimly. "I have not enough money to be able to pay our bills this month."

"I never waste butter. I'd brought it out for cookies I'm going to bake."

"Save on cookies. We must make do with simple food. No food for parties. No more parties."

I rarely interrupted Johnny, but I did this time. "Not even teas?"

"No tea parties. You have to serve cookies at them and maybe a cake."

"Just lemonade wouldn't be costly," I suggested. "Who would hire a carriage to come here for nothing but lemonade?" he countered.

"Could you borrow some money until things perk up? Johnny, you know so many wealthy people, bankers, and diplomats. And your cousins?"

"The cousins! They want to borrow from ME. My friends? I don't want to go to them. But I do have a plan. Remember my old valet? Whom I scooped up in Ghent to work for me while I was negotiating to end the War of 1812? I have not been in communication with him since he left my employ to work for President Jackson in the White House. My former valet has opened a highly lucrative restaurant since leaving General Jackson. Surprisingly, he wrote to me the other day and asked if there was anything he could do for me."

"How could I forget him? Especially when I think of that time when the two of you went swimming naked in the Potomac where the British Ambassador caught sight of you and told people that all you were wearing was a black swimming cap and goggles."

"Well, I have decided to answer him with a request for a loan. After all, I always called him a gentleman's gentleman."

And so he did.

When Johnny's finances improved, the loan was speedily repaid.

Washington, D.C., June 28, 1838

In the House of Representatives Johnny finds ample opportunity to practice his fondness for debating. He impressed me today on one subject in particular, another example of Johnny's flowering as a caring person. He gave an amazing plea for the rights of women. I can scarcely believe what he has gone on record as saying. "Why does it follow that women are fitted for nothing but the cares of domestic life? For bearing children, and cooking the food for a family? Devoting all their time to the domestic circle to promoting the immediate personal comfort of their husbands, brothers, and sons?" He'd barely drawn fresh breath before continuing, "The mere departure of woman from the duties of the domestic circle, far from being a reproach to her, is a virtue of the highest order, when it is done from purity of motive, by appropriate means, and towards a virtuous purpose." All this was thanks to a women's rights group having put forward petitions in spite of the Southern Congressmen's stance against petitions. These had been provoked by a petition to end slavery from women based in his constituency: Plymouth. In recognition of these women's stance, my Johnny had ended by adding: "I do believe slavery to be a sin against God."

Hurrahs for Johnny!

Washington D.C., October 29, 1839

Finally, Charles has accepted in good heart Johnny's position as a Representative in Congress. But it seems he will be less forthcoming in the great fight my old warrior now undertakes as a Congressman to combat the evil of slavery. My son, certainly with his own sights on the Presidency, isn't going to stand by complacently while his father endangers his position as a Congressman by fighting "slavers." Charles knows little about slavery and cares nothing. His only concern is for himself, for his future career. Charles feels that involvement in an unpopular case—concerning a group of slaves among whom are murderers—is anathema for any politician in the United States. Charles is fully aware of the necessity to collaborate with Southern legislators if there should be any hope for him to someday be elected to the Presidency. Charles seethed with fury when he heard of his father's support for those slaves. He feels certain that Presidential ambitions will be dashed as long as his father is fighting Southern voters on the subject of slavery. Saliva drips from his lower lip when he gets on the subject.

While Charles remains in Massachusetts, I am the person closest to Johnny because I am in Washington. I have the day-to-day opportunities to influence Johnny. And I feel deeply about slavery as an evil plague. Anybody who will stand up to stop slavery I will back fully. That person in today's Congress happens to be my Johnny, who seems to be a mark for spite.

Washington's appetite for gossip and back-biting again continues to rear its ugly snout over and over. Our reappearance on the Washington scene prompted a re-hashing of an old calumny from the 1828 election days when he had been smeared by vicious rumors. Johnny had been accused of serving Czar Alexander as a pimp, when he was Minister in St. Petersburg, sending our housemaid Martha Godfrey to be the Czar's whore. In fact, his label during the campaign by many was, "The Pimp of the Coalition." Never happened!

Russia was a police state, where letters sent abroad were scrutinized. Silly Martha had written to an American friend alleging that the Czar was a lustful reprobate. Nothing could have been further from the truth where she was concerned. But yes, Martha had written such a letter. It described her visit to the Czar when she was accompanying our son Charles as a nanny. That was the only time she ever went to The Hermitage Palace. And that visit came at the request of BOTH the Czar and Czarina who were curious to see such a forward girl. When Martha went WITH my son Charles, they spent no more than ten minutes in the presence of the Czar and Czarina.

Such an old story has less merit upon re-appearing. But when has malicious GOSSIP ever needed validation?

Washingtonians, ever eager to tear us down, even decry my liking for puns. But a pun is fun! Some ladies were shocked by my toy-matching-boy pun. Others dislike me for giving double meanings to some of my puns. Oh my, how can I ever please everybody? The answer is: I shouldn't try.

Such vile stuff, this gossip! And it can infect those with the highest power. I'm reminded of the business between President Jackson and Vice-President Calhoun. No sooner had Johnny unpacked his books and important papers here in the F Street house, than he was swept into a new mess deliberately planted by Vice-President Calhoun, already aiming for the top spot in the White House. Like hyenas attacking a vulnerably wounded lion, the gossip mongers fell on a series of letters Calhoun had written almost a decade ago "reprimanding" Andrew Jackson, letters he had published in the United States Telegraph. With President Jackson, you do NOT remain a friend if he learns you ever opposed him, so Jackson's support for a Calhoun Presidency disappeared like a wounded lion's meat down the gullets of hyenas. Andrew Jackson has never forgiven anybody who maliciously spread the old news that his wife was a bigamist when she married him, a woman with two husbands at the same time. Being a friend to the hero of New Orleans—who had taken on the over-whelming forces of the British—is not easy. The smallest slight is enough to be banished from his inner circle. Petty men like these are supposed to lead us?

I've never been a gossip, but I'm human, and I must admit I recently followed one story that gripped Washington several years ago. I'm always tardy hearing these things.

It concerned that same ex-President Jackson and a member of his former cabinet. With ex-President Jackson still complaining about the cruel way his late wife had been treated by scandalmongers, it amazes me that Jackson decided to play the White Knight to defend the reputation of a lady whose name had been well and truly smirched. The lady, a Mrs. Peggy O'Neil Timberlake Eaton, had married the War Secretary in ex-President Jackson's cabinet. It was a legal marriage, although a murky one, because it is widely believed her late husband had committed suicide upon learning that his Peggy had been conducting an illicit affair with Secretary Eaton.

Washington D.C. split up into two groups, one supporting Mrs. Eaton's right to find happiness, the other reviling her name as a Jezebel. Mrs. Calhoun, the former Vice-President's wife led the latter. The rumor escalated to include the suggestion that exPresident Jackson, as a widower, was not motivated solely in clearing the lady's name: he wanted to get her into his bed. Jackson's 1829-1833 cabinet split into two camps copying political parties—Vice-President Calhoun headed the moral party, Martin Van Buren that of the "frail sisterhood." And he was notoriously engaged in canvassing for the Presidency by courting Mrs. Eaton. If his letters had not so incensed President Jackson, surely Calhoun's castigation of Mrs. Eaton would have cost him Jackson's support anyhow.

This story interested me in particular because it eventually drew Mr. Calhoun and Mr. Adams to mend fences which had been damaged during the last election. But that truce was short-lived as Johnny moved on to what he considered important: the ending of the Gag

Rule. It is a challenge that began for Johnny in 1836, and one that will likely take many years to win. On his re-entry to the political arena Johnny believed he could present petitions at will to Congress. Not so. When the Southern states' Representatives gleaned that many of Johnny's newest petitions were aimed at terminating slavery, he was gagged, and Calhoun was one of the reprobates moving to silence him. His petitions were disallowed! In this nation, sworn to uphold the freedom of speech? Johnny is not going to permit such a breach of the First Amendment! For three years now he has fought the Gag Rule to win justice promised in the Constitution. Johnny may have been a loser in the 1802 campaign to be a Congressman; this time around he was not going to be a loser in Congress.

Washington, D.C., November 13, 1840

Even though it can be serious, career-ending stuff, and the fear of it has kept me quiet about my heritage for years, gossip lost its interest when a new serious matter caught my interest and Johnny's as well. That was when we both became obsessed with LA AMISTAD, a Caribbean slave ship with its forty-nine adult Mende Africans aboard who'd captured their owners, killed the ship's captain and cook, yet have become heroes to half of America's people—the half who does not accept that slavery is a just condition. Thanks to many Americans' pride in their ideals pertaining to freedom of the individual, these Mende Africans have become revered as live exponents of the desire for freedom. The Forty-nine Mende adults and four Mende children were captured, kidnapped, and transported against their will to Cuba, and Johnny feels they were justified to kill to regain their freedom! Oh my, what a Pandora's Box of questions this incident opened up for our Southern slave holders!

When I helped Johnny during his terms as Secretary of State, I worked on various projects studying how to end slavery in the United States. And then came this LA AMISTAD case, or simply AMISTAD, as most people say. Johnny and I learned more about the case reading a selection of newspapers during our breakfast hour. We both like the forthright views in the Tappans' New York Journal of Commerce. This newspaper was one of the first to describe the strange wanderings of a battered-looking schooner that kept an erratic course off the coast of Maryland. Being half a Marylander, my attention was drawn to this story from its first appearance.

I know the Tappan brothers to be very wealthy Abolitionists, committed to using their money to end slavery. Lewis Tappan was the friend who provided the cloth for my Jackson Party gown. Both Tappans have made their money honestly, first by importing silks and woolens, then founding this newspaper and laterally starting a marvelous new publication. This newest endeavor promises to amazingly and daringly reveal the stability—or lack thereof—in the business world's companies, exposing in addition the reliability—or lack thereof—of some of their executives. I understand that they intend to eventually grade the businessmen in their files. Johnny feels very enthusiastic about the latter because he never has ceased being fascinated by weights and measures, and this idea of weighing and measuring businesses and businessmen delights him.

The various newspaper articles recounted how AMISTAD had been seized off Long Island by an American Navy patrol boat, the USRC WASHINGTON. Officers counted fifty-three Africans and two Spaniards on board after capturing a Mende scouting party that had gone ashore for water and food. According to the Spaniards, José Ruiz and Pedro Mendez, the Africans' leader, Cinqué, had managed to use a nail to open the lock that secured the chains of the men in the hold. Cinqué had told the men to mutiny. He pursued and killed the captain, while his cohort Grabeau dispatched the cook. Cinqué believed he needed to kill the captain in order to be the Mendes' leader. Grabeau murdered the cook because Celestino had teased him saying there were cannibals in Puerto Príncipe who would eat the Mende people.

The two Spaniards said they would have been killed, but Cinqué decided to have them steer AMISTAD to Africa. The Spaniards knew there were not sufficient provisions to reach Africa. Taking turns at AMISTAD's wheel, they steered for the United States at night and only by day followed Cinqué's directions to go east.

A cursory court had been set up on The WASHINGTON's deck, with a local judge presiding. The Spaniards had declared that Cinqué and Grabeau should be returned to Cuba to be hanged and the other slaves, none over the age of twenty-five, given back to them as their rightful owners to work on Cuban plantations. Oh? Johnny's astute legal eye picked out the glaring fact that among these fifty three

African "slaves" were three little girls and one little boy. Could these children be accused of MURDER?

"No women on board?" I asked, holding up a slice of toast.

"Yes. No women."

"These three little girls, surely they're far too young to work in the fields or in kitchens. They are far too young to be nursemaids." My eyes met Johnny's eyes. We've both lived in Paris. We knew about the brothels there that offered children to pedophiles. Johnny sighed, heavily. He hasn't forgotten our dead baby Louisa Catherine. He cares about little girls.

"I'm going to look into this matter. Remember, dearest Louisa, I worked on the Treaty that outlawed taking Africans from Africa to be slaves. I want to discover if these fifty-three Africans were born in Cuba or illegally shipped there from Africa." When Johnny takes a bit in his mouth, like a cart horse, he proceeds from strength.

There had been a trial on board the arresting ship and a not-guilty verdict pronounced. But, upsets do happen; that verdict was overturned. Johnny learned from newspaper accounts that the AMISTAD people had their next court appearance on dry land in New Haven in January. Johnny was not present. The Africans were given three other lawyers by Lewis Tappan. Two soon dropped out, believing their case was hopeless, leaving the Amistad Africans' future in the hands of a youngster called Roger Baldwin. However, when a second not-guilty verdict, also overturned, was then followed by a demand that a third trial be commenced—this, straight from the desk of the victor of the latest election, President Martin van Buren. He wanted this third trial to take place in the hollowed precinct of Washington's Supreme Court!

Martin van Buren, eager for a Second Term as President, brooked no chance that he could lose the Southern States' votes by allowing the Mende people to escape punishment. As the sitting President, he could channel the next trial to go to the highest court in the land, which he felt would send the Mende to Cuba to be slaves again. He was convinced the Supreme Court Justices would rule against the Mende because so many of the Chief Justices came from Slave States.

Lewis Tappan's prestigious Abolitionists felt that only Johnny could save the Mende Africans. A third not-guilty verdict couldn't be overturned when pronounced from within the hallowed walls of the United States Supreme Court. So Tappan and his colleagues, went to Quincy. There he trapped Johnny, who was sojourning during his summer vacation from the House of Representatives. He implored Johnny to save these unfortunate Africans, already knowing there was a good chance Johnny would, since he had penned a strongly-worded letter in defense of the Mende in the November 1839 issue of the New York Journal of Commerce.

After Johnny was approached by Lewis Tappan to plead for the Mende Africans before the Supreme Court, Johnny "girded his loins" and prepared for battle. Yes, he hesitated for an instant because he doesn't want to be branded an Abolitionist. Lewis Tappan, a leading American Abolitionist, had that reputation go before him. For years Johnny has managed to avoid officially espousing the Abolitionists' cause. It isn't because he doesn't want to end slavery in the United States. He does. And he has had his job in Congress threatened because of it. But the thought of those three little Mende girls in prison determined him to fight for the AMISTAD people, whether or not he would be finally branded an Abolitionist.

I care too. Together we have worked on the AMISTAD case. Johnny stays up until three a.m., night after night. I know he does because we share that marital bed. There, I get kissing, but no fondling. He is too tired, often the hour was too late, and he wants to be up and preparing his brief every morning by five a.m. He goes into battle on two hours of sleep.

For all that Johnny worked, Lewis Tappan also didn't sit on his you-know-what. He had the two Spaniards arrested for illegally buying the

Africans in a Havana barracoon and transporting African born people to be slaves. Mendez—older and cagier—broke bail and returned to Cuba. Ruiz preferred to be in an open jail, assured he would get back the forty-nine "slaves" as his property.

Reading this history, Johnny decided he wanted to meet Cinqué in person and survey the conditions under which all the other AMISTAD people were imprisoned. He was still particularly anxious about the three little girls. I had to wait at home whilst he went without me to Westville near New Haven to check out their jail. On his return, I ran to our front door the moment I heard carriage wheels stop on F Street. I blurted out my question.

"Did you meet the AMISTAD Africans? Cinqué?" "Yes, Cinqué. And I checked on some of the others.

Previously they were incarcerated by a tough jailor, a so-called Colonel Pendleton. He admitted he beats them, but then admitted to whipping his white prisoners too. There are only thirty-six males left of the original Mende; six died on board AMISTAD from starvation. One drowned by his own hand . . . . Forgive me; I shouldn't have mentioned that death. One died recently in the prison, and there was a to-do about burying him according to their African pagan rites."

"The three little girls? Are they alive?"

"I suppose I could say yes, but not LIVELY. They may still be recovering from their treatment at the hands of Mrs. Pendleton, a tiger of a woman. With her, all was NOT fine. I smell a rat. There is something very wrong threatening those little girls. Mr. Baldwin, their lawyer, told me he suspects Mrs. Pendleton was using them as servants—cleaning the jail's premises, including the cells of vicious prisoners. And, he suspects Pendleton was abusing the girls."

"Johnny! Do something."

"I already have. I've instructed that the AMISTAD Africans must have clean, adequate bedding and warm clothes. The girls are to be sent to a secure location, away from prowling men. For what it's worth, at least in this new warehouse in Westville, they are not subjected to tourists paying money to come watch the AMISTAD prisoners paraded around the greens."

"And Cinqué? Were you able to speak to him?" "Through an interpreter, yes, a pleasant African born seaman, James Covey, has been recruited to help in translating their Mende language. Apparently he was born in the Mende country. He says he was kidnapped and dragged to a slave ship, just as Cinqué has told him was what happened to him."

I gave Johnny a cup of hot chocolate. He preferred to get a glass of Madeira. We sat down in the breakfast nook to explore the subject further.

I asked, "What happens to them next? I mean, in the courts?"

My lawyer husband hesitated before answering. He wrinkled his forehead and did that Massachusetts snuffling thing he does. "Strange, this Baldwin, he won two court decisions, both favorable to the AMISTAD people. But both favorable decisions have been set aside because the Government has demanded the case be appealed."

"Appealed? How can that be?"

"These Africans are asking the same question. They say that in their country a decision stands. Not so here. President van Buren is in cahoots with the Queen of Spain over this matter. I can't believe he would be, but he is."

"Martin van Buren is a lame-duck president, he's out, lost in the polls to Harrison. Maybe Harrison won't be favoring the Spaniards."

"This case will probably be settled before Harrison takes office. And it was Van Buren who demanded it go to the Supreme Court."

"Oh, but that's terrible, with all those Southern slave owners sitting as justices—Southerners who will vote those kidnapped people should be returned to the Cubans as slaves!"

"Yes, powerful top-ranking Southerners, who maintain that the South's economy depends on slavery. And, as you know, to some extent it does. How would your Maryland cousins run their estates without their slaves? Louisa dearest, with four million slaves owned in this country, the AMISTAD people face defeat. It will take a miracle to set them free."

"YOU! You, Johnny, must be the miracle."

"With my voice that cracks? My dour face? My lack of . . . Charm?"

I should have spoken up quickly, reassuring him that he had many qualities. Instead, I waited a few seconds, then I took his hand, and for the first time in the forty-four years of our marriage, I kissed his fingers, one by one. I've never kissed his hands before because they had been off limits.

"You must be the instrument of God's justice," I

said gently. "Slavery is against the laws of God."

I went into the kitchen and poured out another cup of chocolate. I drank it down as if it was ambrosia.

Washington D.C., March 2, 1841

Often in the following months I couldn't sleep. I lay awake waiting for Johnny to join me in bed. I mulled over the way many Americans seem to accept slavery. I wondered what I could do to help Johnny in his looming test before the Supreme Court.

For Johnny's part, he missed receiving all those barrages of letters from his father and mother. Abigail had been dead for a little over two decades, and his father had barely managed to stay alive long enough to see his son become the Sixth President. The letters from his parents have been re-read until they are in tatters.

When Charles was away, Johnny receives notes from him, but they are now very disparaging of Johnny's quest for the Golden Grail of liberty for the AMISTAD Africans. Charles still does not want to sacrifice his own future on an altar of Johnny's further successes.

Late some nights, I read the brief Johnny was preparing. It seemed flat or too speechy: without a clarion call, too long. Those old justices would fall asleep, listening to him!

This thought still weighed on my mind one balmy afternoon, exchanging recipes in my F Street kitchen with my daughter-in-law Abby, I thought how unappetizing a treacle tart would be if too much treacle was added. Unsavory, inedible.

"Abby, how much sugar do you put in a Medway apple pie?"

"No sugar. I let the apples speak for themselves."

I felt my mouth quirk up with delight at an idea that might help Johnny! Surely if the Justices heard from the slaves themselves, their hearts could not remain stony.

That night, I asked Johnny if the AMISTAD Africans would be invited to speak to the Supreme Court.

"No. That's been ruled out. A few of them addressed the District

Court in Hartford. Cinqué cried out, 'Give us free.' It didn't help."

Feeling distressed, I needed to take a deep breath before continuing. "So if the AMISTAD Africans can't bring drama to the Supreme Court, what will?"

Johnny shrugged. He didn't try to answer me; he went to his library and poured over books describing past cases. But there had been NO case like this AMISTAD case in those old books.

After a weighty pause, Johnny returned and said, "Sometimes I feel like one of your Episcopalian priests. A priest, on Sundays, can stand at an altar and raise a chalice for Holy Communion and feel elated that God has come down from Heaven. On weekdays the same priest has the low-road job of visiting dying parishioners, some with loathsome sores or stinking bowel movements. What a contrast!

I feel my present job is not so different with ITS highs and lows."

Martin van Buren's last months as a lame duck president didn't provide time for the Supreme Court to convene to rule on the AMISTAD case. Worse, the Supreme Court postponed the AMISTAD case several times. On one occasion it was due to Johnny, whose coachman had been killed on an outing with him. Johnny had held the man in his arms until he breathed his last, and then he'd asked for a postponement. Another postponement came about because one of the justices, James Barbour, had died overnight. It was late February before the initial session began that would determine the Mende's fate.

Early in the morning, Johnny and I had left for the Capitol in a hired carriage to hear the final pleadings for the AMISTAD people at the Supreme Court. I brought his relative, Mrs. Smith, with us because otherwise I would have had to sit alone in the Visitors' Gallery when Johnny took up his place downstairs with the other lawyers on the case.

It was a bitterly cold day. I had a shawl, but Mrs. Smith shivered in her bare-shouldered dress. Fashion has changed radically from motherly draperies hiding bosoms. Now, even the most conservative ladies appear in public wearing revealing gossamer columns with tops that display shoulders and a lot of bust. I've been criticized in the past for being too fashionable. I, too, wore those narrow gowns that burst out around the back and bust like a stalk shows off its flower. Not that day. I went to the Capitol in as quiet an outfit as I could find in my clothes press.

As a threesome we entered the premises until Johnny left to take his position as an advocate. He would follow Roger Baldwin to plea for the AMISTAD Mende people. Johnny bowed to me and to Mrs. Smith as we reached the steps that led to the Visitors' Gallery. Then, he disappeared in the crush of legislators who wanted to hear the Justices' decision.

There were seven Justices, all of them known to Johnny. Some had worked with him during his administration as President. Chief Justice Roger Taney, a sterling character, was in Johnny's Cabinet as Secretary of War.

The speeches took over three hours each. I dearly wish it wasn't the habit of American lawmakers to talk so long. There was no break for food or drink. But I did notice that many of the older men had to make frequent use of the washroom. By the end of the day, there was no resolution. The Chief Justice ordered another session.

A new date was tolled for more speeches. I didn't believe I could take any more. I decided to stay home when next Johnny would go to the Capitol. That appearance fell on February 24, when again Johnny's pleadings were interrupted.

That morning I saw Johnny leave carrying a pile of books, a ledger, and notebooks. How could he juggle all that whilst walking to the Capitol, eschewing a hired carriage to save money?

I went to the kitchen, where Abby presented me with more Medway recipes. I suggested we try cranberry sauce in a different way, serving it on hot apple pie.

"Please, Louisa, restrain from mixing cranberries with apples." Abby wrinkled her pert nose. "Indeed, I prefer learning more about your European recipes."

"How about we try out these Hungarian ones?" I went to my folder and drew out three recipes that the new Minister from the Austrian Hungarian Empire had given me. I knew we had most of the necessary ingredients in my larder. But what really struck me was the AMOUNT of recipes I've collected—too many! There was an avalanche of paper as recipes spilled out all over the floor. Abby and I had to waste ten minutes just recovering them from behind the stove and the dirtied-utensils basin.

All those recipes sparked an idea.

When Johnny returned that evening, exhausted, I gave him a cup brimming with hot chocolate. I had added cinnamon to give it a lilt. "And how did the session go?"

"It was a disaster. The AMISTAD peoples' main lawyer, that Roger Baldwin, just repeated the same arguments he gave before. No FIRE in his belly. I think he's become too popular due to all the newspaper articles about him thanks to this case, and now he has so many new clients we don't count any-more."

"Couldn't YOU have saved the day?"

"God knows I tried. I spoke for two solid hours.

But I noticed that even good old Roger Taney's eyes seemed to be glazing over. Several of the Justices were snoring."

A heavy silence followed. I let it be. Sometimes silence is the best resort. But I was not going to let it be the last resort that night.

Topping up the hot chocolate in his cup, I said quietly, "Johnny, maybe a speech of two hours is too long, although I do know there are many legislators who speak for three, or more."

"The brief I am preparing, for later, could well take three hours."

"I scattered my recipes today. My album was so full that they fell out of their folders. They couldn't be opened without half of the pages spilling away. I imagined how sick too much food can make you feel. Suppose I gave you eight courses at supper because I wanted to try out new recipes? You could get a dreadful stomach ache."

"Eight courses? I would not eat them."

"Exactly. Johnny, while you were at the Capitol today, I studied various cases in your law books. So many words, many of them did not lead anywhere. They failed to get to the point."

"Dearest Louisa, I wish you wouldn't read my law books. You know how I feel about women and legal matters. No woman will ever be a lawyer."

Another heavy silence followed that remark. I let the silence speak for me.

Eventually, I tried another route to get MY point across. "Johnny, part of a little Ditty has been nagging at me all day. My mother used to mouth it to me when I was sent to the parlor to recite for our relations. Be brief, be right, be gone."

"Yes? And... "

I went to Daniel Webster's new dictionary, near us there on the lectern. I looked up the word brief, which has several meanings. I said, "Curiously, one of the word's meanings describes what you are preparing from all these books, 'Concise summary, as of a legal case.' Its other meaning is, 'Short, or concise.' In italics, for BRIEF as a verb, the description added, 'Give final instructions or essential information.' Could you do that in just under two hours?"

A third silence lumbered into the kitchen. The only sound was Johnny making that Quincy snuffling noise with his nose.

Abby came into the kitchen, raised her eyebrows at our silence, and asked, "Shall we try that paprika chicken recipe for dinner?"

I don't expect Johnny to listen to my brief advice. I'm only a woman, and women don't count. I did smile to myself when Johnny told me what Chief Justice Story wrote concerning Johnny's long oration, noting it was, "Extraordinary for its power and its bitter sarcasm, and the dealing with topics far beyond the record and points of discussion." So, Johnny had "dealt with topics far beyond the record and points of discussion." No wonder his arguments take four and a half hours! How could I cue his mind so that he will not repeat that error on his next appearance?

Yes, I am only a woman. But I thought of Egypt's Cleopatra, England's Boadicea, France's Joan of Arc. I don't need to have myself rolled inside a rug to meet Caesar, or fight in battles against the Roman invaders like Boadicea, or command armies to rise up against the English like Joan of Arc. I don't need to ride to Tilbury, like Queen Elizabeth to address her soldiers, expecting the arrival of Spain's Armada and declare to them, "I have but the feeble body of a woman, but the heart of a man."

All I needed to do was to pat Johnny's free hand and say, "Remember to give a concise summary."

Johnny spent quiet time walking in the White House park, meditating. Later, he told me how he could divert his mind watching a soft wind playing through new leaves making them twirl like ballet dancers.

He had started speaking on February 24 and did not conclude his remarks until yesterday, March 1. That morning, Johnny went alone again to the downstairs chamber underneath the Senate. After giving an honorable mention to Barbour's passing, Johnny returned to his subject and spoke for an additional three hours. His final tally was eight and one half hours over this past week.

When Johnny returned home with a quizzical expression on his lips, he admitted to me that he hadn't taken much notice of my admonitions to keep his speech brief. He asked me to be patient to learn the outcome of the day's proceedings.

Late this night, we sat in my kitchen, the warmest room in our house against the cold, March air. Johnny armed himself with his favorite Madeira wine, while I listened as he explained why he spoke for all those hours. "I needed to clarify how the doctrine of CONTINUOUS VOYAGE applies to the AMISTAD saga."

"And what is that?"

"In layman's terms, the doctrine of CONTINUOUS VOYAGE applies because the AMISTAD people had been on a continuous voyage from Sierra Leone in Africa on route to Camagüey, Cuba, regardless of what happened in-between."

"Oh, I guess I do understand." I recognized in Johnny his need to recapture with me the magic of his arguments. Whether I fathomed his meaning or not, he needed me now to support him by asking questions as if I were ignorant of the case and had not been his helpmate in this matter for this past year and a half.

"Moreover, I fought for the principle of HABEUS CORPUS."

"You'll have to explain that one more fully."

"Of course I do. You women really have no mind for legal matters. HABEUS CORPUS relates to the requirement of a legal process to bring a person before a judge or to be put into prison. It makes it essential to investigate the legality of the restraint. It is immensely important."

"Give me an example."

"When Jesus was apprehended in the Garden of Gethsemane, HABEUS CORPUS was already established at that time, and the Roman soldiers had to take him before judges. First he went before Caiaphas and then was taken to the headquarters of the Roman Governor, Pontius Pilate. The Jewish leaders wanted him to die, but only the Romans could order an execution. Pontius Pilate found no legal cause to restrain him, washed his hands, and sent him back to the Hebrew courts. To their everlasting shame, they ignored HABEUS CORPUS, and unjustly crucified him."

He was in full flow now, thrusting with his words as he used to thrust at me! But unlike that loveless lovemaking, he was aflame with passion now, and I wanted nothing more than to fan his fire. "Give me a modern example."

"Suppose a police officer wanted to take you, dearest Louisa, to jail. He would have to have legal grounds to do so, and that is where HABEUS CORPUS comes in again, as it has for the AMISTAD Africans. Not even a President van Buren can follow the recent advice of his Attorney General to deliver people to a foreign power without just cause. HABEUS CORPUS makes it mandatory to investigate the lawfulness of any restraint. Van Buren could not avoid it. Neither could Harrison, nor our new President Tyler. No power can supersede HABEUS CORPUS. If such was not the norm, where would have been the help by which every human being in this Union—man, woman, or child—has held the blessing of freedom? THAT is what I put before the Supreme Court."

We had been speaking for all of fifteen minutes. "And that took eight and a half hours?"

"Your little Ditty advised me to give a summary: To be brief, to be right, and to be gone. I looked at that pile of books and notes I brought with me every day to court and remembered your Ditty. I looked farther, and my eyes caught sight of a copy of the Declaration of Independence framed on a pillar nearby. I repeated its immortal words, 'We hold these Truths to be self-evident, that all men are created equal, that they are endowed by their Creator with certain unalienable Rights, that among these are Life, Liberty, and the Pursuit of Happiness.'"

"Johnny, that's beautiful. Wonderful. And then you left the chamber?"

"Not quite, I reminded the Court that since 1804 when I first stood before it, I was called to the discharge of other duties—first in distant lands and in later years within our own country, but to different departments of her Government."

"And then you left the chamber, Johnny dear."

"No, not exactly, I caught breath again to plead the cause of justice—and of liberty and life—on behalf of many of my fellow men, saying, I stand before the same Court... but not before the same judges.

My eyes seek in vain for one of those honored and honorable persons whose indulgences listened to the sound of my voice. Marshall—Cushing—Chase—Washington—Where are they now? Gone! Gone! All gone!"

"Good. Great! And THEN you left the chamber?" "No. I had more I had to say. I'll give you a concise version. I reminded those Justices present that I pray every member may go to his final account with as little of earthly frailty to answer for as those illustrious dead. I wished, 'That every one, after the close of a long and virtuous career in this world, be received at the portals of the next with these approving sentences: Well done, good and faithful servant. Enter thou into the joy of thy Lord.' And THEN I left and came home."

His words had run out, and so had mine. I could do nothing better than to shower his balding pate with kisses.

Washington, D.C., March 10, 1841

Almost a week passed, and we had no news of a decision by the Supreme Court. The suspense was terrible. I have never eaten so much chocolate.

On March 9, Johnny was summoned to the Supreme Court to hear the AMISTAD Africans' fate. He wouldn't let me accompany him. He shook his head decisively, his unkempt hair sprinkling dandruff.

He explained, "In spite of all those years of being a diplomat, I do not feel I can be sure to control my fury if these poor Africans are denied their freedom. You have been spared my rages lately, dearest Louisa. I do not want you to see me get violent."

"I think you are going to win."

"Thank you for those sweet words, but, NO. The

Supreme Court is stacked with Southern slave owners." "Some of them have set their slaves free."

"The Chief Justice, YES. Maybe one or two others

I have not been informed about. But there is at least one Northerner among them who is also sympathetic to slavery. Do not get up your hopes, dearest Louisa, my dearest friend." Johnny kissed me, put on his cloak and prepared to leave the house.

I know better than to argue with Johnny. There is never any way of winning an argument when we are face to face. He is a professional at arguing, after all. My only victories have been sideways. That is how the French wives manage, and they DO have some say in THEIR households.

Yesterday, when Johnny left for the Supreme Court to hear the final verdict, Washington's temperature had changed markedly, heralding the new coming season. With spring only eleven days away, the birds had returned from their winter holidays. Buds were bursting out on bushes and trees. Early daffodils had unfurled their yellow frilly heads. Clouds had whizzed away like the sails of a defeated fleet.

The Supreme Court was still in its narrow, pie shaped area of the Capitol, downstairs underneath the Senate's premises. Johnny told me later—as he recounted the whole of the event to me—how he entered the room feeling amazed how much business could be conducted in that building.

He had a duty to perform before taking his place as advocate for the AMISTAD Africans. There was a young attorney whom he was to present to the Bar. He took care of that job and found his own proper place as the Defense Attorney. He wanted to make himself comfortable because he foresaw that the Chief Justice would take advantage of this important moment to roll out a long oration.

Chief Justice Taney did take his time. The stage was his, and he was glorying in it. He spoke agonizingly slowly. Johnny could hardly sit still. He kept tapping his foot, as if to urge a horse to gallop faster. There was still the wait for Justice Story to pronounce the Court's decision.

Story wanted to play the roles of all the characters in the AMAZON saga. He started like an old time campfire storyteller, giving the salient points of this case. Grinding on, he reviewed the state of slavery in America. He reminded his listeners that Heads of State had become involved in the AMISTAD case, notably President Martin van Buren and the Queen of Spain. He acknowledged that Cinqué had killed AMISTAD's Captain Ferrer, and Grabeau the cook Celestino. But then he reminded his audience that it had been brought out that American revolutionaries had killed British soldiers in the War of Independence in order to gain THEIR freedom. Summing up, Justice Story intoned his ruling, "There does not seem to us to be any ground for doubt that these Negroes ought to be deemed free. And that the Spanish Treaty interposes no obstacle to the just assertion of their rights."

Those words gave the AMISTAD people their freedom.

JOHNNY HAD WON!

Justice Story continued on with the verdict. Like a jockey who has won a race, but stays in the saddle to make a victory run in front of the stands, Story completed his moment of stardom adding that as the present Government, "had not asked, on final appeal, for an order to return the Negroes to Africa if found free, the Court revised that decree of the District Court."

In other words, the Mende people would get passage back to their homeland. From across the room, a huge grin and a wink was relayed to Johnny from a Federalist bystander.

Still Justice Story was not ready to relinquish the stage. He droned on, "It affirmed the lower court's award of salvage to Lieutenant Gadney against the ship itself."

His voice petering out, his moment of creating suspense over, Story finally, crankily removed his robes and stepped down from his semi-throne, ducking the overhanging curtains around his pulpit as he went. The verdict had been almost unanimous. Only Justice Baldwin had voted against.

There were slaps on the back for Johnny, but he didn't wait for more. He hurried home. And to ME.

He hurtled through our front doorway like a schoolboy who has garnered top honors. "Dearest Louisa, I won! The AMISTAD Africans won. The antislavery people won. Victory! Victory for our side! I must write to Lewis Tappan and laud him!"

Johnny pounced into his library, sat down at his desk and fired away. I stood behind him and memorized each word. "The captives are free. Not unto us! But thanks, thanks in the name of humanity and justice to YOU."

But Johnny was too humble. Lewis Tappan may have been the one to convince Johnny to participate in this crusade, but it was Johnny himself who had proven himself with his deep, enduring care for these people. After he had visited them in prison, two of the AMISTAD prisoners—a young man named Kin-na and one of the girls called Ka-li—wrote letters to Johnny, pleading with him to help them. Both had called him, "Dear friend Mr. Adams." He had lived up to their esteem by proving himself friend enough to win back their freedom.

But it wasn't just them he saved. The ongoing threat of having my illegitimate status be revealed, plus the common knowledge that my father was a bankrupt man who didn't pay my dowry, have combined to keep me in agony until this past year. It was until after Johnny accepted to serve as a lawyer in the AMISTAD case and began pleading for the freedom of those jailed African farmers that I could begin to set aside the agony caused from the shame of my illegitimate background.

To help the AMISTAD's "cargo" of slaves, these Mende people who had lived as farmers before they were kidnapped, Johnny accepted me as a partner to copy all of his voluminous papers for this case. And I did. Thanks to that job, I have begun to feel a real person, of some value.

Washington D.C., July 18, 1841

Money is tight, because there are grandchildren, nephews, and nieces to help financially. I love them all. But most of all, I love Johnny. It is my Johnny whom I want to help the most—with his finances and with every other challenge.

I told a friend, "He's always by my side, now, always trying to please me."

The single bed in my F Street bedroom was given to my widowed daughter-in-law. I returned to our old marital bed that has no bad memories, only empty ones. All that reading of the Tom Jones novel has certainly revived Johnny's libido, and it is directed to ME!

At first I found it difficult to respond in the way Nancy had to her husband's foreplay. My mind intervened to stall any pleasure. I was thinking of what I needed to accomplish to be a complete woman. I felt if only I had a challenge that would crown me as an achiever, the trials of my life will have been justified. But what changes can I hope to accomplish? There looks to be no chance for me to help married women to get the vote, to own property, or to divorce an abusive husband. Those three aims seem absolutely out of reach. What chance can I have of mending any of the abuses women must accept? However our hours of lovemaking are NOT when I should be thinking about women's causes.

Little by little, I have learned to put on the back burner those hopes when I am in the marital bed and Johnny has initiated foreplay. Now I can focus, can concentrate on the foreplay. I will be a suffragette outside of the marital bed, not during sexual intercourse.

I have the example of Britain's Queen Victoria to inspire me. Her Majesty has made it well-known that she is in love with Prince Albert, her husband. Their first child, a girl nicknamed Vicky, was born November last when they had only wed the previous February! The

Queen is already expecting another living proof of her lovemaking. She does not permit the burdens of state to interfere in her happily blessed marriage. I know in my heart that I should put aside my concerns for America's womanhood and put more love into lovemaking with Johnny.

But outside of our marital bed, there is still much that captures my attention on the topic of women and their rights in this great nation. I've followed the careers of those two wonderful women: Sarah and Angelina Grimké. Sisters, they both work for noble causes. I am particularly impressed by Sarah Grimké, with whom I have started a lively correspondence. From her portraits, I have decided she looks like a man. It's said she has no female graces. Evil tongues allege she plays the flat game. She would never have tried that with me!

In any case, I never have met her, but Johnny did. He was presented to both sisters and has taken special care to keep me from meeting Sarah, whom he considers dangerous for espousing women's rights.

What a fabulous brain she has. The theme in her letters is a bit one-sided, like a trumpet—she can hit various splendid notes, but invariably makes the same sound. But I've always liked the music a trumpet makes.

I did meet her younger sister, Angelina. We started our friendship by sitting down together in my upstairs alcove. Her first words to me were, "Slavery in the United States must end."

She wore a heavy wool tweed cape, although it was summer. Johnny had decreed we would soon be leaving Washington for Massachusetts—which was hard on me: to leave a city that was warming for a state that is almost always too cold for me—and I had skimped on my packing to meet Angelina. Thank God I did that because Angelina had more strings to her bow. In addition to her crusade against slavery, she was pushing for women's rights—my own favorite subject.

Angelina, patting her tightly knotted bun, handed me a slim volume she'd written on that subject of slavery in these United States. I nodded with encouragement. I said, "I agree with you entirely."

She continued in a clarion tone, though one that lilted with her Southern drawl, "This nation cannot be contaminated bah such a loathsome custom. How can a nation flourish when such evil persists? Ah want to see more slavery-free states. But the opposite seems to be occurrin' as the new states t' join the Union share that horrible practice with the Southern states."

She continued, continued, and CONTINUED without a stop, like the new railroad trains that have initiated Express locomotives that don't slow for milk stops.

I hoped she would broach the subject of votes for women. She did, although not as promptly as I would have liked. "We women must fight for our rights. Vote, hold of ice, and be lawyers, doctors, and engineers."

Later, in the evening in front of our favorite fireplace, I repeated some of the conversation to Johnny with words he couldn't disdain, "Angelina has enormous energy and determination to get things done. At present her chief subject matter is the wickedness of slavery. She works to end slavery in all its forms, and I believe that is her main passion. She uses arguments from the Bible to urge church ministers that slavery must be eradicated."

Johnny interrupted with one of his favorite platitudes, he honked. "I have always bemoaned the existence of slavery in our nation."

Not quite true. Johnny did address the Senate on several occasions during the brief years he had served there, sidestepping the issue of slavery in order to suck up for votes for his longed-for run for the presidency.

I didn't contradict him. Why bother? Instead, I thought I should give him some favorable information about Sarah.

"Sarah was born in South Carolina to a wealthy family. She used all her resources to launch her books and then to have them distributed in the Southern states in addition to ones in the North. She is a genius in presenting how terrible are the sufferings of slaves in our Southern states and demonstrating how those sufferings are a blight on America's reputation worldwide."

Sarah has also written in favor of women's rights. I decided to leave that very controversial subject for another so-called chat with my difficult husband. Personally, I am fascinated by how the sisters got involved with that most sacred of my dreams.

When next she came to my private alcove, Angelina told me that she started her long trek down the road to freedom-for-women when she met Giuseppe Garibaldi!

"Garibaldi was born in Nice in 1807, when that city still belonged to Italy, or more precisely to Savoia," she began. "He started his career as a sailor, became a sea captain, and then turned into a mercenary, hirin' himself to fight in Argentina. He incorporated many of his ah-deas from those early days, including the use of red shirts. He learned from Argentina's butchers that red shirts do not show blood. All his followers adopted the red shirts ah-dea, enlargin' it t' include red ponchos and sombreros."

Interesting, but that was not really what I wanted to hear. Angelina, nobody's fool, sensed she was losing me, so she plunged into the meaty part, "The ah-deal of a unified Italy had already been raised a decade earlier. But Garibaldi had enlarged on the concept by speakin' out for women t' par-tici-pate in the foundin' of a republic."

Ah! Now, Angelina was getting to what was tasty. Like cutting away ordinary beef and slicing into the sirloin, she added, "He foresaw the power that women could bring t' a nation. T' support his ah-deals, he wrote many novels and non-fiction books. He wrote t' that young Legislator in Illinois who is makin' so many waves, Abraham Lincoln, regardin' givin' all of the South's slaves their freedom. And women, theirs."

Great! But I still longed for her to go further into my favorite subject. She did. Angelina smiled her tight-lipped, toothy grin. "He wrote about women's suffrage, givin' a preview. He demanded that suffrage be accepted by all of America's states, North, South, and those comin' in t' the Union from the West."

I swallowed and hoped for more erudition. Angelina had said her piece for that day. It wasn't until a further occasion I learned that both the Grimké sisters lapped up all of Garibaldi's beliefs, particularly endorsing his concept of women's suffrage. Eventually the sisters wrote books on that subject. But they did more than write about it, just hoping someone somewhere would read what they had written. The sisters proceeded to give lectures. To these lectures they invited both women and men.

Even in our modern day it is not proper to have "mixed audiences," composed of both men and women. The fact that Sarah had joined with her sister to address mixed gatherings got her into big trouble with authorities. What did she do to counteract trouble from authorities? She went to battle like a Joan of Arc, ready to die in flames if necessary. She pleaded with important leaders in our country. She wore the armor of righteousness and convinced more than a few leaders of the intrinsic fairness that women should have equal status with men.

It can be said that Sarah Grimké actually started the fight for the women's rights she practices. Her battle has spread for all kinds of rights, not only the right to publish books and to address "mixed audiences." Sarah is extending the battle to ask that women be allowed to vote. MY own, longtime project. Sarah's sister Angelina, eleven years younger and pretty in spite of her toothy smile, has the airs and charm of a southern belle. She prefers to give lectures. Immense crowds flock to hear her. Both sisters have moved North and joined the Abolitionists' cause, dedicating their lives to end the abomination that is slavery.

Sarah and Angelina have become Quakers. "Quaker" is the popular nickname for followers of George Fox, who refused to bow to his English King saying he would only bow to God and then founded the persuasion correctly called The Religious Society of Friends. In our day these, "Quakers" are best known for helping our Underground Railway transport escaped slaves, moving them surreptitiously through slave states to freedom in Canada.

Johnny went to one of their meetings many years ago, but of it he had to say, "I seldom, in the course of my life, passed two hours more wearily." However, I lately went to a Quaker Meeting and was deeply moved by what they refer to as their Inner Light. One of the Quakers present began to tremble with nerves then stood up and quoted a small section of the Bible, which he compared to a Longfellow poem. This he also recited. I suppose the fact that he had the shakes is why these nice people are called "Quakers."

Washington, D.C., September 6, 1841

On one of the first chilly evenings of the coming autumn, although still in high spirits after the AMISTAD case, Johnny made me shiver due to his disapproval of a book I was reading. I made the mistake of quoting my favorite classic to him as he strode into the tiny alcove. He came carrying his expensive Morocco-bound volume of Cicero's works, which I believe is more of a Bible to him than the one I take to church. He hates it when he finds me reading any book that teaches women that they have rights.

"Women should not be over-educated," he roared. Nor am I to write more books. When the first book I had authored in 1825, Record of my Life or My Story was dumped as garbage, I wrote another opus The Metropolitan Kaleidoscope. I'm certain that many of our friends must have considered it autobiographical. I wrote the story of an overly-ambitious British peer, Lord Sharply, who made his wife a miserable wreck because he was so determined to succeed in politics. The reason I gave my main character the name Sharply, was because Mr. Adams, when he spoke to me at that time, always used a sharp tongue.

I closed the folder that hides the pages on which I've been writing this secret tome and left Johnny at his desk to continue with his letters. I went into the pantry and cut a nice square of cooking chocolate to take upstairs to our bedroom. I carried my candle and the chocolate to my bedside table, and began to undress. I had the cords of my undergarment's bodice in hand, when our door opened swiftly and Johnny crossed the room, tearing off his clothes as he reached the marital bed. He placed me on it, helped me to complete removing my bodice, and began to kiss me in the way my dear Nancy had described was usual with her husband, Walter. All over, EVERYWHERE, again and again.

Delicious!

At my advanced age of sixty-six, after forty four years of marriage, this was the best time. I've learned what lovemaking could really entail. And I like it!

When Johnny finished, and we lay side by side in rapture, I ate my piece of chocolate. Lovemaking's afterglow was better for the sweet, and the delicacy was far better during afterglow.

In recent months, I have sometimes initiated lovemaking. Johnny responded avidly to that. We have had better and better lovemaking. On occasion, I thought this new passionate lovemaking had replaced his need for swimming. He gave up diving every day into the Potomac some time ago. Our sheets have become his new Potomac. But there is far more to this than THAT.

Vitally important to me is how he seems to RESPECT me during our lovemaking. I am no longer like a chamber pot to be used when needed. What has happened to make the difference?

Oh, how I have longed to mutate from my fear of his learning I was born illegitimate! Could he have known all these many years, but now that no longer mattered to my Johnny? Could it be he loves me for myself? For WHO I am! Not worrying about WHAT I am, a bastard. I believe he has evolved into a man of just causes, who will not be influenced to despise me if and when some over-ambitious news reporter goes to London and discovers my parents' wedding took place at St. Anne's in Soho after I was nine years old—a fact, which could ruin his political career. And THAT change in his attitude had the direct effect of impacting his lovemaking to produce exquisite, sublime sensations in my most intimate being. Oh, bliss!

IF Johnny has learned I am illegitimate, how much more wonderful it is to be loved even THOUGH I have a FLAWED parentage, which could be used against him by his enemies in the next political contest. I want to be like a butterfly, beautiful and flying free after escaping the chrysalis of my fear. Butterflies start out as ugly insects, but mutate into one of God's most glorious creatures!

Washington, D.C., January 27, 1842

My dear husband has received many plaudits for the way he'd handled the AMISTAD case.

"May the blessing of many ready to perish fall upon you." Joshua Levitt, a notable Abolitionist, wrote. "Glorious!" that was the one word from Roger Baldwin, holed up in his thriving office in New Haven.

For a week, Lewis Tappan was too busy to be writing letters. He did not even pen his thanks to his partner Johnny who had won freedom "for our humble clients." He was trying to arrange transport for the remaining thirty-six AMISTAD people to return to Africa. Like Johnny, he was particularly anxious about the three little girls' future. Lewis Tappan had a plan for the eldest girl, Mar-gru. He hoped to get a scholarship for her at Oberlin College.

Plaudits from the Abolitionists were more forthcoming than funds for the Africa trip. The AMISTAD men were gainfully employed on farms in Connecticut, while the little girls were given a trustee to oversee their welfare, but they all had to wait out the spring and summer before money could be found for their return trip.

Nine months passed without collecting enough money to charter a ship. Finally Lewis Tappan got news of a missionary ship bound for Sierra Leone, on which he could place the AMISTAD people for a total cost of $1,800. To Mr. Tappan's credit, he did not dun Johnny for a contribution as he was deeply grateful that Johnny had dispensed with charging a fee for his legal services.

The Abolitionists had a Defense Committee that worked the public relations side toward victory on the AMISTAD case, and Mr. Tappan got them to write Johnny a formal expression of thanks "for valuable services gratuitously rendered in rescuing our humble clients from the imminent peril to which they had been exposed."

Charming, but I wish Johnny had not been so quick in refusing a fee. Our larder was not that full. And I have so many recipes I want to try before our stomachs are too old to digest all that fancy food.

"I've received a new recipe from the Russian Minister," I told Mary, the widow of our son John. "It's called kulebiak and is made with the finest pastry, braised spinach, and tender salmon slices. But aren't salmon out of season, and if we could get one from Canada, wouldn't that cost a lot?"

Abby, my other daughter-in-law, had returned to Quincy to rejoin Charles. He was NOT rushing to congratulate his father. No doubt because he doesn't want to encourage Johnny to continue to be a star on the political stage.

Charles wrote Johnny, "It is a great relief to me that your cause is settled and well settled." THAT was all he had to say.

Johnny's reply to Charles reeked of bitterness.

"The agony of soul that I suffered from the day that I pledged my faith, to argue the cause of the Africans, before the Supreme Court, until that when I heard Judge Story deliver the opinion and decree of the Court, was chiefly occasioned by the reprobation of my own family, both of my opinion and my conduct, and their terror at the calamities which they anticipated they would bring upon them."

No fool, my Johnny, doting father that he is, he can still see through Charles and not like what he sees. But I did not dwell on that problem when I had the pleasure of enjoying the company of my two favorite daughters-in-law. We talked food.

Johnny did make one attempt to help the AMISTAD people to get a free trip back to the Ivory Coast. He asked Daniel Webster, Secretary of State during President Harrison's short term, if he could provide a public ship for them. Webster's answer? No!

There was the same answer but with a sneer when Johnny approached President Tyler's Government. That slaver would never provide anything for the AMISTAD people. Never. Nor was the Government obligated to do so under an 1819 law because these Africans had not been illegally imported into the United States.

In order to raise their $1800 fare, the Abolitionists had scraped up theater engagements for them as entertainers. They were put on display like animals in a circus. The girls were made to sing for pennies, the younger men, Ka-Le and Kwong turned cartwheels and walked on their hands, which wouldn't have earned them a cent if they hadn't been part of the AMISTAD Mende group. Mr. Barnum's Tom Thumb Show had acrobats who could achieve far more daring feats. It was all the publicity motored by the AMISTAD case which provided any chance for these Africans to lure paying customers.

Johnny and I kept abreast of all that was happening to them.

Their eastward crossing of the Atlantic finally took place on THE GENTLEMAN, the missionary ship which had been scheduled to leave these shores in November. The passage was duly paid for the AMISTAD people, including the three little girls. Two of the missionaries who were sailing had wives, and I felt confident they would look after the girls.

How wrong I was. Elizabeth Raymond and her husband were going to Africa with the AMISTAD people because they wanted fame. They have hitched their wagon to the AMISTAD stars. The other woman, Tamur, was the wife of the Negro missionary. Later, after months in Sierra Leone's poor little capital Freetown, she deserted him to take up the life of a prostitute in Liberia. She learned there was money to be had for women of that ilk.

Lewis Tappan received letters from Sierra Leone that were extremely contradictory. First he heard that Cinqué was elated to be back in Mende country. Then Mr. Raymond wrote to say Cinqué had left Africa for Jamaica. From Reverend Stevens came a letter stating that Cinqué had run off with a pagan woman and deserted the Sierra Leone mission for a life more suited to the Bible's Sodom and Gomorrah.

What was Lewis Tappan or any of us to believe?

Washington, D.C., February 7, 1842

Johnny initiated a crusade in Congress to stop the Gag Rule, a continuing thorn in his side these past six years. He'd taken a dangerous stance, using his enemies' speeches to defeat them. I don't know if it was a clever move, but when Johnny presented a petition from citizens of Georgia by demanding that he himself, Congressman Adams, be relieved of chairing the Foreign Relations Committee, it proved to be a ploy that caused more trouble. For days now he has held the floor, haranguing his colleagues with decidedly un-brief remarks about the abomination that is slavery. He fought on, declaring he hoped the day would come when "slavery and war will be banished from the face of the earth." Plaudits have begun to flood in. Johnny is acclaimed as one of the greatest of the men who had fought against slavery.

Today, the Representatives voted 106 to 93 to table the censure of Mr. John Adams, if only to quiet his mouth.

Washington, D.C., August 1, 1843

A year and a half ago, President Harrison's Inauguration took place amid much ballyhoo, noise, and fireworks. Johnny had sent his regrets. He had an excellent excuse not to attend what with the AMISTAD decision still hanging like Damocles' sword, but it was a tradition in the Adams family not to attend Inaugurations. Johnny's father had avoided Thomas Jefferson's. Johnny had boycotted Andrew Jackson's and van Buren's. And I boycotted Johnny's own.

Johnny had anticipated attending many a reception and dinner in Harrison's White House. That was not to happen. Harrison, attempting to demonstrate he was a working man, had gone hatless to his Inauguration and caught a cold. Whilst President Harrison steamed his mucous membranes and sipped honey drinks to alleviate pains in his chest, Washington's street cleaners had barely managed to clear the mess made of spent fireworks and empty ale bottles left by merrymakers celebrating his Inauguration. A congressional steward rapped on our front door shortly after with a note to advise Johnny that President Harrison's cold had developed into pneumonia.

Within three weeks he was dead.

Gone from the White House was a friend! Into the White House sauntered Vice President Tyler, announcing in no uncertain terms that he was in charge and demanding the full title of President.

Tyler is the member of government whom Johnny detests most.

Johnny went into one of his worst rages. "That slave-breeder. That viper!" He used dreadful epithets, none that I dare write here. Oh, I knew we'd not be going to any of Tyler's White House receptions.

It hasn't been possible for Johnny to avoid Tyler entirely, including a dramatic run-in this morning. Johnny has been very pleased to be invited to have a photograph taken at the new Daguerreotype Studio. He fancied himself as the first President to have a Daguerreotype photograph, even though it's likely Harrison was, though no one can produce the proof.

This morning was the day he'd booked for his appointment at the studio, and I'd chosen a new wrap-around tie for him to wear and his newest pair of ankle boots. I sent him off to the studio with his head held high.

Hours later he returned with his eyes ablaze, the tie askew, and his new shoes scuffed as if he'd kicked at a door. "That slave-breeder Tyler showed up at the studio to be first to have his picture taken!" Spit hit the walls of our hallway.

"What did you do?"

"I raced him. I recalled how I'd ridden to victory in that Point-to-Point when I was Minister to the Court of St. James. I accelerated my pace, pulled out in front of him AND GAVE HIM MY BACK."

"So, you got into the studio FIRST!"

"I almost didn't make it. That wily fox tried to show me his heels. After all, he's twenty years younger, and he might have succeeded. But I noticed the floors were being newly waxed, and I chose the unfinished side. He slipped, lost his footing, and, to correct his stance, had to go behind."

"And you left him in the waiting room whilst taking the dark room for your daguerreotype!"

I held out my palm for him to give me the finished product. His picture was encased in a beautifully-carved, velvet-encased frame that opened like a locket.

I stared at the image, shocked at what was reproduced there. Who was this man with the sunken chest, cavernous eyes, sullen mouth? This isn't my round-faced, straight-shouldered, jolly-lipped lover!

I raised my eyes to his and realized that, yes, they have grown into his skull. His cheeks have grown into an almost invisible neck.

Why haven't I been aware of the changes in Johnny? Is lovemaking so magical that I haven't noticed any differences other than that his special member hurts me less because it is shorter and softer? Or is the hurting minimal now that I almost welcome it as I grow so wet where it matters?

I clicked shut the locket-like clasp and gave Johnny my bravest smile. I said, "Wonderful! You certainly will always best that slaver Tyler."

Inside my heart I felt tremulous. Is my husband's energy fading? Has he grown old before I became aware? Will he die before I realize he could be fatally ill?

I handed him a half-glass of Madeira. I determined I will cut down on his drinking wine, substituting it for fresh fruit juices. I will oversee that he eats more nutritious foods. I'll get him to bed earlier. Oh, yes!

But must I cut down on lovemaking?

Not this night! We celebrated the daguerreotype "victory" in the way he liked best.

Washington D.C., September 2, 1843

Sitting at my loyal Chippendale desk, using my old weathered pen, I wrote my own Declaration of Independence: I will not be driven from my aims.

I believe women are equal to men. Yes, I'll sing out that women should be able to vote! I believe they should be owners of their own bodies and not have to bring into this poor world baby after baby, until the woman's body is used up and she cannot produce more.

Daughters must have a chance to blossom and become complete flowers.

Had my daughter lived, she would have had to endure the life of a woman of today, which would have meant multiple pregnancies, with probably a loveless marriage arranged to suit a Mr. Adams-type and his ambitions and no rights of her own.

I want the world to change from its dismissal of women's just causes. As Johnny says he wants to represent our entire nation, I say I want to help all the women of every nation to get their just rights. I know that it means hard work and dedication, and I'm prepared to give this mission just exactly that.

Sarah Grimké has encouraged me to do what I did best in the past: give parties in my F Street home. After Sarah got into trouble for addressing "mixed" audiences composed of the two sexes, men and women, I decided I could help out on that score.

I could give parties for both sexes. Instead of frilly teas for women only, I invited acquaintances of both sexes to come to my SALONS, again every Tuesday. Diplomats, lawmakers, industrialists, and outstanding personalities from the concert and theater worlds all mingled over Madeira or whiskey. Like a captain at the rudder, I kept the conversation to my two favorite topics: ending slavery and getting equal rights for women. Sarah Grimké expanded her lectures to add equal rights for women. Why shouldn't I at my parties?

Washington D.C., December 21, 1843

I was discussing the entire problem of slavery with my friend Angelina, one sunny autumn afternoon when we were sipping tea together next to my new modern stove that has so many improvements over the old one.

"Angelina, will the United States ever rid itself of slavery?" I have become so fond of asking her such questions, just to hear a Southern voice speak against slavery.

"Ah lahke t' believe it will. Too bad there has never been a man t' make a real difference 'bout slavery."

And that was when I had my own my personal epiphany. I began to tremble, but not from horror. A pure joy washed through me.

I spoke out, "Oh? Surely you cannot mean that! Jesus Christ made a huge impact. It was after HE preached that all peoples were free children of God that slaves broke their chains and eventually even destroyed the Roman Empire."

Angelina was hushed. For once she couldn't utter a word. Instead, she left her chair to hug me.

We stayed clasped together until one of her three children came to her skirts to plead for more cookies. Then, she found her voice. "Yes, yes, yes." She said to me, while extending a hand to count out three cookies and hand them to her eldest babe. To me, she added, "Of course, you are right. Jesus Christ with HIS teachings broke the long tradition of slavery that had been the bulwark of the Romans. With so many slaves willing to die for their beliefs, the Roman army could not win against the barbarians from the north."

We ate the remainder of the cookies in a joyful contemplative silence. But, from that day forward, I started to go regularly to the nearby Episcopal Church where I could receive Communion, as it was the American branch of the Anglican denomination into which I have been baptized.

Johnny received many hate letters due to the successful outcome of his labors for the AMISTAD people. One of the first came from an anonymous writer, who penned, "Is your pride of abolition oratory not yet glutted? Are you to spend the remainder of your days endeavoring to produce a civil and servile war?"

I believe that was a particularly unfair criticism because Johnny has always been so against wars of any kind. Was not his first triumph the Treaty of Ghent, stopping our War of 1812? I know I have dwelt on that, but it's the truth.

The AMISTAD people have touched his heart. Those Africans have lit a fire in America against slavery, where before there were merely sparks.

Johnny has long detested slavery as practiced in the United States, agreeing with Roger Baldwin, that it diminishes the national character. Mr. Baldwin even wrote to Johnny to praise him for saving that character "from reproach and dishonor."

Letters began to arrive for Johnny with requests from responsible anti-slavers to propose that he petition the House of Representatives to make changes to laws that upheld slavery.

Johnny thought long and hard over those requests. He began to ask ME what he should do. What a turnabout! Not only did I encourage him forcefully to follow through with his fight against slavery, but to start with the petitions immediately. To urge him on I offered to go to Congress again to sit in the Visitors' Gallery.

At one time I was loath to make use of that Visitors' Gallery. Over the years, I mistakenly thought that ladies who go there are show-offs who merely want a venue where they can display their newest fashions. Several years I've been put off to the idea of returning to the Visitors' Gallery because I watched one silly woman or another preening herself in a hat over-decorated with feathers or wearing a dress cut too low over the bosom. It occurred to me that the flightier ones might be going to the Visitors' Gallery to pick up men. Earlier, in Paris, I learned that it is not only legislators who use those hallowed halls to make assignations, but women are prone to do the same.

It was my friend from South Carolina, Angelina Grimké, who encouraged me to overlook the flirtatious women and concentrate on what the Congressmen had to say. "Our time WILL come when we, too, shall be Members of Congress and can present petitions. We SHALL get the vote. We SHALL be as free as those Negroes your husband liberated. Meanwhile, women must learn how t' act as Members of Congress against the day when we too can enter as Representatives."

Angelina is a different type from her sister. Sarah isn't interested in homemaking crafts. She prefers the pen.

One day, I invited Angelina into my kitchen to teach her my recipe for grilled croquettes. I'd checked in my pantry earlier that morning to be sure I had all the right ingredients. My recipe calls for three cups of cooked chicken, cold; four slices of ham, cold; two cups of bread crumbs; salt and pepper; nutmeg, grated; one teaspoon mustard; one tablespoon ketchup; half-pound butter; one egg yolk, beaten; drippings, for frying; parsley sprigs, for garnish; and radishes cut to look like roses. Chop up the chicken and ham together, very fine; add half the bread crumbs, salt, pepper, grated nutmeg, mustard, ketchup, and butter. Knead all together until it resembles sausage meat. Form into cakes. Dip in the beaten egg yolk, and coat thickly with remaining bread crumbs. Fry the croquettes in drippings until light brown. Serve hot, garnished. Makes four servings. I was so busy breading the croquettes I almost missed Angelina's point.

She spoke in that soft Southern accent that I've long enjoyed at the Maryland homes of my cousins, "We mustn't wait until men are willin' to GIVE us the vote. We will grab it on our own. But meanwhile, we must become privy t' the customs of the House—learn its rules—t' abide by them later and not make fools of ourselves through ignorance of them. Louisa, please go t' the Visitors' Gallery as often as ever y'all can. Promise me y'all will."

Angelina ate her chicken croquettes with gusto, cleaning her plate in what I felt sure was not a ladylike thing to do for a Southern Belle. I handed her the recipe that I'd written out earlier, and saw her to my front door in plenty of time before Johnny would return from the House. I well knew he wouldn't tolerate either of the Grimké sisters, and he would worry that their ideas for liberating women could be contagious, that I would follow their lead.

The Grimké sisters told me horrible tales about slaves who were murdered for some small disobedience. They collected the stories from newspapers, meaning they were authentic and in the public domain.

Angelina whispered, with tears in her pretty eyes, "There was one young African runaway slave whose owner gripped her throat with red-hot tongs and burned her until she died, still sayin', 'Missie don't.'"

Another of Angelina's gory tales came out of Richmond; it told how her owner flogged a fifteen year-old slave girl, and when that didn't kill her a hot iron was put on her back. She pulled away to jump out a three story window to her death. Angelina added, "A more common punishment is meted out by tyin' a slave to a tree, settin' it on fire, and burnin' the slave alive."

I buried those stories in my heart and didn't pass them on to Johnny. He has his own friends to whom he listens. I followed Angelina's cue and got my pass for the Visitors' Gallery.

On my new visit to the House of Representatives I discovered that Johnny often uses it as his private club. He has a favorite chair to doze in, exactly as he does at home. The Madeira wine is less expensive there, served at a discount to the legislators, and it is a very good Madeira!

I fitted in there unostentatiously with the less exuberant women. Yes, there were so-called ladies who would shout out, contradicting legislators as they pirouetted on the floor. Even my husband received his share of nasty catcalls.

Johnny has looked into the current situation for slaves who've escaped from Southern owners to make their way to so-called free-states up North. But, according to the Constitution, those escaped slaves can be returned to their, "rightful owners," which is why my Abolitionist friends help runaway slaves go on the "underground" railway to Canada. Quakers and other Abolitionists gather up escaped slaves to hide them in wagons, then smuggle them across the New York border to Canada.

In my alcove, one night in late December when nightingales sang sweetly in the woods, Johnny repeated to me some extremely well-spoken phrases he wrote a few years ago, "The world, the flesh, and all the devils in hell are arrayed against any man who now in this North American Union shall dare to join the standard of Almighty God to put down the African slave trade, and what can I, upon the verge of my seventy-fourth birthday, with a shaking hand, a darkening eye, a drowsy brain, and with all my faculties dropping from me one by one, as the teeth are dropping from my head, what can I do for the cause of God and man? For the progress of human emancipation? For the suppression of the African Slave Trade?"

He interrupted himself to take three deep breaths, and then continued: "Yet my conscience presses me on, let me but die in the breach."

Johnny still keeps to his long-winded style. What can I do to correct it? Nothing. I tried, and he paid no attention. I do not want to turn into a nag. Not now, not when we have come to such blissful lovemaking both in and out of our marital bed.

Washington D.C., March 10, 1844

Year after year Johnny sloughs on with his petitions, even when most of them are never accepted. He cannot be stopped from presenting the petitions, so he continues without abating, in spite of the curses shouted down on him. To stop him, the enemies of these petitions continually invoke that hated "Gag Rule," which still batters Johnny in Congress. It was Johnny who'd invented the nickname "Gag Rule." My auburn hair now has streaks of white, which I don't deplore. I consider them distinguished. My walk has slowed, but I can still go fishing, and I've become quite the terror of the local fish, as I am now most proficient with my rod.

One afternoon when I was seated in the Visitors' Gallery of the House of Representatives to hear Johnny's NEWEST reasons to attack the Southern congressmen, a middle-aged gentleman grabbed the empty seat next to mine. He was dressed in the latest fashion, with no Beau Brummel fripperies. His hair was cut short in the new style, and I noticed that his shoes were highly polished and of good quality. He was handsome in a sportsman type of way: I imagined he could be adept at racing horses.

What he said was embarrassing, even insulting. He had a marked Southern accent, possibly from Georgia. "Hi, y'all, yo' sho be one pretty gal. Ah's seen y'all out-fishin'. Y'all sho knows how to toss the line.

Where'd y'all learn t' cast lahke that?"

I couldn't resist replying, "England. I was born in England."

"Sho 'nuf? Ah recognahzes thet English ac-cent." I'd given him an opening. He smiled broadly, edging closer to my left thigh.

What in Heavens' name was happening?

Here I was, a woman in her sixties! Did my hat hide the streaks of white in my hair? Should I remove it—and the gloves that hide the gnarled veins in my hands? I didn't. I smiled in return. Good grief! Was I behaving like those loose women who made assignations in this Gallery? Did those exquisite nights of lovemaking show in my face? Illuminated it, or what?

A flash of intuition hit me. I remembered how in Paris a woman married to a high-ranking member of the French Government had entered into a love affair with a German officer who had fought Napoleon. Her husband lost his position, and that couple had to go into exile to escape the backbiting from his political enemies. I thought this same ending could come if I encouraged this Southerner. I had a feeling he wasn't flirting with ME; he was obeying orders to ensnare me to end Johnny's career in the House of Representatives.

Could this handsome, engaging Southerner be a human trap sent to entangle me and ruin Johnny? I wasn't so stupid as to ignore that possibility.

Feigning a coughing spell, I rushed out of the Gallery and stayed in the women's washroom until Johnny ended his speech. Then we hurried home together. Did I tell him of that possible entrapment? I didn't. Do other wives tell such secrets? In my life, all secrets are indelibly entwined.

At about this time, I was in the habit of going to church every day. This helped me in a variety of ways. Formerly, church-going had been a trial. I had suffered from doubts ever since I returned to England from our exile in Nantes during the most fraught years of the American Revolution. I had made fun of the ministers in churches, giggling with Nancy at perceived mistakes. The French nuns of my Nantes convent drilled into me that I would go to Hell if I ventured inside a Protestant church. But when we moved back to London and I was sent to a British boarding school, I was made to go to a local Protestant church. I fainted there; I was so terrified at the prospect of immediately going to Hell. I have a vivid imagination, and I'd conjured up the devil's flames scorching me. My teacher and the school nurse had quite a time reviving me.

And there was also that special steaming hot day on August 22, in 1785 when I accompanied my parents to the church of St. Anne in Soho, Westminster, in Middlesex, when they went through a marriage ceremony. I recall how strongly my father inscribed his name JOSHUA JOHNSON in the marriage register and how cordially the parish minister acted when presenting a plume to my mother to record her name as CATHERINE NEUTH. For my mother it was a glorious day of vindicated patience, having finally achieved the status of a married woman after having given my father five daughters. But in the midst of her joy was the imposing atmosphere of the church itself. Those spaces—so sacred for others—were often stifling for me.

On the evening of my brief flirtation in the halls of Congress, I turned once again to my long-held method of calming my nerves. I sought among my more complicated recipes to prepare a feast. I chose a recipe for beef Wellington to embellish our supper. The British Minister's wife gave me the recipe; it was similar to preparing Koulibiak, rolling out puff-pastry and lining it with slices of beef, except there was no call for spinach. For the beef tenderloin, I went to the butcher myself the day before. When it was ready and we were seated at our long table, Johnny shook his head. He didn't like the look of my beef Wellington?

"Dearest Louisa, I'm concerned about something I noticed in the Capitol today."

Oh, God! Had he looked up toward the Gallery and seen me fluttering eyelashes at the Southerner? Surely Johnny with his weakened eyes couldn't have captured that long-distance play. To distract him, I whispered, "Don't you like the beef Wellington?"

He stared down at his dish. "Too demanding on what's left of my teeth. But I have more important concerns. I fear the Southern Congressmen have decided to get me out of the House of Representatives, no matter what it takes. Dirty tricks, or whatever."

DIRTY TRICKS!

He HAD seen me with the Southerner! I felt speechless, agonizing!

Johnny continued, "It is well-known that I hate duels. Did I not write the Prentiss-Adams law against dueling? I won't participate in one, no matter how bad the insults. And even the worst of those Southern Congressmen wouldn't dare court the reprobation he'd earn for challenging an old man. Cowardice, that's what people would call it."

I swallowed. I was beginning to see light at the end of the tunnel. "No duel. Surely not."

"Did you not tell everyone how shocked you felt that Russia's greatest poet, Alexander Pushkin, was killed in a duel? You called it 'murder.'"

"It WAS murder, and what a loss for Russia."

"I don't think anyone would dare challenge me to a duel. Those Southerners will try to get at me in different ways. Maybe try to poison me. Didn't you say we are invited to a fish supper at the home of a Georgian troublemaker? A rotten oyster could do the trick."

I was safe. Johnny had gone on to other suggestions.

I said, "We're very careful when I serve oysters here. I have a barrel full of sea water brought in and keep the live oysters in it to clean them out of any impurities, feeding them good quality flour."

"Yes, dearest Louisa, you do. Often times, I've checked on that barrel and thrown out any oysters that are suspiciously open. And I have no intention of eating oysters at that man's house, even if I DO accept his invitation. No, I've thought how poison could be administered. Possibly, in my coffee at the Capitol. That way suspicion would fall on hundreds of people. Easier for the killer to go unnoticed."

"Johnny, I'm quite of a mind not to go to any more parties in private homes, and you should avoid having coffee in the Capitol building. I don't know how I'd go on living, if I lost you."

Johnny hadn't touched the beef Wellington. I went to the larder and brought out a lamb jelly that I knew his rotted teeth could handle.

He ate that, and we went together upstairs and to bed. But that night neither of us started the kissing. We were both too upset.

Johnny mused on about Adams family history, "I also recall from family records that my ancestor Henry Adams' only daughter Mary wed another England-born founder of a community: George Fairbanks, a Captain in the Royal Artillery Company before embarking for what was then called 'Northern Virginia.' There, Captain Fairbanks kept a concubine who gave him three children, one born the same week that his wife Mary Adams gave him a son."

Oh? I listened, but my thoughts wandered. I couldn't help wondering if my descendant of Henry Adams had ever kept a concubine! My Johnny who still reads Don Juan. That Mary Adams sounded like a good wife, she certainly gave her George Fairbanks male descendants, two of whom became Congregational Church ministers. Yet, her George's concubine gave birth the same week as she did! At least I didn't suffer that humiliation!

Washington, D.C. July 7, 1844

Johnny was not going to stop presenting petitions.

Last night in my alcove I asked him, "What about the Constitution promising Free Speech?"

Johnny had researched the Constitution's ruling and felt confident that its wording did not interfere with presenting petitions. "No, dearest Louisa, the Constitution does not exactly guarantee freedom of speech," he explained over a goblet of his favorite Madeira wine I still kept under my desk for him.

We were avoiding parties, and I hadn't told him that my main reason was to be sure I wouldn't meet up with that Southerner who'd tried to seduce me.

Johnny still loves giving long explanations on any subject. "The Constitution prohibits Congress from ABRIDGING freedom of speech. Those who wrote the Constitution, the Bill of Rights, weren't giving people rights; they were simply protecting those that already existed."

"I don't know what that means," I said, merely to give Johnny the pleasure of elucidating.

"It means that people's rights are inherent, and they pre-exist government. Our wise forefathers who wrote that immortal document were insuring that government could not take away such rights."

"Would you like some more coffee?"

"Yes, half a cup. But not so strong, please. And let me finish. I'm proud to say that Sire de Quincy was a signer of the Magna Carta. Yes, way back in 1217. England's Magna Carta guaranteed due process of law, Habeas Corpus, freedom from unreasonable searches and seizures, the right to counsel, the right to confront witnesses, and trial by jury."

"Wasn't the Magna Carta written to curtail outrages perpetrated by a tyrant, King John?" I wanted to let Johnny know I've studied my history books.

Johnny left that subject to tackle a new one. “Today, in Congress, I was compared to an ancient Greek who had been a great hero, but one who had a flaw—too much pride in himself—and who was therefore courting disaster.”

I had nothing to say to that. Johnny did have a lot of pride. But surely, he deserves to believe he has achieved a great deal in his life. Maybe he hadn’t been the best of Presidents. But he WAS very good at settling wars by signing treaties. I kissed him, we went to bed, and we DID make glorious love.

Washington D.C., December 3, 1844

Today tolled the end of the Gag Rule. Johnny's long battle against it ended when Congress voted 108 to 80 to agree to Johnny's conviction that it was an abomination and repealed it. Thanks to my brilliant challenger, there will be no more gagging in Congress when the subject of ending slavery is presented in a petition.

We celebrated quietly at home in our cozy kitchen—Johnny with Madeira wine whilst I enjoyed a cup of my hot chocolate. We could hear some reveling outside on F Street. Yet another rowdy crowd was voicing praise for newly-elected President James Polk. A Jacksonian candidate, he trounced Johnny's erstwhile friend, Henry Clay, in the bid for the top office.

The Polk faction continually held parades and public meetings to prepare the public for James Polk's Presidency. He was the leader of the so-called Liberty Party.

Johnny remarked in a curdled tone, "I don't think he knows what LIBERTY means."

"I agree! Isn't he a slaver?"

In Massachusetts, the Liberty Party candidate, who'd hoped to defeat Johnny to become a Congressman, garnered only 850 votes, while Johnny won over 8,000. That outcome came as a pleasant surprise for Johnny.

Putting aside his wine, Johnny added, "I never expected to win ten times the votes as my opponent garnered. I'd almost become resigned to losing to him and going back to private life. Now, even though I know my physical strength is going, I intend to fight on in the House until I become the head of the anti-slave movement in this country."

"Oh yes, dearest Johnny. Oh, yes!"

"Our son Charles is a rising star in Massachusetts. He's already equaled poor George's record by being elected to the local House of Representatives. Next, he aims to be a Senator. And maybe an Ambassador? We'll watch and see how he does. I may go to visit him in his Boston home, after the House goes into recess."

Washington, D.C., March 8, 1845

Johnny has made good on his plan to visit Charles, leaving me alone in our F Street home. At least by the time he left I didn't have to listen to any more rowdy groups yelling out compliments to that slaver, Polk. He's now been inaugurated, and again Johnny skipped the Inauguration ceremony. I suppose at this point I should be grateful he attended his own!

Washington D.C., May 24, 1845

Yesterday afternoon as I sat in my alcove looking out at an apple tree that is in full blossom, it made me ruminate about the happy marriage between Charles and Abby. I've always been loath to speculate on the sex life of my children. Oh, I'd learned that George had been a naughty man, getting Eliza pregnant and maybe other girls! Before young John died, I did wonder if John and Mary enjoyed marital coupling: I'm afraid I doubt Mary could have enjoyed it when I recollect what an alcoholic John became before his demise. It has been a great consolation for me when Charles and Abby moved to Washington D.C., adding a residence in the Capital to their Boston, Mount Vernon Street home.

Johnny has made peace with Charles following that bitter time in 1841 when Charles behaved in so selfish a manner towards the AMISTAD Africans.

Sipping his wine, Johnny commented, "Charles was astonished to learn that Mr. Abraham Lincoln had remarked in a private room at the House of Representatives that 'like father like son,' how much

'Charles resembled' Congressman Adams." My Johnny!

Personally, I don't see the resemblance. Charles has the same amount of ambition, but something's lacking towards achieving it. I've begun to doubt he will ever be President of the United States. He hasn't the fire. He has "fire in his belly" for it, but not the fire of wisdom.

Abby is always prompting me to tell jokes to my Johnny. Really, he likes hearing jokes, but cannot remember the end line if he tries to pass one on. He often jested before that his memory was failing him; now, he means it.

I know in my heart of hearts that Johnny wants one more fight in Congress. He keeps referring to it. "I still want to kill my lion."

Sitting in our kitchen whilst his manservant Ben Andrews packed Johnny's summer clothes for the Boston trip, I listened attentively whilst Johnny railed against President Polk.

From Tennessee—as was his mentor, Andrew Jackson—Polk shares that ex-President's view on the annexation of Texas. The idea of a huge new slave state coming into the Union dismays and infuriates Johnny. "It isn't that I can't sympathize with the frontiersmen needing help in cutting down trees, uprooting them to clear fields or create grazing ground. I have a farm; I understand those needs. But I PAY my farm hands. They are freemen and can quit and move on if that suits them."

"Have some of my rice pudding." Hoping to quiet Johnny to spare his blood pressure, I produced a bowl of that healthy dessert for him, "It has cinnamon and nutmeg in it. It's easy on teeth."

"No rice pudding. I know it's good for me; that's why I hate it. Listen to me dearest Louisa, Henry Adams, the first Adams to come to America, brought his eight sons and daughter, Mary, to what was a raw place. Seven of his sons and Mary liked Massachusetts. They stayed there and married and had progeny. But one son couldn't accept the frontier way of life. He wanted to go to London to the shops and taverns and theaters. He left what was then called the Northern part of Virginia and was never seen again. Henry's second son, Joseph, was my great great-grandfather. If I'd been descended from that foppish son I'd be living in England. But I'm not. I understand that the frontier life is hard, and I would be proud of the Texan men who take on that life if they will forgo having slaves. Otherwise, annexing Texas would be an abomination. We will have another slave state in the Union, which adds up to another threat to its survival."

"Survival of the Union," is still one of Johnny's favorite subjects. I ate my rice pudding in silence. It had too much nutmeg. I decided to change its recipe.

I said, "It's more than Texas, isn't it? Aren't you concerned about Missouri and maybe Oregon?"

"Yes, and all the vast amount of Mexico that Sam Houston's men are claiming; we could go to war over that."

"Is there anything you can do about it?"

"I intend to do plenty. I was looking through my diary and my old correspondence preparing to refute a calumny the Democrats and Liberty Party people have raked up claiming that in 1817 I'd stupidly ceded away Texas at the time, when in those days there would have been no question of a war over it."

"Johnny! Everyone knows you hate war. That you are a genius writing treaties."

"I am going for the jugular. I will call out those Jackson people on the bold and baseless lies they've invented. The spirit of freedom and freedom from slavery: this dispute with the slavers can take this nation into a deadly conflict of arms. The annexation of Texas to the Union is the blast of the trumpet."

"Is that what you are going to say in Boston to the rally of the Young Whigs Club? Charles won't like such strong words."

"Yes. And yes again. The trouble with Charles is he pussyfoots when he SHOULD use strong words."

Johnny went into the larder and brought out two apples. He cut them up and shared them with me. The threat of war over Texas didn't go away as easily as I disposed of our apple cores.

Johnny had more to say before we went to bed. He told me that in Congress that day he'd called the slavers by their correct name. "I was reviled by a Southerner who took exception to two petitions I'd put forward. The first was cannily from nine unnamed women, the second from slaves. That Southerner's shouts were joined in a clamor of others demanding that Johnny not put forward a petition from prostitutes. Yes, the Southerners had taken the bait."

"Tell me the whole story."

"The Southern congressman whined, 'I did not say they were prostitutes. I have not said I know those women.' There, I'd hooked him like a trout in a raging stream I countered, 'I am glad to hear the honorable gentleman disclaim any knowledge of them, for I'd been going to ask if they were infamous women, who it was that had made them infamous women. Not their color, I believe, but their masters. I have heard it said in proof of that fact that in the South there existed great resemblances between the progeny of the colored people and the white men who claim possession of them. Thus, the charge of infamous might be retorted on those who made it as reflecting on themselves.'"

"Johnny! How brilliant! And then what happened?"

"Noise. So much noise I couldn't make out another of the insults, so I came home."

We did finally go to bed, and Johnny hadn't lost any of his virility for having created so much agitation in Congress.

Washington D.C., June 21, 1845

Former President Andrew Jackson died in Nashville on June 8. I learned of it late, in mid-June, because Johnny was still in Boston, and ex-First Ladies are not important enough to be regaled with important news.

I didn't shed any tears for Jackson. Being born a Britisher, I've always detested him for killing so many British soldiers during the Battle of New Orleans, which battle should have been unnecessary because my Johnny had already signed the Treaty of Ghent ending our War of 1812 with Britain. If that wasn't enough reason, I've been an enthusiastic supporter of our native Indian tribes and therefore hated how he treated the Creek Nation after he slaughtered its braves during the Battle of Horseshoe Bend.

I long to share comments with Johnny about all the praise and laudatory reviews showered on Jackson during memorial services. I learned that Johnny had gone into one of his rages when he heard that Boston had given $1,000 for a memorial for Jackson, bitterly alleging, "Jackson was a murderer, an adulterer." I need to know more, but Johnny is in Massachusetts, where he is celebrating a promise from Harvard University that it will build an astronomical observatory. I understood how much that means to Johnny, who dreams of seeing a man on the moon! But it doesn't get any easier to be lonely just because of growing older.

Washington, D.C., December 10, 1845

When Congress re-convened I invited Angelina Grimké to go to its Visitors' Gallery. Her stern, prim face was not one to invite compliments from any seducer. I thought Angelina could provide help against any further attempts on the part of the Southern "gentleman" who'd tried earlier to seduce me.

She talked in a deep voice all through several of the Congressmen's speeches until a House page was told to "go and keep that woman quiet."

Angelina was telling me stories about the great women who were founding a premier group for women's rights—not a popular subject in Congress at any time, but much less so when bleated out by Angelina's formidable voice. "And don't discount those frontiers-women in Texas," she said of a sudden, almost gaily. "They wear trousers and go out on the range to help round up steers. If a war comes, those women will shoot as straight as their men."

I groaned. Johnny couldn't abide the Grimké sisters for their bold talks to mixed audiences, and would most certainly despise Angelina the more for lauding the possibility of war to let the women in Texas show of what they were made. And here in Johnny's "Private Club," the House of Representatives!

Angelina Grimké liked the sound of her own voice, and no young page would be enough of a barrier to stop that flow. "Mark my words, the people of the United States WANT THIS NATION TO GROW BIGGER. If it takes a war, then so be it."

Her remarks didn't escape the speaker's notice. Again a page was sent to stop Angelina, a senior page, and this time Angelina was escorted OUT of the Capitol. No such treatment was administered to me because the speaker happened to be my husband.

I decided to follow my guest to the steps outside the premises. There, I invited Angelina to continue her stories, but in the confines of my kitchen or alcove.

Angelina chose to go into Johnny's private library, where I used one of Johnny's best crystal goblets to serve a glass of Madeira to calm her embarrassment. Whilst she drank her wine, I admitted to her that I've met Margaret Fuller, who speaks out for women's rights and founded The Conversations. In 1840, about the time I wrote my second book, Record of a Nobody, I went to Boston ostensibly to buy some woolens and attended one of her Conversations. I'd read The Dial, the Transcendentalists' magazine of which Margaret was Chief Editor. Of course, I hid that magazine just as carefully as Johnny had hidden his three copies of Tom Jones. What I like is that this group believes there is a creative energy in the universe, an "over-soul" to which mankind is linked by his divinely inspired intuition.

"One of the Great women is Margaret Fuller," Angelina agreed, lowering her usually booming voice to a whisper, yet still maintaining that unmistakable Southern drawl. "She unconditionally accepts women as the equal of men and rejects any demands for strict uncritical conformity to religious or social creeds. Just lahke Ah does. There's other Great women in her group. Ah par-ti-cularly lahkes Elizabeth Peabody, who has a bookstore that sells Transcendentalist lit-er-a-ture, and her sister, Sophia, who married Nathaniel Hawthorne, who wrote The Scarlet Letter."

It isn't that I've been sneaking behind Johnny's back to be with these ladies who are agitating for women's rights. I just don't want him to have a temper tantrum sparked by this subject. At this point in his advancing years, I know that such an attack could seriously affect his heart.

Angelina took out her humiliation at the Capitol on me by giving me a scolding for the use of too long, too-complicated, too-fanciful words. She sweetened her pill by alleging I need to improve my talks to our women by choosing words they can easily understand. "Y'all needs to learn that many of the women who come fo' hearin' about our rights are women who never had a chance to read these books of your husband's in this here library."

"My husband doesn't allow me to read most of them," I said, getting her point without acknowledging it.

"Y'all needs to use short words. Fo'get those three-syllable fancy ones. Try findin' words that have German, not French roots. They hit home best. HOMEY talk, that's what our women lahke."

I went into the kitchen to fetch cheese and biscuits to accompany the Madeira. When I returned, I found Angelina leafing through a hand-tooled, Moroccan leather volume dedicated to the triumphs of Roman Emperor Marcus Aurelius. She slammed it down on a side table where a few drops of Madeira had been spilled. Oh, I hoped against hope that there would be no Maderia stains on the book's Moroccan leather. I said nothing, busily spreading cheese on the biscuits.

Angelina ate several, patting the book with her free hand. "Our women don't care about Roman Emperors. They want to be lawyers, engineers, doctors. And they want to keep the money they earn that now goes into the bank accounts of their husbands. Y'all can make those aims clearer with short words. Say after me: take, not REQUISITION; save, not CAPITALIZE, in love, not ENAMOURED."

I repeated the shorter words, and when Angelina had eaten all the biscuits and cheese, she left. I know I will take this language lesson to heart, but I wasn't sorry to see her leave me that afternoon.

When he returned this evening, Johnny and I again took up the task of sorting through his mother's letters, putting them in order. One of her letters to Johnny as a young boy told him to learn to control his temper. He hadn't been able to then and cannot now. Johnny still worries from the fear that he never knows when he will go into a rage.

While I read Abigail's old letters, I was intrigued to find one to Johnny's father On the Need to Free Women from Their Chattels. I like best the way she'd put it, "And by the way in the new code of laws which I suppose necessary for you to make, I desire you would remember the ladies, and be more favorable to them than your ancestors. Do not put such unlimited power into the hands of husbands."

And that was written before the Declaration of Independence!

The furious pace of the women's liberation movement was going ahead like a locomotive on one of the new amazing trains. I worry that the women are moving too fast. I fear that a scandal might come along to ruin all their hard work.

I have not had to wait long for trouble to raise its ugly head, for it has already begun. One of our leading women, Elizabeth Cady, refused to marry the man her father had chosen for her. Yet she managed to get the rejected fiancé's acceptance to permit her to wed the man she favored, Henry Stanton, in 1840. At her wedding she refused to promise to "obey" as written in the marriage vows. She used her maiden name combined with her husband's surname. She never calls herself Mrs. Henry Stanton. Elizabeth insists her marriage is one among equals. "I cannot bear the name of another." Keeping her own name was a symbol, she explained, because: "women—like slaves, who also had no names of their own—were mere chattels, with no civil or social rights." Of course, that brought down condemnation from churches all over the country—condemnation that carries on still today!

More recently, Elizabeth launched the delicate subject of divorce originating with the wife. Sarah has been the most prestigious woman to raise banners that called for women to own the money they earned and not to have to give it to their husbands. Her leadership has been followed by many women who demanded the right to have bank accounts, to sign legal papers, and to own property.

I stay abreast of these clarion calls, but I suspect it will be in a different way that I manage to make my own small contribution to one woman's freedom.

Washington, D.C., May 13, 1846

Much as I love collecting recipes and experimenting with them, I don't fancy spending long hours over hot stoves and washing dishes or pots and pans. Now in my seventies, my back gives me twinges when I stand too long chopping up nuts or sorting ingredients.

A dear friend who owns a slave called Julia, decided to ease these unpleasant tasks for me by sending Julia to my house as hired help. I have been asked to pay her a salary, which I am glad to do.

What a situation! I've always been active in the anti-slavery movement. Even my mother-in-law, Abigail, whose own mother had kept two slaves in her house, had never contemplated having a slave. Yet I didn't want to insult the kind friend who meant well. Quietly I welcomed the "slave" into our F Street house. Very quickly I found out that this woman had bought the freedom of her children, but had not enough money to buy her own. She needed $400 to purchase her Emancipation Papers. She saved $275, for that purpose. It wasn't enough. My heart went out to Julia, and I schemed how to help her gain her freedom.

Meanwhile, a problem arose when I wanted to take Julia to Quincy with Johnny and me for the summer. The District of Columbia was "slave" and Massachusetts was "free." It contravened the Washington D.C. law to take a slave from the District of Columbia to Quincy. Obviously, as the wife of a congressman and ex-president, I couldn't break the law. It seemed I would have to leave for Quincy without Julia, but I knew that her owner could sell her at any moment.

Hadn't the Northerners heard many terrible stories about slaves being "sent down river?" But that was not the reason I scraped up the $125 that Julia needed. I did it to help one woman to be free. Free from slavery, free of at least that terrible shackle.

My one brother had died and left me a small inheritance. Johnny had not taken possession of it, and I reckoned I could use some of those few dollars to top up Julia's emancipation money. I was very artful in broaching that subject to Johnny. Although he hadn't taken possession of my small inheritance, he still kept an eye on it. So I labored the subject of taking Julia to Quincy, knowing already that was not acceptable. One "No" from him could possibly bring about a "yes" later.

So I said, "I would like to bring Julia with us. She could finally teach me how to make her millefeuilles pastry."

"A slave? To Quincy? Surely, you know better than that. It is against the law to bring a slave from a slave state to a free state. I MAKE laws, I do not permit members of my family to BREAK a law."

Petulantly, arguing when I knew it could be useless, I moaned, "But your mother's mother kept TWO slaves in Massachusetts."

"In other times, my dear. Forget this Julia. Another cook can teach you how to make a better pastry."

"Johnny, I know you caused a near-riot by accusing slave owners of adding to their holdings by begetting children off the women slaves. Julia has been threatened by her mistress to return Julia to their plantation where the master has twelve mulatto children."

"My dear, that is none of your business." "Oh? I intend to MAKE it my business."

I put a cotton robe over my nightgown and stormed out to go downstairs to the kitchen.

Julia was there, cleaning pots. Her tears were mingling with the dish water. I drew her trembling fingers from the basin, and said, "Somehow I will block your return to your old plantation."

"Cain't be done, Missy Adams. Ah b'longs to the Cahtuhs. Ah's b'n prayin' somethin' terrible to b' able t'earn me 'nuf money t'buy mah freedom. But y'all knows as Ah's sho't one hundred 'n twenty-five dollahs." Her tears now came accompanied by rasping gasps.

I have difficulty understanding her Georgia accent. Earlier, in our conversations over the pastry board, she explained that her Mammy spoke Gullah, which had tainted her own use of the English language. When I worked out she had re-iterated her shortage of funds, I said, “That is a lot of money.”

No comment from Julia. She nodded, though her head dipped so low that it touched her chest. She pulled away her hands from mine and dragged herself toward a shelf where a can reposed. She shook out a waterfall of coins from it. Among these was a gold sovereign that I knew had been a gift from another of the ladies for whom she did her moonlighting jobs. She held up the gold sovereign, finally gulping out a few words. “If’n Ah goes back t’ the plan-ta-tion, please Missy Adams get this to mah chillun. Ah’s bought THEIR freedom. They’s with Missy Monroe’s daughter.”

“I promise, I will. But Julia, tell me more about your children. Who is their father?”

“They’s chillun bah Mastuh Cahtuh. He done took me down t’ the hut on ourn lake; twice. Fu’st tahme when I be fo’teen. Mah Mammy done warned me could happen, soon’s ah got the monthly bleedin’ even though Ah’s been his own chile.”

Incest! Thinking I might vomit on my clean kitchen floor, I sat down and breathed hard. Her children were her own half-sister and half-brother!

My thoughts swirled as wildly as leaves in a storm. Could I raise my hundred and twenty-five dollars? Would Mr. Adams even permit me to discuss using my inheritance? This latest revelation made me more determined than ever to save Julia from returning “down river.” To more incest!

Julia continued, “Ah b’lieves as Ah goes t’ Hell if’n Ah kills mahself. But Ah plans t’ drink bleach if‘n Ah’s ordered t’ go to the lake hut ag’in with Mastuh Cahtuh.”

I shook my head to reassure Julia that she was not going to Hell. Internally, I firmed my resolve; one way or another, I would convince Johnny to help me free this much-abused woman. I took her hands again in mine and said, "My brother left me some money in his will when he died. I have one hundred and twenty five dollars I can give to you. I have to leave in a few days for Quincy with Mr. Adams, but tomorrow I will go with him to his bank and have the bank send what is necessary to where it must go to buy your freedom."

Julia stood where she was, gasping at me. Then slowly she sank to the floor, her patchwork skirt doubling as a prayer rug. She caught at my cotton robe's hem, and kissed it. I released it from her grasp and strode out to the parlor, feeling truly elated that I had helped at least one woman escape her bondage.

Washington, D.C., August 12, 1846

My Johnny has persuaded Congress to bend to his will yet again! In 1829, the illegitimate son of the Duke of Northumberland, who called himself Smithson against the will of the duke's legitimate heirs, decided to make a large monetary offering to the United States to create an important museum. Various States of the Union, greedy, jockeyed to get that money for their own purposes, and for years that money has been fought over like wild dogs vying for meat! At last, my experienced debater took on the fight to grab back the money for which it had been intended, and—lo and behold—Johnny wrested it back. The battle has raged for several years, but thanks to Johnny the museum became a reality on August 10. Our nation shall at last have the Smithsonian Institution, a treasure I hope will last for generations!

Perhaps, like me, Johnny is beginning to feel his age and see the need for ways to preserve all that we have amassed, such as my volumes of cookery. Johnny's body is failing. He used up much of his energy to battle against a war with Mexico, and he saw his hopes dashed when our army invaded our neighbor to the South. It is a sad time for Johnny. In Europe, he oversaw the rout of Napoleon's armies and his exiles to Elba and St. Helena. He signed the Peace Treaty of Ghent that ended our War of 1812. What a blow to his ego that he's failed to stop the war with Mexico.

He suffers, thinking that slavery will extend to any territories grabbed during that war. He feels outraged that slavery is also extending to parts of the mid-west. Johnny worries again how extending slavery could affect the balance of power in Congress, with more slave states coming into the Union with their added votes.

Now he smiles less than ever.

Today he decided to take his favorite walk along the Potomac. In its waters there were two men cavorting, splashing plumes of water like children do. When Johnny arrived at his favorite jump-off spot, he couldn't resist it. He stripped off his business clothes and dove in. He swam for two glorious hours.

When he returned home I noticed that his hair was wet and there were droplets on his face.

Appalled, worried about the ebbing state of his health, I asked, "Have you been swimming?"

"Yes, dearest Louisa, indeed I have."

"Would you like to warm up with a cup of chocolate?"

Johnny shook his head, took my hand, and led me upstairs and to the marital bed. For a man who rarely smiles, he sent me a huge grin. He stripped me of my clothes, and we made beautiful love.

If there was a recipe for lovemaking, it should begin: Take a partner who has just bathed from head to toe, smother with kisses, add ingredients to taste, slowly heat, and serve while hot. It should end: top with a piece of chocolate for the afterglow.

Washington, D.C., May 23, 1847

In August, 1846 we finally went together to Quincy for a few weeks. There, Johnny accepted the unanimous nomination at the Whig Convention of the Eighth District of Massachusetts to return as its Congressman. This time he won with a majority of 1,800 votes over contenders.

After that triumph, Johnny went on to his usual visit with Charles and Abby at their Mount Vernon Street house in Boston. I traveled with my daughter-in-law Mary Hellen Adams, John's widow, and their only surviving child, Mary Louisa, to Washington. To our gratification, we were told Mary Louisa had been selected to be Queen of the May a few months earlier.

On a walk through Boston with his friend, George Parkman, intending to see the new facilities at Harvard's Medical School, Johnny suddenly couldn't take another step. His legs buckled underneath him; he'd had a cerebral hemorrhage. With the help of George Parkman and two other friends, he was dragged back to the Mount Vernon house where he remained scarcely conscious for several days.

Johnny, being Johnny, wrote about that dreadful time in a missive he titled A Posthumous Memoir. Posthumous! He wrote, "I date my decease and consider myself, for any useful purpose to myself or to my fellow creatures, dead."

He wasn't. At seventy-eight, he was still able to return to Congress. To his gratification all the members present rose to stand in his honor. Enemies vanished. They gave up insulting him or even baiting him when he rose to speak.

Johnny said to me after one day in Congress, comfortably seated in our kitchen, "I'd die if I gave up my public life."

He didn't. He attended both sessions of Congress that winter. He responded to roll calls. He voted. He did stand up to speak on one subject. He fought a proposal to amend the civil and diplomatic appropriations to provide a $50,000 indemnity to the owners of the AMISTAD for the libel adjudged against their ship and its self-liberated cargo of mutinied "slaves."

Johnny reminded the House that the Spanish Minister had insisted on the rendition of the Africans not as slaves but as ASSASSINS. Raising his voice, which was becoming rasping and feeble, he spoke out more clearly to underline his final words, "He wanted to have them tried and executed for liberating themselves." Pausing for a succession of deep breaths, Johnny fought on, "There is not even the shadow of a pretense for the Spanish demand of indemnity. God forbid that any claim should ever be allowed by Congress which rested on such a false foundation." Johnny had to stop again before continuing. "The demand, if successful, would be a perfect robbery committed on the people of the United States. Neither these slave dealers, nor the Spanish Government on their behalf, has any claim to the money whatever."

That amendment insulting the AMISTAD people was defeated, thanks to Johnny.

He was thinking about his own money as well that winter. He wrote his will and left me the bulk of his estate, after the payment of debts, to be shared with Mary Hellen Adams, Mary Louisa Adams, and our surviving son, Charles. Johnny kindly remembered other relations in his will, among them nieces and other grandchildren. He gave a small annuity to his mother's niece, Louisa Catherine Smith, who had spent most of her life with us.

Like his own father, Johnny placed a burden on his son of taking care of the Adams family home and estates in Quincy. He specified what he wanted done with his books and personal possessions. Johnny knew exactly where he wanted everything to go.

But I am not ready for him to go.

Washington, D.C., December 12, 1847

Summertime meant Quincy for both of us. We went there in June. Our Fiftieth Wedding Anniversary was duly celebrated in the Adams homestead, but the food wasn't very good, which I suppose by now is tradition for that house. Those Puritans went all-out to provide wines, because they know how much Johnny favors them, but they never asked me for one single recipe that would have benefited the paltry spread on their table.

The summer didn't end without the now-annual separation, while Johnny went to Boston and I returned to Washington.

After Boston, in November, Johnny finally got some recognition for his anti-slavery posture. When he was traveling from Boston, he stopped in New York, where he received a resolution by the executive committee of The American and Foreign Anti-slavery Society.

"Resolved: that Messrs. Arthur Tappan, Rev. Christopher Rush, Arnold Buffum, Lewis Tappan and Rev. Luther Lee attend upon the Honorable John Quincy Adams now in this city, on his way to Washington, and express to him the thanks of this committee for all that he has done in Congress and elsewhere on behalf of the Anti-slavery cause, with their most respectful wishes for his health and usefulness during the approaching session of Congress and while his valuable life be preserved."

Goodness gracious, but those gentlemen are so long-winded. I didn't like the word "while" his valuable life be preserved. Thank you, but why that word?

At the December session of Congress Johnny managed to present several petitions, each one draining his strength more. I know he cared particularly for the one that asked for peace with Mexico, but he sounded very short of breath after asking for it.

Washington, D.C. January 1, 1848

New Year's Day 1848 has not been exactly jolly. I made a wonderful new Polish dessert, a paczki, which the Polish Minister's wife sent to me. The recipe is simple because the main ingredients are the same as I choose for making doughnuts. It mandates that the over-sized doughnut should be cooked in hot oil and, when sizzling hot, should be stuffed with puréed fruit. I found it delicious, but maybe all that sugar hurt Johnny's few remaining teeth.

Johnny struggled through the meal, but limped to his desk later to pen a letter to Charles. He praised his efforts, offered him his paternal affection, and ended with an admonition that he should keep a clear conscience and "never despair."

I've hesitated to write this down before, but I do want to remind the family that Charles was the most successful of our sons. And it was Charles who lived with ME until he was ten, whereas his brothers spent eight years without living with me, and then another four without me while getting their education in Boston. Both of those sons died young and were addicted to alcohol: THE BLAME CANNOT BE LAID TO ME.

Washington D.C. January 18, 1848

Johnny passed his eightieth birthday last July and was still deeply involved in every aspect of political affairs in the House of Representatives. He particularly deplored the danger of pro-slavery territories demanding to become states of the Union.

He liked the backwoodsmen and enjoyed meeting with some of them. "I admire that Representative from Illinois, Abraham Lincoln," he mentioned last night, a cold evening, when he joined me in my alcove.

I brought out the decanter of his favorite wine, and he sipped from a glass of it while I wrapped him in his ready blanket. I ate a cookie while I covered my own knees with the shawl I kept for that purpose. My knees are giving me trouble, and I have twinges from my hips, too. But I listened attentively, while munching on the cookie. It was a delicious almond-flavored cookie. My wonderful chef had made it that afternoon, her hands dancing so that the powdered sugar flew around like snowflakes.

"You said, Abraham Lincoln?"

"Abraham Lincoln," Johnny took two more sips. "He's an odd sort. But has a certain charm, which I understand woos voters. His wife's maiden name was Todd, and it SHOULD have been spelled without the T because she really is Odd. She is a tiny, pinch-faced woman. He is too tall, rather ungainly, and has a large mole on his face. I wonder how they fit together in bed—he so tall and she so short."

I suppressed a light laugh, imagining the Lincoln's in a marital bed. "But you like him."

"I do. He votes along with me on anti-slavery bills and on the construction of highways and canals."

"I remember you said he believes that someday all slaves in America will be free."

"Correct. And thank God, because now we have an added threat to saving the Union. Those new proslavery Representatives in Congress do not seem aware how dangerous the chasm has become. And some of the pro-slavery states are not all that new. Did I not sign the Adams-Onis Treaty in 1818 that eventually brought Eastern Florida into the Union? How could I have foreseen that slave owners from Georgia would move down there and take their slaves with them? 'Georgia-crackers' we call them. Violently pro-slavery. That treaty has been a thorn in my side ever since Clay discovered how the Spaniards slipped in a section giving extra land grants to them."

I looked down at the floor. I well knew how humiliating that Clay-inspired "discovery" was for Johnny. In those pre-election days when Clay was juggling against Johnny for the 1825 Presidency, Clay had almost derailed Johnny's chances with his announcement that Johnny let the Spaniards slip in their predatory extra sentences.

In those days I was more intrigued by what was going on in Greece than in my husband's political woes. I reveled in accounts of how the brave Greeks took up arms against their masters in Turkey and how one of my favorite poets, Lord Byron, had entered into that fray. What a hero he turned out to be! I was scandalized by his incestuous affair with his sister. Less so, with the adulteress mess he caused in Lady Caroline Lamb's life. She had called him, "mad, bad, and dangerous to know." And then he died of pneumonia after swimming to the Hellespont. Thank God my Johnny hasn't drowned on the many occasions when he takes risks whilst swimming!

Too bad that Lord Byron was an adulterer, but I'd been immunized from that sort of tale when I lived in Berlin and in St. Petersburg where adultery was widespread among the aristocracy. Of course, it was TOO MUCH when Lady Caroline, besotted by love of Lord Byron, dyed her skin black to be able to appear as a naked slave carrying the palanquin he used for his famous entrance to you-know-where. And she with a similar position to mine as wife of a future British Prime Minister!

I was ready to go to bed, but Johnny had more to say. He might have been thinking about his failing health because he turned to me with a wide-eyed expression. "Louisa, I have changed my beliefs. I now hold there is an after-life."

What a turn-around! I felt blood rising to expand the beatings of my heart. How wonderful that Johnny had shared those precious words with me!

Calmly, not overdoing this very special moment, Johnny finished the wine in my decanter.

He fell asleep in my alcove. Soon after, I too fell asleep there. Not a good idea, because my old bones really needed the cozy warmth of my bed's blankets. But last night, my joy warmed me.

Washington D.C., January 27, 1848

On a chilly winter day, my Johnny made his tired way to the Capitol alone in a carriage. Requesting time to speak, Johnny launched into a negative stance as regarded a resolution presented in Congress relating to the return of exiled General Santa Ana to Mexico.

In his fading voice Johnny demanded that President Polk communicate as to what instructions he had relayed to army officers or to Minister John Sidell concerning General Santa Ana. Johnny took exception to the use of American assistance, at a time when General Taylor's army was pushing from the Nueces to the Rio Grande. Johnny's aim was to raise the question of whether President Polk had conspired with Santa Ana to overthrow the de facto Mexican Government on the eve of the war and to plumb whether President Polk had not helped the Mexican dictator to go back to Mexico to make a favorable territorial arrangement with the United States. President Polk had resisted giving Congress all the relative papers. Johnny believed that the House had every right to demand to receive all of those pertaining to this question.

In the virile debate that followed, my Johnny managed to say, "I think the Members of the House ought to sustain, in the strongest manner, their right to call for information upon operations in which WAR AND PEACE ARE CONCERNED. They ought to maintain their right, and maintain it in a very distinct manner, against the assertion of the PRESIDENT OF THE UNITED STATES."

Hooray, for my Johnny. With those words he's killed his lion!

Washington, D.C., February 13, 1848

Johnny has begun to reminisce on past events. Today, he spoke of when he went with his friend Justice John McLean to a reception for the Mayor of Washington. He recalled he'd been invigorated from that event, and although very busy with problems in Washington, he went to lay the corner stone for the Smithsonian Institution, garnering on his way kisses, including many kisses on the lips from ladies who crushed through crowds to laud him.

My naughty Johnny, still taking delight from those sex books he loved to read! One lady had started it all by kissing him—meaning for her kiss to laud on his cheek—but Johnny moved his lips to hers and continued to do just that to every other woman in that long line of ladies who had only queued to congratulate him for a good speech!

On the Friday, he attended Congress and voted on the floor for a bill to help the heirs of the Naval hero of the War of 1812, John Paul Jones.

Washington D.C., February 14, 1848

Johnny's health continues to deteriorate. Sadly, Charles described his father as "an old man" after he last saw him. When I try to keep Johnny at home and in bed, he complains he'll die if he cannot go to Congress. After feeling wobbly on rising, when I urged him to go back to bed he immediately announced he felt better. He dressed and left in a carriage, without inviting me to accompany him.

In the past months my social life hasn't palled—in spite of Johnny having "good days" and "bad days." We've entertained friends, and I plan to go to the Washington Birthday Ball in eight days. I got busy looking through my clothes press to choose a gown for the grand event. Clothes, though, were not uppermost in my mind when Johnny returned from the House. Hurrying to locate his decanter that he might savor a glass of Madeira, I joined him in his library.

Johnny had been using his voice all day, but that didn't stop him from launching into the story of Mr. James Smithson, for whose scientific institution he had battled in Congress. Johnny told me that James Smithson was the illegitimate son of Sir Hugh Smithson Percy, the first Duke of Northumberland, and a mistress whose family name was Macie. His mistress didn't have much of a name when compared to Smithson's ancestor, the legendary Hotspur Percy, the most famous of his father's line. On James' mother's deathbed Miss Macie asked James to take the name Smithson, whether the Percy family liked it or not.

I shivered, thinking of all those long years ago when I visited my grandmother MISS Mary Young, whose mother had given birth to twenty-two illegitimate children. What chance did my mother have in a family of twenty-two bastards to escape from the vise of illegitimacy? My adorable mother, who had been so unsure of a family name she had misspelled, Nuth writing Neuth on occasions! Nuth being a name she thought she could use. Why? Thinking that the man who had engendered her was a Nuth? Or had she gone through a mock marriage with a man called Nuth before meeting Joshua Johnson? And yet she rose to be an admired hostess to the Americans in London, and eventually married the brother of the Governor of Maryland!

I tried to control my shivering. I knew I MUST NOT give Johnny any reason to wonder what had caused it. I bit my lips until I tasted blood.

Staring at me intently, Johnny put down his glass of Madeira, handed me his rather soiled kerchief stained from his customary snuffling, and quietly said, "Illegitimate, like you, my dear. Of little consequence these days, when what a person DOES is what matters."

Oh, Johnny knew! He must have known all those long fifty years of our difficult marriage! Papa's butler Chivers must have got to him! Johnny knew, and now he didn't give it any importance?

I had so often prayed that someday this could happen. It finally HAD!

But there was more to come, on that other topic that had so bruised me through the years.

Johnny said, "About the lack of what you call 'love in lovemaking' I must tell you the truth of why I behaved as I did. My problem, if I may dub it that, started when I went to The Hague to be Minister to Holland. I had left America with my heart in turmoil, forbidden by my adored parents to marry the girl I loved, Mary Frazier. She and I had sworn to never love another. Highly emotional young man that I was, I engraved that promise on the bark of a tree near her home. We visited that tree many times. I am a man of my word and believed, after that, how it would be dishonorable to love anyone else, ever. When I kissed her, or touched her privately, she would go alight and respond to me avidly. At night, alone in my Spartan bed in Boston I would think ahead to our wedding and how we would make glorious love together. In Holland, when a college friend of mine wrote to me that Mary had wed another, I had one of my worst furies. So angered was I that I determined to find a wife in Europe to even the score. But the girls in Holland were of no use to me; few could speak English well, and most were fat and graceless. I went to England with the intention of finding a suitable bride. I had a mental list of what her qualities should be: speak English well, and maybe French—the Diplomats' language—play music tolerably, know the art of entertaining with dinners or balls, and be family-oriented. I took it for granted that my future spouse would respond to my physical approaches. Mary Frazier most certainly had! Very much so!

"I met Nancy, and you. Nancy made it clear from the start that she found me physically repugnant. You made jokes and seemed to flirt with me. You spoke French, played the pianoforte superbly, and had been brought up watching your mother give dinners and balls. Your mother chaperoned us so adroitly that I never had the chance to test if you would respond to me physically. I left London for Holland thinking you might do, and fell into your mother's web. I returned imagining there would be time for us to be left alone for me to test your responses. No, that did not transpire. Instead, I was rushed into a wedding within two weeks of my arrival in London. Our wedding day was filled with partying and traveling. I was quite drunk when we went to our poor little marital chamber. When I thought to take you in my arms to caress you, I received a look of horror from you. Assured you were a virgin, I thought it quite normal for you to be a trifle frightened of what should come to pass.

"I determined to not let that anger me, went into the bed, and fell asleep, and the spooking began. There, between pillow and blanket was Mary Frazier. Certainly, I had dreamed of her many times before, but never as I did that night when her ghost and I made wild love. It was the same for the next three nights. SPOOKED, as we went from one miserable inn to another. The fourth night, in a decent bed, I made my initial cautious probes under your nightgown. You showed no desire whatsoever for me. That sent me close to a temper tantrum. By the fifth night, fortified with enough wine, I decided to penetrate whether you liked it or not. You didn't like it. Merely, tolerated me. You seemed to be gritting your teeth like a girl obliged to play ice hockey when what she preferred would be a quiet walk. Well, I had married partly to start a family: I wanted children. I wanted to alleviate my natural physical desires for sexual intercourse. So nightly I soldiered on. And the spooking never ceased. There, always, between pillow and blanket, was Mary Frazier. Not until our son George died did SHE leave."

He paused for a moment to let all that seep into me. Then, he explained further, "I know, dearest Louisa that you wondered WHY early on I acted coldly to you in the marital bed. Now I am ready to admit that I had retained great affection for that first love of my life, Mary Frazier, and through the years could not make love without seeing her face. She had died young, soon after we had parted, and somehow I was imprisoned in her ghostly arms. Towards the end of your first trip to the United States

I did tell you that my first love was a Mary Frazier, because I feared evil tongues would twist the story on your arrival in Quincy. Or you would see the tree where I had carved my promise of eternal love for her. I failed then to explain how deeply I was involved in being spooked."

Oh, my! So, at last I understood about that, too. How many years of reciprocal love from me he had wasted!

Johnny continued, hoarsely, "Dearest Louisa, I want to apologize to you for my cold attitude all those years. Thirty years, when I should have been adoring you! But at last, after George's death, when I saw how tenderly you tried to help me in spite of your own agonizing pain, I knew I loved you. By then I could barely remember Mary Frazier's face or recall her voice. And you were here with me, so caring and kind. And I was reminded what I promised when Reverend Hewlett married us, 'That with my body I thee worship.' I feel ashamed that I failed you for so long."

Oh, Johnny, dear husband! Again I said nothing. My heart was too full of love for him.

Washington D.C., February 20,1848

Today being a Sunday, Johnny managed to attend two church services. Oh, he is certainly thinking of an after-life.

This evening, I gave a reception at home for several of our friends. Johnny was pleased with it and went to each of them to say a few words. But to one he mentioned, “I don’t expect to live out the session of Congress.”

Revived after two glasses of Madeira wine, he even wrote a poem for a girl from Springfield, Massachusetts, which I interpreted as quite flirtatious. She only asked for his autograph, but he went further. The last bit of the poem went, “Alone the poet’s numbers, in iron inspiration glows, Or with the poet slumbers.” Did he mean sleep with the poet?

Later tonight, I read to him Wilberforce’s “Sermon on time.” I didn’t want to bore him that much, but from Sarah Grimké I’ve been prompted not to accept just anything that Johnny might throw my way. Flirting, with a girl at HIS age?

My Johnny was having doubts as to the validity of some of our church’s teachings. “I cannot think that Christ was sent by God to atone for humanity’s sins.

I cannot believe in a doctrine of atonement. But how shall I contradict Saint Paul?”

“You must depend on BELIEF. I do. Just believe it is so.”

“I reverence God as my creator. As creator of the world. I reverence him with holy fear. I venerate Jesus Christ as my redeemer—and, as far as I can understand the redeemer of the world. But this belief is dark and devious.”

Later, Johnny echoed my thoughts expressed in that book I wrote in 1840 calling myself a nobody. Somehow Johnny got an idea that he’s FAILED in life.

I knew he'd written earlier that God did not grant to him "conceptive power of mind." Oh, my. Too bad that he hated hot chocolate. THAT could have calmed him.

Johnny got into bed, but wouldn't lie down straight. His bald pate bumped the headboard. But he cleared his throat, about to continue.

I tried to pour oil on his mental wounds "But

He has, my dearest," I assured him.

"No. I have not improved upon the scanty portions of his gifts as I might and ought to have done."

"Dearest, you accomplished so much."

"Not in comparison to a Shakespeare or a Cicero.

I think about the wonders I could have accomplished if God had bestowed on me the irresistible power of genius and the irrepressible energy of will. But I have failed, I did not receive those blessings."

What could I say? I said nothing. This was getting too complicated.

Johnny kept flaying the subject like a cruel horseman who whips a dying horse. "If I'd been awarded great talents my diary would have been, next to the holy scriptures, the most precious and valuable book ever written by human hands, and I should have been one of the greatest benefactors of my country and the world."

With his voice finally gone, and Johnny beginning to snore, I smoothed his blanket and straightened the top sheet of our bed. I didn't climb in beside him. What was the use? I went into my alcove, wrapped myself in my shawl, and rewrote portions of a speech I intended to give. I shortened the three-syllable words to one, wherever I could. I don't aspire to be a famous writer, but I do want to follow Angelina's advice regarding language and practice cropping my words.

Washington, D.C., February 23, 1848

On February 21, a cold Monday morning, Johnny had one hand shaking from palsy.

"Johnny, your hand is shaking! Are we back to the palsy? What can I do for you? Get the doctor to come to see you?"

I tried to urge him to stay in bed for a cure. No, he wouldn't stay in bed. I decided to bring him light food on a tray. It was a bitter February morning. I brought his breakfast into my alcove which had the best of our two fireplaces. I spoon fed him one of the recipes from Martha Washington's Booke of Recipes. It was for a chicken broth he could digest. I hoped that might give him strength.

There was to be no doctor called. No, he would not stay in my alcove. Over my frantic objections he called for a carriage to go to the Capitol. Suddenly he had an elastic step and sped downstairs.

Was there a kiss for goodbye? No. Was there a wave from his palsied hand? No. I accepted that, as it was his usual custom all these fifty years when he left our home.

Oh, but he'd made me so happy a scant week ago with his declaration of love—on Valentine's Day no less!—and admitting that he's always known I am illegitimate without caring a snap.

With the carriage waiting to collect him, Johnny made his careful way out the door, holding tightly to the doorknob with his good hand. I scurried to where his collection of coats hung from pegs. I tried to cover him with his greatcoat that had a three layered short cape. No, he climbed into the carriage wearing nothing warmer than his usual black suit, threadbare from his years in Congress.

Delivered to the Capitol, he had to carefully manipulate all those steps. The coachman who'd brought him was astonished that he went up them as quickly as he did.

Inside the House of Representatives, Johnny took his usual seat. He listened attentively to the roll call and statements on government business, which took most of the morning.

Later, when the Speaker asked for ayes and nays for a resolution to be tendered by Congress to the generals who should be getting decorations and thanks for the campaigns of 1847, Johnny voted in a surprisingly strong voice: "No!" He sounded as loud as a homebound sailor shouting from his crow's nest perch, "Land ahoy."

The Speaker asked whether thanks to the generals and their troops should be granted a third reading. Fifteen feet away from Johnny, an Abolitionist reporter noticed that my husband's face had turned purple. The reporter, seated at the Press table, had been studying Johnny's face to guess how he would vote. The reporter next saw Johnny's lips working as if to say something, then Johnny's right hand started shaking wildly as he tried to pull himself up from his seat. Like a barnacled old Massachusetts whaling ship of the last century fighting the tide, Johnny struggled.

Johnny had slumped to the left before a Member of the House shouted out, "Mr. Adams is dying."

Congressman David Fisher, from Ohio, who sat next to Johnny, caught him before he hit the floor. Many members came forward to crowd around him, but a physician warned them away to give Johnny space to breathe. Johnny was laid on a sofa carried in by colleagues. The House adjourned, and when the news reached the Senate, it adjourned.

Four physicians advised that he be moved to the Rotunda, then to the Portico. The Portico was too damp and chilly, so my dying darling was taken to the Speaker's Room.

Johnny managed to revive enough to ask for Henry Clay. Why? Henry Clay had been an enemy. Was he inspired to spend his final moments forgiving an enemy? Johnny clasped hands with Henry

Clay and then asked to give his thanks to the "Officers of the House." Johnny said, "This is the end of earth, but I am composed."

Finally, after all that, I was summoned to come to the side of my dying husband. I brought my good friend Mary Elizabeth Cutts with me. I knew I couldn't survive the coming scene alone.

Johnny's eyelids never flickered. Never. There were no final words for me. He was beyond speech.

He lay there throughout February 22, barely breathing, in a coma. I was permitted to remain at his side all night in that stately building.

The Washington Day Ball was canceled, as were all festivities in the city. Johnny, who had wanted to represent "the entire nation," did garner its affection as he died.

He breathed his last at twenty minutes past seven in the evening of February 23. He used to love to go swimming at that time in the old days!

The Speaker announced Johnny's death the next day. What resounded with me was how he ended his recognition of Johnny's sixty years of service with the words, "The crowning glory of his character was his devotion to the Cause of his Redeemer."

No mention was made of Johnny's devotion to me these last few years. The public still believed we had a bad marriage and that there was no love lost between us. How wrong the political world was on that account. I'd never loved Johnny more than I did on the day of his death. My heart felt it would rip apart from loving him so much, and that fact helped me—like when the water of a river flows better after a dam breaks.

Still, I needed plenty of solace from the Redeemer.

Washington D.C., March 4, 1848

Thousands of people queued to view his casket, laid out in his beloved House of Representatives. His funeral ceremonies were of the grade usually reserved in other countries for royalty. The seventeen gun canon salute for an ambassador boomed out over the Potomac from dawn until noon on this vile Saturday. At that hour President Polk entered the House, taking his place on the Speaker's right. Polk's arrival was followed by Justices of the Supreme Court, top officers of the Army and Navy, Senators, and the Vice-President.

Charles, Mary, and her daughter Louisa with a nephew, Isaac Hill Adams, filed in last. They had to listen to a lot of sermons, thankfully interspersed with a choir singing hymns from the ladies' gallery.

Next day, a committee was formed to send a representative of each state and territory to accompany Johnny's remains on their journey to the Congressional Burial Ground, where the remains were to rest until they could be transported to Quincy.

So much, so late.

There was even a parade with military companies. The Committee of Arrangements, the Committee of Escort, and foreign diplomats all rendered homage to my husband.

I wasn't at any of these hollow, meaningless, show-off ceremonies.

I left it to the Committee to accompany his casket to Quincy. I might have gone along, just to see the groups of people who lined along the railroad track to pay respects. But I didn't. I just simply couldn't in so much turmoil. My emotions were in too much of a flux.

Boston, that had snubbed him when he had his downfall losing his second bid for the Presidency, now turned out with hypocritical plaudits. Like an old whore who pretends she'd liked her longest loyal customer, Boston gave more hypocritical praise of Johnny's career in an over-crowded Faneuil Hall. He was lauded as, "Born a citizen of Massachusetts, died a citizen of the United States."

Charles, who lived in that city on and off, may have been pleased with a plaque recording what George Washington had said of my Johnny, "John Quincy Adams is the most valuable character we have abroad and the ablest of all our diplomatic corps."

Nice, but I didn't want any of that panoply. Instead, my kitchen seemed more comforting. I sat there for many days, recalling the good and the bad evenings I spent with Johnny, trying out recipes. The bad days all dated from when we first lived on F Street, before George died. We'd spent stupid years, despising each other's ways. Memories of the other, later, wonderfully happy days full of reciprocated love, were what kept me going.

Washington, D.C., January 1, 1849

I changed.

For better or worse, that is for those who record my life to decide. I AM RECORDING NOW that I lived to do good and to be good, but I like happiness. It is the right of men in the United States to look for the pursuit of happiness. But what about the women? WE cannot look for happiness?

I believe our right for happiness will come, if only as Mr. Abraham Lincoln likes to say, "Someday." In my widowhood I decided to have fun, go to parties, give parties, go to theaters and concerts, and help the cause which I've embraced: more rights for women. Will I achieve SOMETHING worthwhile before it is my time to join Johnny in his resting place?

I go to church every day. Prayer certainly helps. I have additional help from an unexpected quarter. A new church organ was installed in the loft of the little chapel I favor. It was paid for by subscription, and I gave my share. The old organ dates from the mid Eighteenth Century: its music sounds like the bleating of sheep. This new organ is so large—and its pipes so heavy—that it overwhelms the space allotted to it. The floor had to be shored up to prevent it crumbling into the cellar, which could have given the parishioners a preview of falling down into Hell.

What helps me is the organ's sublime sound. Formerly, I thought that a harp created the most blissful sounds. Not any longer, not after hearing that organ. Its VOX HUMANA has the perfect clarity of the voice of a ten year-old boy chorister. When all the pipes are reverberating towards a crescendo, and its music swells to lift my heart as if to Heaven, I know I have to be like that organ and send out MY SONG to the world outside.

I was not to bleat any longer. No whining that I am a Nobody. I must sing loudly and perfectly. I determined to fill my lungs with all the oxygen needed to call for happiness for all women everywhere in every way.

With her letters to me, Sarah Grimké introduced me to many more of the founders of the pursuit of women's rights, which ultimately SHOULD bring happiness. In Sarah's letters she wrote of Elizabeth Blackwell, the first woman to get a medical doctor's degree. Through Angelina I met Susan B. Anthony, who repeated in my parlor her notice of war on men, "The old idea that man was made for himself, and woman for him—that he is the oak, she the vine; he the head, she the heart; he the great conservator of wisdom, she of love—will be reverently laid aside with other since exploded philosophies of the ignorant past."

Should I agree with that? It won't be exploded so reverently in MY house.

To my kitchen came Dorothy Dix, who demanded the reform of prisons and insane asylums. She's been campaigning for that for ten years until she finally persuaded Congress in 1848 to introduce a bill providing Federal support for such institutions. But do you think a man like President Polk would accept that? Never. He vetoed it. I hoped her bill would at least be the inspiration for reforms later.

By Christmas, I had redecorated my famous parlor, famous for the ball I gave all those many years ago for General Andrew Jackson, ostensibly to help Johnny mend political bridges with Jackson, but really because Johnny had conceived a scheme to pacify Jackson through the flattery of giving a ball for him.

On New Year's Day 1849 I gave a party by myself for two hundred of MY friends. First and foremost was Angelina Grimké. Angelina, married, and the mother of three children, leads a contingent of ladies working for women's rights. These were not frivolous show-offs, the type of lady who wants her name on an engraved list but does nothing. One of them had managed to get New York to pass the MARRIED WOMAN'S Property Act. What a coup!

Among the two hundred were dozens who had attended the Seneca Falls Women's Rights Convention in July. I particularly liked Mary Wollstonecraft, who had the idea that "and women" should be added to the Declaration of Independence's Rights of Man. These ladies from the Seneca Falls Convention gave out a statement where they claimed, "The history of mankind is a history of repeated injuries and usurpations on the part of man toward woman having in direct object the establishment of an absolute tyranny over her."

Johnny would have surely gone into one of his rages over that. But he wasn't in my parlor; he was resting in peace. Elizabeth Cady Stanton declaimed part of the ladies' Bill of Rights. Instead of poetry, or a piano concert, I entertained my guests with the newest of the new: the fight for women's rights. In my parlor I heard, "Man has denied woman the inalienable right to vote, compelled her to submit to laws she had no voice in making, made her, if married, civilly dead in the eyes of the law, taken from her all rights in property, even to the wages she earns."

Mr. Henry Stanton, who's been very supportive of his independent wife until that evening, complained aloud when she read out what was probably the most important point, "It is the duty of the women of our country to secure to themselves their sacred right to the elective franchise." Very wordy. What Elizabeth should have said, was, "Women must get the vote." Then maybe Mr. Stanton would have kept silent.

We need the backing of men who would help our cause. They were few and far between.

Horace Greeley's Tribune newspaper, while cautious about agreeing that equal political rights should be given to women, did concede that, "However unwise and mistaken the demand, it is but the assertion of a natural right and as such should be conceded."

Hooray for Horace Greeley!

We women are on the march.

My daughter-in-law Abby, who came to my party, was hesitant to smile acceptance to any of the demands. She must have been thinking: What would Charles say? What, indeed!

Abby, who is a profoundly-intelligent woman, could not but agree with Lucretia Mott's premise that centuries of repression and lack of advanced education may have caused some women to appear of inferior intellect. But Abby had to concede Lucretia made sense when Lucretia declared, "Suppose, for the sake of argument, that women weren't on the whole as bright as men. That would be no reason to deny them their basic human rights. Does one man have inferior rights than another because his intellect is inferior? If not, why should a woman?"

My daughter-in-law, nieces, and one grandson helped me to pass the desserts, which were as unusual as the rest of my New Year's Day party. I served cakes from two recipes given to me by the Polish envoy's wife. One was called favorita, and I made it by rolling out pastry, coating it with jam, individualizing with a cookie-cutter, and serving hot and garnished with powdered sugar.

When I handled that rolling pin, I thought of how that kitchen tool was the only weapon many women had to protect themselves from abusive husbands. The next time a rolling pin was mentioned as a weapon at one of my soirées, I brought out a rolling pin from my kitchen to show men in the audience what one looked like.

A woman guest cried out from the rear of the room, "Hit a man on the right shoulder, then he can't use his paralyzed right arm to hit you back!"

After my guests had left, and I was relaxing in my bedroom, Abby came in with a clipping from a newspaper. It had nothing to do with women's rights. It was an advertisement placed by the redoubtable showman P.T. Barnum. The advertisement invited the paying public to a concert in New York by Europe's greatest soprano, Jenny Lind, the Swedish Nightingale. "Let's go hear her," she said.

I was exhausted from making speeches at the party and the entertaining of unfamiliar guests, but I agreed immediately.

"When is this concert?"

"Next year, at the beginning of 1850. I'll make all the arrangements for a carriage and seats on the train to New York. Will you buy the tickets for the concert?"

"Of course, I will! And I don't care if my women's rights friends consider that frivolous."

I went to sleep recalling that time I took Charles to the theater at Versailles Palace and how angry Johnny had been that I'd spent the household money to go there. Didn't he chastise me, "I could have bought a fine pair of boots with that money." He did. And now I accepted that he was quite right: Johnny had needed new boots.

With hindsight garnished with the love I bear now for Johnny I still hold true to my dream of winning freedom for women. But will I truly help women, or fail whilst trying?

Washington D.C., June 16, 1850

A year and a half has passed since I last dipped a plume into my silver-topped ink pot and continued to write. In 1840 I'd penned my "NOBODY" book, detailing the loneliness that continued to plague me eleven years after Johnny and I had left the White House. At that time I thought of myself as a Nobody although I was an ambassador's wife three times, wife of a Secretary of State, and First Lady of these United States. I'd sent the book to our youngest son, Charles, who is now a State Senator. He changed its title and then killed it.

Charles has grown even more full of himself and is proving to be as ambitious as ever his father was.

I fear he will always resent the political successes his father achieved.

I will leave this secret diary to Angelina, not to Charles. She can decide whether or not to release it to the public.

I suffered a stroke in the spring of 1849. Temporarily, I lost the use of my right hand and arm. For a few months now I've been walking with a cane. But when the cool air of autumn arrived, I started to enjoy carriage rides in the countryside. I "girded my loins." I prepared to go to New York to hear Jenny Lind, and I threw away my cane.

Jenny Lind's concert was sublime. Little Jenny Lind, petite in every way except for her enormous voice, enchanted me and all those people who had slept outside the Garden Theater on its sidewalk in order to get tickets. Abby had reserved ours soon after she'd seen P.T. Barnum's advertisement. We had marvelous seats, which was great because my hearing seems to be failing.

My women's rights friends didn't criticize me for going. They laughingly admitted they were jealous of my having enjoyed such a special evening.

But there was more than just an evening to write about in my secret diary. I managed to build enough courage to take a ship to Long Island Sound, over the same water where my darling George had drowned in that terrible year, 1829.

At that time I had plumbed the depths of misery when I learned of George's suicide.

That same year I'd been reviled by one of Johnny's enemies, calling me a would-be aristocrat who chased after European royalties. I'd countered that lie with my article on "Female Character," printed in both the Saturday Evening Post and in the United States Telegraph. How unimportant that calumny seems to me these days. Now only George's death, Louisa Catherine's, John's, and Johnny's can touch my newly-reformed heart.

After Johnny's death I seem to be a stronger person. I actually enjoyed the trip on Long Island Sound. I could hear the splash of waves against the prow, where I stood like a girl on her first boat trip and thrilled to the glint of sunshine on the breakers' foam. I tasted the salt of their spray. I watched with delight as seagulls swooped to grab up minnows. When our ship's horn warned of approaching vessels,

I neither covered my ears, nor thought the sound lugubrious. Like a kite in the wind, I felt I was soaring. Pleasure, was the order of that day.

All was not joyful where boats were concerned for some of the women in my life. An 1850 drowning hit the women's rights movement.

I was much impressed by one of the most attractive of the founders, Margaret Fuller. She'd been an editor and became a very good writer. She could speak and write in German, a rare quality among our group of intellectuals. Her book Women in the Nineteenth Century stood out like a lighthouse. She was allied with Sarah Grimké in pleading with ladies to visit prisons and insane asylums.

We've been taught from the New Testament to visit prisons to help those in need. I should have been propelled to follow that advice. But

I couldn't. My upbringing, the years when my parents instilled in me the ways of frivolous ladies, had stunted my soul to where I never followed that call earlier. I couldn't do it at Margaret's direction now. But I did read her book with intense enthusiasm.

Margaret, once having left America for Italy, became involved there with the Roman Republic. She backed a renowned Liberal, Joseph Mazzini, founder of La Giovine Italia—Young Italy. She also lived through the three-month siege of Rome, during which time she ran a hospital. Wonderful woman! Margaret penned a superb book on the history of the Roman Revolution. But why did she leave America? Horace Greeley had installed her as the literary critic of his New York Tribune! Horace Greeley described her as one of the best writers in the United States. He was awed by her work in introducing French and German authors, among them the outstanding poet Goethe. And yet Margaret left the United States to go to live in Rome. Why? Was it due to falling in love with an Italian Marchese that kept her in Italy? A leading member of the 'women's movement' had left the type of job for which we had been fighting? Oh, my. And for the love of a man! It was reported that she married her Marchese secretly and had borne him a baby.

In May 1850, Margaret embarked for the United States with her husband and child. The voyage was uneventful until their ship was hit by a storm of near-hurricane force off Fire Island. Fire Island was that same island where the AMISTAD had been impounded. Margaret's ship was grounded on a sandbar, fifty yards off Fire Island. Rescuers arrived to help the women to disembark. Margaret refused to go without her husband and child. "I see nothing but death before me." She called into the wind, "I shall never reach the shore."

Whilst she was speaking, the ship's mast broke and crashed down. A ship's steward grabbed her child and jumped into the sea, attempting to save the baby. Their bodies were washed up, dead, within minutes. Neither Margaret's body—nor her husband's—were ever found.

That was a horribly gruesome story for me.

All these years later, I still mourn George, who disappeared into those same waters.

Washington D.C., August 13, 1851

With my heart following new directions, I soldiered on with the women's rights movement. I don't accept ALL their teachings. I am ambivalent on the subject of debasing LOVE BETWEEN A MAN AND A WOMAN. I cannot agree that MARITAL LOVE is harmful to our cause. No, not after the last blissful years I had with Johnny.

There were leaders in the women's movement who decried marriage. True, as things stand now, a woman loses all her possessions when she weds. Her husband can sell everything she has, even her clothes. When women DID have the vote in Massachusetts during Colonial times in the 1750s, only unmarried women could vote—that meant the widows and spinsters. So some of our followers were eschewing matrimony.

In my own home I was a witness to the sad, unfulfilled life of Johnny's niece, whom we called "an old maid." As a young girl, she had a rosy-cheeked face full of smiles. But little by little, as a permanent spinster, over the years she had dried up like a plum turns into a prune.

I also have reservations about the Temperance issue, where wine and all alcoholic drinks are considered bad. Having lived so many years in Europe where wine invariably accompanies dinner and having been married to a man who so much enjoyed his three-a-day glasses of Madeira, I would be a hypocrite if I backed the Abolitionists' co-movement, the Temperance League.

Goodness gracious, I've known of several prestigious Americans who were connoisseurs of wine. President Thomas Jefferson annually imported close to three thousand bottles of European wine. My father-in-law enjoyed many a tipple with him, savoring those wines. Martha Washington's Booke of Recipes included domestic wines made from blackberries, cherries, gooseberries, or lemons. Her recipe for hippocras contains two gallons of white sauterne and one gallon of chablis.

Even the New Testament teaches that Jesus turned water into wine at a marriage in Cana. How could these Temperance ladies think they had a right to counter that?

Cruel tongues still flay me. There are women in Washington who like to recall that I introduced silk worms to the mulberry trees in the Capitol's garden and who complain I harvested the silk to make a gown for myself. What small minds, scraping a bucket of legend to find something to criticize!

There are men who should know better than to belittle worthwhile improvements in the way we live. For instance, I don't respect doctors who fought the use of a new discovery, chloroform, which is such a boon to women during childbirth. I read that Britain's Queen Victoria had made use of chloroform when her last baby was born, Beatrice, and was A GREAT SUPPORTER. She'd knighted the doctor who invented the anesthetic, Dr. James Simpson, although his church excommunicated him. Many churchmen believed that women must suffer during childbirth because the scriptures wrote, "In sorrow shalt thou bring forth children." Imagine that! Having endured four complete childbirths, one stillbirth, and seven miscarriages I can hardly be expected to agree with those churchmen!

As is my custom when I feel depressed, I tried out a new recipe to bolster my self-confidence. My grandson Henry, who loves cookies, was in the kitchen with me one morning recently, and he helped me prepare the ingredients: half cup butter, one cup sugar, two eggs, teaspoon vanilla, one cup flour, teaspoon baking soda, teaspoon vanilla, teaspoon cinnamon, half teaspoon salt, three cups uncooked oats, and one cup raisins. I beat the eggs with the vanilla and then put all the ingredients together in a mixing bowl. When I turned to check the oven was not too hot, Henry asked, "Grandmother, should there be eyes in these cookies?"

"Eyes, you mean raisins?"

No, they weren't raisins in the cookies; what Henry referred to were the eyes of a live mouse that had been trapped in the mix.

I gave the mouse its freedom by scooping it out with a measuring cup and then placing it outside in the garden. I hope it lived. I don't think I'd got around to beating the mix too hard.

We dropped the batter on cookie sheets, and I placed them in the oven. After ten minutes the cookies were golden brown, and I removed them to put them on a wire rack. Henry ate his cookies with gusto, but I gave mine a miss. I love new recipes, but the flavor of mouse was more than I could stomach.

Washington D.C., May 15, 1852

With winter's blasts gone, I still keep to my bed.

I long to go for walks in these balmy days. I want to welcome the trilling baby birds and thrusting buds. But without Johnny to please or hope to get compliments from, I've let myself grow plump. The extra weight makes it harder to leave my bed.

Thoughts of what I must accomplish kept my mind sharp.

I AM torn between giving more time to the founders of the women's rights group or to a newer group that is allied with the anti-slavery faction. I have always been against slavery, having heard William Wilberforce speak out against it in England when I was a girl.

I keep myself calm by reading the books I never had time for earlier or by writing poetry. My fingers long ago grew too stiff for the harp or piano. And stuck in my bed, I cannot get to a musical instrument, can I?

My daughters-in-law and nieces clamor around my bed. After he offered to come too, I sent a message to Charles, discouraging him from arriving at my house, writing that, "Old persons know best what suits them." I don't need a man crowding my bedroom. Not now, not when Johnny has been dead three years.

Angelina Grimké came, although she had a mob of children pulling at her skirts. Angelina was full of good news. She met a woman called Esther Morris who is thinking of taking the pioneer road to the Territory of Wyoming. Esther Morris believes that in Wyoming she could get the legislators there to pass our dreamed-of law, giving the vote to women. Angelina prompted Esther Morris to tell Wyoming that New Jersey from 1776 to 1807 had permitted unmarried women to vote, and therefore, A PRECEDENT HAS BEEN SET.

But even a newly independent New Jersey, free from being part of a British Colony, was not willing to give the vote to married women.

By 1807 New Jersey had rescinded allowing even unmarried women's right to vote. Hopefully now in 1852, women will get to vote in Wyoming, and if not now, then in the future, surely!

Angelina knew that Wyoming's Governor was not averse to listening to women pleading for their rights because he'd admitted that—as a young man in Ohio—he sneaked into a women's convention that copied the Seneca Falls deliberations in 1840.

"It may take time," Angelina said, "maybe as much as ten or twenty years. But I foresee that Wyoming will be the first of all the territories to give us the vote, and for any woman—married, or unmarried—to have rights to her property. We WILL win, Louisa. I promise you. And if you doubt me, you should meet Esther Morris. She's big in lots of ways. All of six feet tall."

I don't doubt Angelina. But I don't want to meet this Esther Morris. Not if she stands six feet tall, when there's little enough space now in my crowded bedroom.

The winter months dragged by, although I enjoyed watching the snowfalls. I liked to catch the glint of sunlight on the swirling flakes when any pale ray peeked by my window.

When the first robins arrived, announcing spring from a branch outside calling out their notes while they leapt from twig to twig, I thought I felt well enough to write a poem.

But the day when Abby brought me pen and paper, I couldn't compose a stanza.

I did manage to tell each and every member of my family that I love him or her. How could I do less when the mother robin was outside feeding her young? Expressing LOVE is the best food for MY people.

I feel at peace. My daughters-in-law love me, my grandchildren love me, and even Charles in his difficult way loves me. Most important, I can finally love myself. I will not title this work Diary of a Nobody: Part Two, because I don't believe I'm a nobody now.

Yesterday, Angelina Grimké came to visit at my bedside. She gave me all the news of the advances in the women's rights movement. She finished by saying, "Louisa, when we get the vote—and we shall—you will be thanked for all you did to achieve it. You were a founding member of our great crusade.

We value your part in this, not because you were the First Lady of the United States when John Quincy Adams was President, but because with your superior intellect, you could recognize our special needs. The need for entertaining Congressmen and other power brokers and the need to love all the women in this business, whether poor or of color or elderly! You, Louisa, you are a very special person."

Early this morning, I called for Mary. She has always been very close to me, being my sister Nancy's daughter and my dead son John's wife. "I don't feel well," I told her. Nothing more, I didn't want to alarm her.

To make the tolling appear less serious, I added what she was accustomed to hearing, "Please bring me some hot chocolate and my diary." When Mary returned I scribbled FOR ANGELINA on the diary's cover.

I took up my bedside pad of paper and a pen and sit here now, trying to write out my last recipe. "Take two arms, wrap around loved one, hug until satisfied, purse lips, and kiss."

How I wished I knew that recipe on the day I married Johnny.

Louisa Johnson Adams died at noon on May 15, 1852, at the age of seventy-seven. She did not die a NOBODY; she had vindicated her long life by buying the freedom of a slave with her own money and by being a founder of the Women's Rights movement, which eventually gave the vote to all female citizens of the United States of America.

www.ingramcontent.com/pod-product-compliance
Lightning Source LLC
LaVergne TN
LVHW050926080826
845145LV00001B/222

9781623860219